From the moment he first hear[d] [at the age]
of twelve), John Chilton was o[ne of the]
dedicated jazz fan. He began p[laying the tr]umpet and
became a professional jazz musician, working for four
years in Bruce Turner's Jump Band before leading the
Feetwarmers, who toured the world with singer George
Melly for thirty years.

Throughout his musical career John has combined
trumpet playing with writing books about jazz, including
highly praised biographies of Sidney Bechet, Coleman
Hawkins, Billie Holiday, Louis Jordan, Henry 'Red' Allen
and Roy Eldridge.

In *Hot Jazz, Warm Feet*, he not only recounts the story of
his music making and the joy of jazz research, but also
poignantly writes about his wartime evacuation, the fun
and frustrations of national service in the RAF and life
on the road with George Melly, who described John as 'an
anecdotalist of genius'.

Also by John Chilton

Roy Eldridge: Little Jazz Giant

Ride, Red, Ride: The Life of Henry 'Red' Allen

Sidney Bechet: The Wizard of Jazz

*The Song of the Hawk: The Life and Recordings
of Coleman Hawkins*

Billie's Blues: A Survey of Billie Holiday's Career 1933-59

Let the Good Times Roll: The Story of Louis Jordan

Who's Who of Jazz: Storyville to Swing Street

Stomp Off, Let's Go: The Story of Bob Crosby's Bob Cats

Teach Yourself Jazz

A Jazz Nursery: The Story of Jenkins' Orphanage Band

*McKinney's Music: A Bio-discography of
McKinney's Cotton Pickers*

Louis: The Louis Armstrong Story (with Max Jones)

Who's Who of British Jazz

Hot Jazz,
Warm Feet

John Chilton

Hot Jazz, Warm Feet

Northway publications

Published by Northway Publications,
39 Tytherton Road,
London N19 4PZ, UK

www.northwaybooks.com
email info@northwaybooks.com

Edited by Ann and Roger Cotterrell with Sallie Choate.

Front cover photo of John Chilton by Robert Carpenter Turner. Back
cover photo of Bruce Turner, Bill Coleman, John Chilton, Steve Fagg
and Wally Fawkes at New Merlin's Cave, 1971, by Harry Diamond.

The publishers acknowledge with thanks the kind permission of copyright holders to reprint the photographs used in this book. Permissions
have been sought in all cases where the identity of copyright holders is
known.

A CIP record for this book is available from the British Library.

ISBN 9780955090837

First published 2007.

Printed and bound in Great Britain by Cromwell Press Ltd, Trowbridge,
Wiltshire.

For my grandchildren:

Louis, Jack, Nathaniel, Samuel and Gabriel

Contents

1. Evacuation   1

2. Rustic Joys   14

3. National Service   30

4. Fleet Street to Swing Street   45

5. From Butlin's to a Jump Band   59

6. Life on a Liner   76

7. Living Jazz   91

8. Finding Fawkes and Meeting Melly   110

9. On the Road Again   133

10. New York, Sydney and Beijing   153

11. The Frith Street Charm School   176

12. A Jazz Scrapbook Comes to Life   194

13. Pals and Personalities   216

14. A Gig with Slim   229

15. The Good Old Wagon Stops Rolling   240

Index   261

1

Evacuation

The sound of horseshoes scraping on concrete plagued my early childhood nights. The metallic clatter didn't originate in a manor house stables, it came from the hooves of dray-horses quartered in the railway yards of London's Euston Station, close to Levita House, a large block of council flats, one of which housed my family. Each and every night the nags, weary after hauling consignments of coal all over London, stretched the stiffness out of their legs by noisily kicking at the hard floor of their stables.

We moved into Levita House in 1936, when I was four years old. I have scant recollections of our previous home on Holborn's Bourne Estate, but both my brothers (Tom born in 1917 and Ron born in 1927) had clear memories of the cramped, bathless conditions my family endured there. My father, Thomas Chilton, a singer and tap-dancer (who worked under the stage name of Tom Elliot) had been part of various music-hall acts, juvenile troupes and concert parties before being gassed during army service in World War One. His ill-fortune was later compounded when he contracted pulmonary tuberculosis; both his father (a cab-man) and his grandfather (a french polisher) died before I was born.

Both my parents were born in London: my father in 1892, my mother (née Eileen Burke) five years later. My mother was a kind and affectionate woman whose lively sense of humour helped her deal with the fact that she was a born worrier (a trait I inherited). Her father, a printer, (born in Ireland) died in the 1920s, her mother (a domestic servant) survived into the late 1940s. Despite my father's health problems, which meant he could no longer do professional stage work, my mother never became despondent. She, like my father, loved the music-hall tradition – a trip to the nearby Holborn Empire was guaranteed to dispel any trace of gloom. Dad's chronic ill-health meant he spent long periods in convalescent homes on the South Coast. When he was well enough he worked sporadically, sharing the driver's cabin in a van that delivered magazines – but there were many weeks when he was too ill to work.

My father was a patient man who rarely raised his voice; he bore his illnesses without complaining and was always intensely interested in the progress of his three sons. On the front page of his scrapbook he pasted the dictum, 'Never starve a child of praise.' My mother was also even-tempered but a rare surge of rage occurred when my brother Tom (then about nine) swapped my father's beloved tap-shoes for some goldfish, the deal having been brokered by a 'totter' who wheeled a barrow around the streets offering preposterous exchanges. As soon as my mother found out about the one-sided barter she scoured the locale until she found the wandering dealer. Fortunately the shoes hadn't been sold and were still displayed on the barrow. My mother had to buy them back for considerably more than the price of goldfish but she was happy to do so.

Despite the penury, Mum and Dad bought a piano on hire purchase (or 'the never-never' as it was then known) – at that time the owning of a piano was a status symbol among the working classes. There was no money available for any of us to take piano lessons but we were encouraged to amuse ourselves at the keyboard whenever we felt like it. However none of us developed any great desire to play anything more complicated than a single-line melody. This didn't mean that the piano wasn't used; a stream of club entertainers and 'turns' dropped in to see how my father was and, with minimal encouragement, sat down at the keyboard and warbled a song or two. As a small child I thought that this was the done thing when visiting and for a while imagined that everyone was capable of unselfconsciously presenting an entertaining song.

At five I started at a local council school but, other than being impressed by the sight of a huge ledger in which the teacher entered my name, I remember little of those early school days. I know that I could read by this time, having been taught by my mother – comics being the primer. Details of lessons floated away, but from this same period I still have detailed memories of the films I saw and where I saw them and I have a vivid recollection of my father telling me of the death of George Gershwin in 1937. The names of boxers, footballers and show business icons stayed firm in my head but other more useful facts and figures were relegated to the back of my mind. The event most clearly imprinted on my memory from this period concerned the only time in my life that I was ever in trouble with the police – I was six years old.

During the 1930s it was still the custom for undertakers, making an initial call on a bereaved family, to leave their top hats at the foot of the stairs, as a mark of respect for the recently departed. Bizarrely they kept up this tradition even when visiting a large block of flats. Wending our way home from school, a young pal and myself, to our utter surprise, came across something we had only ever seen in the movies – a silk top hat. Knowing nothing of the undertakers' time-honoured practice we were mystified and excited. We picked up the shiny topper and admired its leather and silk interior. My friend claimed that as he had seen the hat first it was, by rights, his. I disputed this and hung on tight to the treasure. In no time a tug of war developed, I pulled fiercely at the top section and my rival firmly gripped the brim. The hat was not designed for such rough treatment and soon split into two sections.

The rending ended the bickering, my pal took the brim and wore it as a sailor's hat, and I utilised the other section as an over-size black fez. Full of delight we ran up and down a passageway, acting what we took to be appropriate roles for such headgear. When boredom eventually set in we con-ceived the idea that if the brim were stuffed into the fez we'd have a pretty good replica of a football. We kicked the bun-dle to and fro for several minutes before both of us were simultaneously struck by the same thought: such a hat must belong to a person of some importance, and he would soon begin searching for it. Feeling confused and guilty we split up and I decided that I would get as far away from the scene as quickly as I could. I made for Euston Station and meandered around that area for what must have been two hours – a long time (even in that innocent age) for a six-year-old to be over-due from returning from school.

Eventually I made my way back to Levita House and, sensing trouble, slowly climbed the three flights of stairs and tapped on the door of our flat. The instant I saw my mother's face I knew that the game was up. My guilty look was immediately apparent to her. She sat me down and in a severe voice asked what I knew about the recent destruction of a valuable hat. My immediate confession placated my mother, but to underline the severity of the incident she described in full detail how the bareheaded undertaker, accompanied by a police constable had visited her an hour earlier, my accomplice having already confessed. The undertaker listened to my mother's pleas for forgiveness and, probably swayed by the obvious lack of affluence, said he would forget about the loss of an expensive hat providing I was severely reprimanded. My mother certainly made me aware of my wrongdoing and I was emphatically punished by being forced to abstain from reading any comics for two weeks, a woeful experience for me.

Gradually the affair melted into family anecdotage, no one being more amused than my Uncle Archibald (a bluff Royal Navy petty officer) who, some years later, on his death bed, summoned up a last burst of humour by telling me that in no circumstances was I to kick the undertaker's hat at the impending funeral. That same uncle had visited Russia at the time of the 1917 Revolution and the letters and envelopes he sent from there were all proudly kept. My parents were led to believe by a newspaper article that the Russian stamps on the envelopes were worth a small fortune. As a result these philatelic treasures were regarded as collateral of the first order that could be used to raise cash in a family emergency. The day came when money was very badly needed and my parents took the stamps to a well-known dealer in the Strand, who, in a matter-of-fact way, said they were only worth a few pence each, a valuation echoed by another near-by stamp shop.

I continued to take a lively interest in events that occurred outside, rather than inside, the classroom and precociously observed the growing preparations for a war with Germany. Neville Chamberlain's September 1938 waving of the Munich 'peace in our time' agreement made an impression on me as did the subsequent issue of gas masks, the digging of trenches in London parks and the hideous moan of the newly installed air raid sirens. Wardens wearing tin helmets with the letters ARP (Air Raid Precautions) painted on them would suddenly blow three blasts on a whistle to signify that we must practise donning the uncomfortable, sweat-inducing rubber gas masks issued to us as protection against the possibilities of enemy planes dropping poisonous gas. A new word entered the everyday conversations at school: evacuation. Although war had not been declared, the threat of German air raids on central London was made clear to parents, and the majority of them (including my mother and father) agreed that their children would be safer as evacuees in the countryside. The decision didn't affect my eldest brother, Tom, who was soon to join the RAF, but it meant that Ron, aged twelve, and me, aged seven, were sent to safer locales and, because we attended different schools (Ron having recently won a scholarship to Holloway County Grammar School) we would not be travelling to the same destination.

The parents of every evacuee were given printed instructions detailing what their offspring needed for the journey to their new homes. These included gas masks, a change of clothing, sandwiches, an apple and a label giving the name and home address of the child. No one could forecast the exact date that the exodus of youngsters would take place but everyone was told that they should be ready to leave at an hour's notice. At first, every parent strictly observed the requirements but, as the days of high alert drifted into weeks of uncertain waiting, the satchels of food and clothing were often left at home. The tearful morning farewells that our mothers shared with us gradually changed into affectionate cheerios as the sense of imminent danger abated. Then, one morning in late August 1939 we were called into the school playground and told, without further ado, that all of us children, with or without satchels, would be leaving immediately to begin life with foster parents. Like all of my class mates I was too stunned to cry. There were no mothers to wave goodbye as we marched crocodile fashion to the nearby main line railway station to begin a train journey that had the air of a mystery tour since none of us, including our teachers, had any idea of our destination. Apprehension temporarily disappeared as we posed for an American newsreel crew who were filming the departure of hundreds of children from many schools. We cheerfully pressed our noses against the carriage windows as we waved to the camera.

The government had foreseen the problem of distributing the evacuees, and *Evacuation, Why And How* (issued in July 1939) made it clear that they could not reveal in advance the destination of the departing children. Eventually we reached Burton Latimer, a Northamptonshire village, where we were put into the hands of local billeting officers, many of whom had only recently been press-ganged into the role. Children can usually spot uncertainty in an adult and, young as we were, we quickly realised that confusion was rife. Our teachers were obliged to hand us over to these local custodians who lined us up in groups of a dozen or so and then set out to find homes for us. The lack of strategy and pre-planning meant that we ambled along behind a middle-aged woman who radiated anxiety. We reached West Crescent, which consisted of a series of small council houses, and our guardian began banging on doors and ringing bells to ask whoever came to the door if they would take in an evacuee, in what she described as 'the present emergency'. Interest perked up when a weekly payment of seven shillings and six pence was mentioned and gradually our party was reduced to six, five, four and then three: myself and two sisters who would not be parted. Eventually the girls were taken in by a kindly woman who had small children of her own clutching at her skirt. I realised with dismay that we had come around the Crescent back almost to where we started the trawl and I still hadn't been placed in a billet.

In succeeding years I sometimes pondered on why I was the last youngster on offer and came to the conclusion that it was because I was, as a child, very fat. This was long before fears grew about juvenile obesity, but I suspect that potential foster parents seeing my plumpness equated it with an expensive appetite and, with the imminent prospect of food rationing, one that would be difficult to satisfy. Whatever the reason I felt hurt and frightened. Then, at the last door to be tried, I was accepted by Mr and Mrs Crisp, who had a small son aged about five and thought I would be company for him. My relieved minder wrote down the address where she deposited me and was gone in a flash. Mrs Crisp ushered me in and asked if I was hungry. I certainly was, not having eaten for several hours. She left the room and returned with a large plate held aloft. My spirits rose, then fell as she lowered the plate to reveal sliced beetroot, only beetroot, nothing else, not even a crust of bread. 'That'll get your weight down, my lad,' she said cheerfully.

On the following morning all of the West Crescent evacuees were gathered together and marched to the local school. There we were reunited with our teachers and with other evacuees whose billets were scattered in different parts of the village. A semblance of stability was established as our names were entered in a register. We were told that school proper would start on Monday morning and that we would have to make our own way there because the billeting officers would be busy greeting new arrivals. Most of Saturday was spent exploring a wooded spinney where we London boys and girls climbed trees for the first time in our lives. On Sunday morning several of us went to a nearby park where we asked some local boys if we could play them at football. They accepted the challenge somewhat grudgingly and the result was a mud-splattered draw. We left the recreation pitch dishevelled but happy, but as we strolled out of the gates we were approached by an old couple who said, with some agitation, 'Mr Chamberlain has just said that war has been declared. You had better go home to your mothers straightaway.' Our happy mood vanished, not at the prospect of international strife but because the mention of our mothers jolted us into realising that we were far away from home.

I sent details of the Crisp family's address to my parents and got an immediate reply from my mother which also included a sixpenny piece sewn on to a piece of cardboard. Mr and Mrs Crisp weren't cruel or unpleasant, and their small son accepted my arrival affably – happily there were no further servings of beetroot. Mr Crisp was a self-employed shoemaker who cut out leather shapes from pungent hides and sold them on to a Northampton shoe company which stitched them together and added a sole and heel. Some of my school friends were billeted with tyrannical landladies, but despite the absurd way we had been distributed I was not aware of any of our group suffering sexual abuse, certainly no incidents came to light during the long talks we had in the school playground. Neither were there any signs that a lack of supervision was inducing any savage type behaviour. My particular clique all pulled together and helped each other with shoelaces and neckties, as well as keeping one another cheerful; several of the girls acted as kindly 'little mothers' wiping noses and cleaning the wax out of various boys' ears.

A regime was established whereby we made our way to school individually, and this led to my first big Burton Latimer trauma. I had always been terrified by dogs of any shape or size. In London I usually had to avoid them one at a time, but on my journeys to and from the country school I seemed to be surrounded by half a dozen growling, un-collared dogs. I soon became a nervous wreck but I couldn't bring myself to tell my pals of the problem; instead I wrote to my mother for help. As a result she wrote to the school's headmaster asking if he could arrange for an older boy to accompany me to and from school. I have never worked out whether the teacher's course of action was that of a perceptive psychologist or a heartless commandant. He read out my mother's letter at assembly and asked for a volunteer to protect 'a certain boy' on the morning and afternoon journeys. Several goody-two-shoes put up their hands and the headmaster arbitrarily selected a boy of about twelve. Although my mother had requested that my name would not be mentioned, the head pointed at me and said in a loud

voice, 'You'll find Chilton over there, fix up details with him.'
This was a low spot in my early life; every face at the gathering turned towards me as a collective snigger filled the hall.
I went scarlet with embarrassment. I met up with my young protector after school and we set out on the ten-minute walk to West Crescent. Half way there, just before we reached the usual gathering place for the feral hounds, he said unceremoniously, 'This is as far as I go,' and with that he turned and left me stranded. The shame of my recent humiliation was still coursing through me, and this helped me to be determined not to buckle as the canine pack came towards me. I walked in a straight line towards them and almost fainted with relief as they trotted disinterestedly past me. I was suddenly cured of my crippling fear of dogs. Whether by accident or by design the headmaster's tactics had worked.

This was the period of the 'Phoney War' during which Britain and Germany girded themselves for the coming battles by sitting tight while amassing stocks of aircraft and munitions. The heavy air raids, forecast to begin from the moment that war was declared on the 3rd September 1939, didn't materialise. During the early weeks of the war, parents were not encouraged to visit their evacuated offspring for fear of unsettling them just as they were taking root in a new environment, but by the end of 1939 most of us had been visited by our mothers. Burton Latimer was about seventy miles from London but it seemed to us evacuees as though we were in a distant land and the sight of parents was very reassuring. Early in 1940 I had to leave the Crisp household because Mrs Crisp was expecting a baby and would not be able to look after three children. A local billeting officer arranged for me to be placed with another landlady in a different section of Burton Latimer. I felt sad at the change and with some trepidation became one of Mrs Marsh's charges.

My apprehension was justified; ill-treatment began within an hour of my arrival and it continued throughout my stay. Mr Marsh was never mentioned and I suspect that he had fled from his harridan of a spouse long ago. For whatever reason, Mrs Marsh was sadistically cruel and embittered. She had no children of her own, but filling her house with evacuees (none older than eight) brought her economic advantages and provided a supply of targets for her warped aggressiveness. As a seven-year-old I thought of her as an old lady, but looking back I realise that she was probably in her forties.

Five of us were billeted with Mrs Marsh: three boys and two girls. We weren't given enough to eat and all the boys were made to sleep in the same bed. One of the little lads habitually wet the bed soaking all of us. Mrs Marsh knew who the culprit was but pretended she didn't, thus giving herself the excuse to cane all three of us. We were commanded to come home immediately after school and made to stay in until next morning, whereas on Sundays we were put out of the house after breakfast and not allowed to return until it was time for an evening meal. These restrictions were carried out regardless of the weather – fortunately the worst of the winter was over. We were all too terrified to tell our teachers, and no one from the billeting authorities checked on our well-being – we were also forbidden to write to our parents. The principal place of work in Burton Latimer was the Weetabix factory and at that time the smell of that popular cereal pervaded the local atmosphere. As a result I came to associate the aroma with my misery and for years after I couldn't bear to be near a packet of that product. Eventually

I was 'cured' by the sight of my children enjoying Weetabix for breakfast.

Grim though our situation with Mrs Marsh was, one incident provided us with pure merriment. During one of our Sunday 'shut-outs' we chanced on a group of men attempting to do military drill with broomsticks. They were all in everyday civilian clothes but each of them wore an arm-band marked with the letters LDV. They were the Local Defence Volunteers (the forerunners of the Home Guard). We couldn't stop giggling at these adults, who were, so we thought, imitating children for the fun of it. However, the man who was shouting out the drill instructions did not see the funny side of the situation and with some menace told us to shut up and move on. We didn't need telling twice but as soon as we were out of his sight we became convulsed with helpless laughter.

On another Sunday during the late spring of 1940 I was again forced to trudge the streets, this time in heavy rain. I had lost a lot of weight so my wet clothes hung heavily on me. The mother of another evacuee, visiting her son in Burton Latimer, saw my plight and told my parents as soon as she returned to London. Within hours of learning of my sadness my parents despatched my brother Tom, who was awaiting call-up into the RAF, to Burton Latimer. He imme-diately called on Mrs Marsh to tell of his decision to take me back to London. I was saved.

2

Rustic Joys

The administrative details concerning my return to London were soon sorted out and I went back to attending my previous school in the King's Cross area, but, because most of the pupils were still evacuated, the classrooms were only about a quarter full. Those still attending the school consisted of youngsters whose parents had not allowed them to be evacuated, plus a small number of pupils who, like me, had returned to London. I didn't know any of the teachers but they all seemed kind and helpful. The first difference I noticed was that thick gauze had been pasted on every window in the school, to prevent them being shattered by bomb blast. Within weeks of my return the Battle of Britain started. It was the wrong time for a child to be in central London but I was in no fit state to be re-evacuated. Yet, despite the tension that filled the air, I gradually began to put on weight and resumed a more cheerful outlook, happy to join other children in collecting the jagged pieces of shrapnel that fell to the ground during the increasingly frequent air raids.

The school routine was constantly disrupted by the German daylight attacks. When the warning siren wailed, all of the children and the teachers assembled in the largest classroom, the windows of which were piled high with sandbags. The children sat on the floor and read or listened to a teacher telling a story. When the 'all clear' sounded we returned to our own classroom, but were often forced to repeat the whole routine again within half an hour. The frequency of the German air raids (day and night) continued to increase dramatically, so for safety, my mother took me each evening to the King's Cross underground station where we were allocated a two-tier bunk-bed on one of the platforms. A fine spirit of camaraderie existed down 'the tube', despite a lack of fresh air and the uncomfortable heat generated by hundreds of people (without bunks) who slept on newspapers spread along every square foot of space on the various platforms. When a regular bunk dweller failed to appear it usually meant that they had become a victim of the blitz. I slept fitfully during our overnight stays below ground and one night tumbled out of my lower bunk and rolled dangerously near to the electrified track – still live because the last of the night trains was still running. Thereafter the side of my bunk was bound with thick twine each night to prevent me rolling on to the track. As night ticked away the heat became nearly unbearable; even if the cold water taps were left running the flow of water remained unappetisingly hot. Because of his respiratory problem my father could not sleep in the subterranean fug and he remained at home in our flat.

By this time my brother Tom had entered the RAF He had attempted to volunteer for the Royal Navy but, having told the medical examiner that he'd had rheumatic fever as a child, he was immediately rejected. Undeterred, he walked into a nearby RAF recruiting office and, without mentioning his childhood health problems, was passed 'A1' and served with distinction throughout the duration of the war. My other brother, Ron, had been evacuated with his school to Yardley Gobion, a village in south Northamptonshire. There he learnt about the hazards of the ceaseless air raids on London and enterprisingly went round the village in an effort to find a family who would be prepared to take in his eight-year-old brother as an evacuee. Happily, his enquiries were successful and within days, my father, despite his health problems, accompanied me via Wolverton railway station and rural buses to the home of the Horton family, as kind and nice a quartet of people as one could ever find. They were to fill the role of benevolent and caring guardians for much of the next five years of my life. The family consisted of Mr and Mrs Horton, then in their late fifties, and their two sons Frank and Charlie, both bachelors in their late thirties. There was nothing untoward about the single status of the sons; both were happy to be part of a family that radiated kindness, honesty and decency and they saw no reason to move on. I met them all on a late summer's day.

My father introduced me, I sat down on a sofa and, clearing my throat, I blurted out a brief, dramatic confession, 'I've got sweaty feet.' With an almost Dickensian flourish Mrs Horton sang out, 'Why bless the boy. We've all got them.' I was instantly at ease with the family and remained so throughout the coming years. Although I was in the heart of the countryside the nocturnal sound of horses' hooves didn't reach the Hortons' cottage, nor did the aroma of breakfast cereal spoil my days.

Whereas Burton Latimer was an urban village with lots of shops and a cinema, Yardley Gobion was positively rural, with a village green, three farms, three general stores, a post office, a butcher, a baker and two pubs. It had no factories, but as the war became more intense many of its young men and women commuted to nearby towns to work for munitions manufacturers. Few people from Yardley had ever visited London, which they referred to as 'The Smoke'.

The folk of Yardley were intensely proud of their band, which had taken part in national championships at London's Crystal Palace. Mr Horton had been a star cornet player with the eighteen-piece band, which had already disbanded for the duration of the war by the time I arrived in Yardley. Although he had one of the lowliest jobs in the village (he was its road sweeper), he possessed a fine, natural dignity. He was staunchly in favour of the Labour Party and got joy from reading William Connor's 'Cassandra' column in the *Daily Mirror*, which often contained criticisms of various eminent politicians, even the nation's indomitable leader Winston Churchill.

Even those Yardley villagers who worked in modern factories retained the expressions and rustic ways of country folk, acutely aware of their rural traditions. By their example I was soon aware of how the changing seasons governed the planting and harvesting of crops. I learnt how to tell a beech tree from an elm, a chaffinch from a bullfinch, a roach from a bream. But not long after I had settled in with the Horton family I was made acutely aware of nature's cruel streak.

The Hortons decided that a regular supply of eggs would help supplement the meagre amount of food available via ration books and to this end they bought seventeen prize young pullets from a Northampton dealer. Many of the villagers awaited with interest the arrival of these pedigree fowls with interest, but none was more fascinated than me. The young hens arrived on a Saturday and I spent most of the day watching them closely – they seemed to grow before my eyes. I got up early next morning to observe their progress through the wire netting that surrounded their pen. I raced through Sunday tea to return for yet another peek. This time the scene that greeted me was horribly distressing. Although only ten minutes had passed since my previous check-up, in that time a huge rat had burrowed into the pen and wantonly killed every one of the young creatures. I ran as fast as I could to the tea table and, almost incoherent with shock, told the family as best I could what had happened. Frank and Charlie raced to the pen but were too late to save any of the pullets. Mr Horton followed on and began clearing up the carcases noting that all of the chickens had been killed by a sharp bite to the throat – none of the killings were for sustenance. For the Horton family the shock of the incident was compounded by the fact that the carnage had deprived them of a good slice of their meagre savings, but even so they remained philosophical, being well aware as country folk of nature's profligate ways.

I was just old enough to realise how quaint some of the villagers' customs were; one being the Sunday ritual when everyone took their lunch to be cooked in the huge ovens of the village baker, Bill Swain. When the two pubs (the Coffee Pot and the Packhorse) closed at two, the men of the village walked to the bakery to collect the metal trays that contained their cooked roasts. A small group of children always hung around the bakery at this time because Bill, a kindly fellow, gave the youngsters a crisp, savoury treat consisting of the strips of dough he had used to seal the oven doors. The children also enjoyed viewing the procession of their elders carrying the hot lunches, particularly those who had taken one drink too many. Icy pavements always produced scenes of pure slapstick – one slip and a man and his Sunday lunch sailed in different directions.

My evacuation to Yardley Gobion was timely. Within weeks a German bomber, on a night raid, scored a direct hit on Levita House, in a failed attempt to target the three big railway stations (Euston, St Pancras and King's Cross) near-by. As usual my mother had taken her nightly place in the underground station, but Tom, on leave from the RAF, was visiting Ron and me in Yardley – otherwise he would surely have been a casualty. My father was not so fortunate; he was in the flat and suffered severe injuries and shock, having been buried for several hours beneath rubble. His health had been poor for many years but thereafter he was a permanent invalid. The fatalities included ex-school friends of mine who had not been evacuated. Sad to say, looting took place, but the scavenger who picked over the meagre contents of our flat had some heart because he took only one of the two pound notes that were tucked away in case of an emergency.

Everyone in Yardley Gobion soon learnt about my family being 'bombed out' and I received a lot of sympathy, partic-ularly from my fellow pupils at the Church of England School. The school's usual complement was increased con-siderably by the arrival of various evacuees from as far away as Ipswich. The three teachers who made up the school's staff managed to control and educate their charges under difficult, cramped conditions. The headmaster, Mr Baker, left soon after I was enrolled but not before he made an indelible impression on my memory. I was not unduly forget-ful but, somehow or other, during my first week at the school I broke the golden rule and left my gas mask at the Hortons' cottage. That morning Mr Baker burst into our classroom shouting, 'Gas attack! Gas attack!' I realised instantly that I had forgotten my gas mask and my heart began pounding as I followed the rest of the children into the cloakroom. No one else had forgotten their gas masks and each child made straight for his or her peg where the protective item hung. I sprinted to my peg even though I was all too aware that it was empty. I remember thinking, 'I'm going to die,' and resignedly accepted the situation, determined not to let my classmates know I was terrified. I turned to face the headmaster to see if he had noticed I was the only one without a gas mask but he was looking fixedly at his wristwatch. With a loud sigh he said to the assembled children: 'You are just as slow as you were last week. You must get quicker.' The alert had simply been a test, a rehearsal for what could have been an enemy attack; my thoughts of impending death had been totally unnecessary. The incident didn't make me braver but it did impart a certain fatalism – and I never ever left my gas mask behind again.

Mr Baker was soon replaced by a temporary headmistress who in turn was superseded by a truly remarkable, unforgettable teacher, Eric Clayton Jones, a man who inspired every pupil he ever taught. By the time he arrived I had made friends with three local lads: Ron Allen, Malcolm Johnson and Geoffrey Brown. Each of us benefited from his eccentric but highly effective methods. His philosophy, 'Learning is Fun', certainly produced results: Geoff became a wing commander, Malcolm a successful designer and Ron a high ranking police officer. Through his own perpetual enthusiasm Mr Jones succeeded in getting his pupils to gain pleasure from literature, music, epic poems, fractions, gardening, history and life itself. Out of his own pocket he bought the *Children's Newspaper*, *National Geographic* and *Wide World*, undreamt of reading fare for a village school. His antennae always sensed the moment when children were about to get bored and to counter this he would suddenly abandon the lesson in hand and begin narrating a chapter from an adventure story (*The 39 Steps*, *Lorna Doone*, *Prester John*, *King Solomon's Mines*, etc)

Without ever revealing which party he supported he'd encourage us to think about and discuss politics (looking back I think he was more of a Liberal than a Socialist). Years before the average household possessed a telephone Mr Jones stressed that phones would become part of everyday life. Accordingly he would drive a small party of us to a call box in nearby Grafton Regis and from there we'd telephone the call box in Yardley and speak to our classmates. Perhaps his most startling achievement was in getting everyone, from juniors upwards, interested in listening to music (dwelling mainly on Beethoven, Bach, Mozart and Mendelssohn). He was a proficient violinist who spoke of Jascha Heifetz and the young Yehudi Menuhin with infectious enthusiasm; what he lacked in technique he made up for by being able to sing accurately an entirely different melody from the one he was playing – a rare gift.

Mr Jones and his wife regularly invited boys and girls from the school to visit their small holding at Old Stratford, some three miles from Yardley. There the couple grew all their own vegetables and their own tobacco. He loved bestowing nicknames on his pupils – as a result Ron Allen gained the mysterious sobriquet 'Knicky Knocker', Geoff Brown became 'Doc', Malcolm Johnson 'Morecambe' and me 'Tubby'; these nicknames were used in and out of the class-room. Mine was easily understandable because I was, once again, an overweight child. To be plump in those days was thought desirable by many country people who often used the expression, 'he looks fat and well.'

Mercifully Yardley Gobion was never the target for German raiders, though a landmine fell to earth in a field a couple of miles from the village. But if a reminder was needed that a violent conflict was still in progress, one only had to look towards London during one of the all too frequent night raids that the Capital suffered. From fifty miles away a red glow in the sky was easily visible, showing that the German incendiary bombs had done their searing, destructive work.

By the summer of 1942 many American servicemen drove through the village, and through the skies above in huge bomber aircraft. I witnessed a terrible drama involving two of these flying juggernauts. Mr Horton had suddenly been taken ill, and, as Yardley had no resident doctor, a physician was called from a nearby village. The medic wrote a prescription stressing that the patient was to take the medicine as soon as possible so this meant a journey to the nearest chemist (in Stony Stratford). Both of the Horton's sons were away so I was asked to take a bus into the town and to get the prescription dispensed before the chemist closed at 7 pm. This I did, but as there wasn't a bus back until 9 pm, and the situation was urgent, I started to walk the three miles back. It was a clear moonlit evening with every star visible, and as I neared a local landmark called the Three Beeches I could see for miles across the meadows. There on the distant horizon I saw two giant American planes seemingly on a collision course, totally unaware of each other. To my horror they met head on. The resultant explosion showered the sky with luminous patterns that resembled a grotesque firework display. Although I was well away from any of the flying particles I ran as fast as I could into Yardley. The cottage door had been left ajar and I tumbled in, shaking uncontrollably, startling Mrs Horton. 'Two planes have blown up,' was as far as I got before my trembling hands dropped the bottle of precious medicine which smashed instantly on the stone floor of the cottage. Fortunately Mr Horton soon recovered but no details of the calamity involving the two planes were ever reported in the newspapers, even though the explosion was heard for miles.

We children were given special holidays from school so that we could help the war effort by gathering in the grain harvest and assisting in picking up the crop of potatoes and mangel-wurzels – this last endeavour was to bring me woe. A machine churned the mangel-wurzels out of the ground and we youngsters followed on picking up the swede-like roots and throwing them on to a horse-drawn cart that moved between the furrows. One day I picked up a particularly large, rounded specimen, and to show off to my classmates I lifted it above my head, uttering the name 'Charles Atlas', a famous strong man of that era. I threw the root with all my might aiming it to drop into the half-full cart. I completely misjudged my own strength and the vegetable, weighing about two pounds, sailed high over the cart and out of sight. A split second later we heard an enormous groan, I ran round to the back of the cart and beheld a scene that resembled Arthur Devis' painting depicting the death of Nelson. There stretched out on a muddy furrow was the foreman of Charlie Weston's farm, one Mr Phillips. The weighty mangel-wurzel had hit him on the top of his head knocking him clean out. One of the farm labourers cradled Mr Phillips in his arms and mercifully the victim gradually came to his senses. His eyes flickered open as he said, with some feeling, 'Whoever threw that bloody mangel is sacked.' Thus ended my employment as a harvester. Many years later I became friends with Mr Phillips who never lost an opportunity to jovially remind me of the incident by saying, 'Here's the fellow who tried to knock some sense into me.'

Although I was barred from any further gathering in of mangel-wurzels I took part in rat catching for farmer Charlie Weston. Labourers were given the task of climbing on the top of wheat and flax ricks and pitchforking the sheaves into a threshing machine. Dozens of rats, who had spent months resting and nesting in the ricks, were suddenly exposed and leapt out of the ricks in a desperate attempt to find a new home.

To stop them getting away a fine wire mesh about three feet high was placed all around the rick-yard. The rats ran in circles desperately trying to find an escape route only to be met by a half-dozen of us youngsters armed with stout sticks intent on killing the swarming rodents. To stop myself feeling faint-hearted about this slaughter, I told myself that I was avenging the wanton carnage that had ended the lives of the prize chickens, but I discovered that the old adage about rats turning on their pursuers when cornered was all too true. One particularly big specimen realised I had trapped him and turned on me with eyes glinting and teeth showing. I lost my nerve and ran, and in an instant the rat had sunk its teeth into my thick sock. Mercifully one of the labourers got his pitchfork and in two swift movements knocked the rat off my leg and then speared it to death.

Charlie Weston, a celebrated ex-rugby player, then in his fifties, prided himself on toughness and agility, two qualities he demonstrated when it came to catching rats. He would squat on all fours with the rats circling him, and then, with lightning reaction he'd catch a rat by the tail as it ran near him. Then he would hold the wriggling creature against a large plank of wood while a labourer skewered the life out of it. I was fascinated by this amazing feat of hand-and-eye co-ordination but was never tempted to try it. We got three pence each for every dead rat we handed in at the end of a threshing session – the remains were counted and then fed to the pigs. By this time my mother was a fairly regular visitor to Yardley Gobion and I well remember her turning alarmingly pale when I acquainted her with this last detail.

One year (I think it was 1942) a terrible drought looked like decimating the grain harvest, and some of the village dignitaries, at the behest of local farmers, decided it was time for young and old to pray for rain. Accordingly we all gathered in the village church and fervently appealed for a downpour. Lo and behold, just as the congregation was leaving the church the heavens opened and a mighty deluge fell. I expected some kind of spontaneous celebration but instead I heard one farmer say grumpily to another, 'Too bloody late.' His comment helped me to understand why ordinary country folk believed that farmers were never satisfied.

In 1943 there was a positive lull in Germany's air attacks on Britain, so in July, during the school summer holidays, I went to London to visit my parents. I say London, but by then my mother and father (having been bombed out) were renting a semi-detached house in the suburb of Kenton, Middlesex. My brother Ron was with them, having left Yardley Gobion through economic necessity – the wages he could earn by starting work would help my parents' financial plight. He joined St. Clement's Press in London, thus put-ting his foot on the bottom rung of a ladder that eventually took him to being the chairman and chief executive of the vast conglomorate, IPC Magazines.

I had a happy summer with my family but, just as the stay was scheduled to end, I contracted hepatitis (then called yellow jaundice) and was admitted to St. Bartholomew's Hospital. I was quite seriously ill but gradually improved and was discharged by a doctor who said I needed clean country air. So I returned to Yardley in November 1943, but after being there for only a matter of days I was recalled to Kenton where my father's health had taken a distinct turn for the worse. He died in Edgware General Hospital on the 23rd of that month. He was a much loved if slightly distant figure, intelligent, lucid and kind, whose inability to follow a show business career never blighted his appreciation of talent. My mother, who had cared for him for so long, was terribly upset, but relieved that my health was improving.

After various examinations I was pronounced well enough to start at the local Claremont Avenue School, Kenton, in December 1943. I was grieving for my father and I missed my friends in Yardley. My diary of this period conveys a feeling of misery, noting that the Germans had resumed heavy bombing of the London area: 'Bad air raid, eight German planes shot down,' was a typical entry (from the 21st January 1944). Another was, 'London's Bourne Estate badly damaged, hundreds of incendiaries dropped,' and later, 'First daylight raid since July'. My mother viewed the worsening situation with alarm and decided it was time I returned to the safety of Yardley Gobion. So, in the spring of 1944, I again became a member of the Horton family. My departure meant I narrowly avoided the onslaught of the V1 flying bombs (doodlebugs) and the even more lethal V2 rockets.

During my absence from Yardley, a Wellington bomber manned by Canadian airmen had crashed very near to the village, killing all the crew. None of the villagers was injured but I returned to find them in deep grief. Yardley Gobion, like most other towns and villages throughout Britain, had its own Home Guard unit, and as an adjunct it was decided that an Army Cadet Corps for boys of twelve upwards be formed (one had to be seventeen to join the Home Guard). So, in 1944, together with several other lads from Yardley I went to a depot in Old Stratford to collect a khaki uniform. Our designated task was to act as messengers, but we were also taught to fire rifles and sten guns. The threat of a German invasion had passed but I later wondered if we youngsters would have been called into action, as the Hitler Youth Movement were, if the enemy had landed. In fact, no sooner had we been trained than the Home Guard disbanded, so we were not called to be part of the nation's defences. Our clique of lads went back to playing sport on the local recreation ground, some cricket but mostly soccer.

In the winter of 1944 we were due to play a school football team from Potterspury, but because of severe frost the pitch was unplayable. I returned home in a bad mood, angry and thwarted at not being able to take part in the match. I entered the Hortons' cottage and irritably flicked on the radio, just for something to do – and my life was changed forever. The music that came out of the radio literally entranced me, I had never heard anything like it before. I stood motionless until the piece ended; then I heard the radio announcer say, 'That was "I Thought I Heard Buddy Bolden Say", by Jelly Roll Morton, featuring Sidney Bechet.' This was my introduction to jazz. I fell in love with it there and then and went round asking everyone in the village what they knew about jazz and drew a series of blanks. However I did find out that a shop in Stony Stratford sold jazz records.

Next day was Saturday so I went there, found the shop

and immediately began quizzing the male assistant about jazz. There was no point in buying a record because no one I knew in the village possessed a gramophone. The assistant was very patient considering the absurd nature of my questions, but he eventually tapered off the interrogation by selling me, for one penny, a catalogue that listed all of the HMV recordings then available. I pored over it again and again, happy to see it contained a photograph of Sidney Bechet. I vowed that I would begin a jazz scrapbook as soon as possible, allocating first page prominence to Bechet. I began listening avidly to any radio programmes that might contain jazz, noting down the title of each piece as well as writing a brief critique of the performance. From this auto-didactic approach I came to the conclusion, without any guidance whatsoever, that Louis Armstrong was the supreme jazz musician – a viewpoint that I have never considered it necessary to change.

But compiling a scrapbook and analysing radio perform-ances didn't satisfy an urge that began blazing within me – I felt that to get closer to the world of jazz I had to play an instrument. As soon as Mr Horton heard me say I wanted to play a musical instrument he and his wife put down the money for a secondhand cornet on the proviso that I pay them back at sixpence a week – a strategy that would encour-age me to make regular use of the instrument. Despite his former prowess, Mr Horton couldn't demonstrate for my benefit. Sadly he could no longer play the cornet, having lost all of his front teeth in a bizarre accident. In earlier days musicians of the Yardley band had organised an annual hundred-yard race in which each entrant had to continue to play a coherent melody throughout the sprint, the winner being given a bucket of beer as the prize. One year, during the race, another musician had stopped abruptly in front of Mr Horton, the bell of whose cornet disastrously hit the man's brawny back with such force that it knocked out four of Mr Horton's front teeth and finished, forever, his music making.

Because of the long tradition of Yardley Gobion's prize brass band, almost everyone in the village, male and female, had some knowledge of brass playing, so I didn't want for advice and encouragement. A neighbour gave me a basic tutor book and someone else gifted me a mouthpiece. Mr Horton gave me guidance. Both his sons had played briefly without developing a passion for music; nevertheless they too urged me on, and in a sympathetic atmosphere I would sit at the kitchen table practising the cornet while the rest of the family sat nearby reading their newspapers. No one was more delighted to hear of my involvement with the cornet than Eric Clayton Jones. His practice of abruptly stopping a lesson to read to us was now occasionally supplemented by him saying, 'Tubby, go home and get your cornet so that you can give us a tune.' It was all marvellously encouraging.

3

National Service

In May 1945 Yardley Gobion, like everywhere else in Britain, celebrated VE Day, marking the end of World War Two in Europe, but for me and several school chums the day nearly turned into a catastrophe. One of the lads had been to Whittlebury Woods seeking moorhens' eggs and found, to his surprise, that the guardposts, usually manned by soldiers of the King's Royal Rifles, were all empty. He looked into a tent and saw a stack of small canvas bags in which there were foot-long sticks of a substance that looked like solidified glue. Out of curiosity and mischievousness he brought a couple of bags back to Yardley where he met up with a few of us idling on the village green. He showed us his find, but none of us had any idea what we were handling though one boy suggested they might be something used to light fires when the soldiers were on patrol.

Equipped with a box of matches we went down to the Grand Union Canal, a few hundred yards away, to test this theory. Something told us that we should stand back a distance after the stick had been lit, but even so we were totally surprised by the loudness of the resulting bang. We still hadn't realised that we were playing with highly dangerous explosive fuses. We became excited by the power we had at hand and a spirit of recklessness took over. Using several sticks tied together we blew a tree stump out of the ground. I picked up a stick, lit it, and attempted to throw it into the hedgerow, but I was slow in letting go and as a result was blown sideways as it exploded in the air a few yards from where I stood. I wasn't hurt but I was completely deaf in one ear for a week. My foolishness cooled everyone else's daring and the few sticks remaining were thrown into the canal. All of us involved kept the affair secret, and somehow I managed to hide my temporary deafness.

The end of the war meant I would soon be leaving Yardley to return to Kenton, but before my departure, together with almost everyone in the village, I attended a victory celebration dance held in the school on Saturday 19th May 1945. A local dance band was doing a satisfactory job but some of my friends kept calling on me to perform a number. I was cajoled into playing, secretly pleased that I would have the chance to show off in front of a classroom sweetheart. If I had known that I was going to play at the dance I would have brought my cornet. Instead I was persuaded to borrow a trumpet and a mouthpiece from a member of the band. This was a mistake, as a trumpet mouthpiece is much larger than that of a cornet and I found it extremely uncomfortable when I tried blowing into it. It was like attempting to run fast in boots that were four sizes too big. As a result I couldn't find the starting note for a piece called 'There Goes That Song Again' and had to play a scale to get my musical bearings. As almost everyone present knew about playing brass instruments, hearing me undertake such an elementary move caused several people to laugh out loud. Scarlet-faced I managed to struggle through the tune, but the experience made me apprehensive about playing in public for a long time afterwards.

A few days later, I packed my bags and said goodbye to my school friends, to Mr Jones, the villagers and the Horton family. I promised that I would never forget them, which turned out to be true, and I said I would often return to Yardley Gobion, which was also an accurate pledge. Just before I left them, Mr and Mrs Horton gave me back all the sixpences I had paid them as instalments on the cornet – a typically kind gesture. So, with my cornet and my jazz scrapbook in my suitcase I arrived in Kenton and was given the warmest of welcomes by my mother and brother Ron. Tom, demobilised from the RAF had married a Scottish ex-WAAF, Ina, and was about to start a family. Within a week I was back at Claremont School. This time my stay was a happy one and I soon dropped in with a football and cricketing crowd, who also loved going to the cinema, cycling and larking about with girls.

None of my immediate circle was interested in jazz. In this respect they were like most teenagers of that era, but I was able to listen to my jazz records at home on a wind-up gramophone, playing the discs over and over again in the hope that family and neighbours would be converted. But sport was also a big factor in my life and I was filled with admiration for Denis Compton's triumphs at cricket and soccer. He lived close by in Kenton and one day I bumped into him – literally. I was out on my bicycle and carelessly turned into the middle of the road without looking, straight into the path of an oncoming car. The driver immediately jumped out to check on my state of health. I wasn't hurt, just shaken, but as soon as I saw that the motorist was Denis Compton I was on my feet and asking for his autograph.

I thoroughly deserved the angry look he gave me, but he didn't refuse to sign. A few weeks later I enjoyed meeting another two all-time heroes of mine at a charity cricket match: the comic actor Will Hay (whose films still give me pleasure) and the great West Indian cricketing all-rounder Learie (later Sir Learie) Constantine.

During the Easter 1946 school break I revisited Yardley Gobion and was taken by Mr Horton to see my first game of professional football. It was a match between Northampton Town and Walsall. Sadly the home team lost 4–1, but in spite of the score line I sided with Northampton Town and ever after always checked their results and followed their progress. Mr Horton was disappointed that I hadn't brought my cornet with me. He had hoped to check on my progress, but if truth be known I had got out of the habit of regular practice and without tutoring I had made no headway. Most of my thoughts were connected to the fact that I was soon to leave school (at fourteen) to start work.

Happily my school reports had been good and through brother Ron's efforts I was granted an interview for a junior post at St. Clement's Press. As a result, one morning in August 1946 I travelled by underground to Holborn station and walked to the offices where I was due to meet Mr Levin, the director of staff. Ron had stressed that I must appear confident and polite – I was to make sure I gave a firm hand-shake. A secretary ushered me into Mr Levin's office and said he would soon be with me. The door opened and in walked a suited figure. I jumped up and pumped the man's hand and asked if he had a pleasant journey. He looked total-ly confused, and he had every right to be, for he was not Mr Levin – he was a mechanic there to service the typewriters. Mr Levin entered just as the muddle occurred. I had stepped off on the wrong foot, but I settled down and got through the interview without further mishap, and stayed with the company for a couple for years.

My tasks at St. Clement's Press were not intellectually taxing. I was the office boy in the order department. My main jobs were to keep everyone supplied with cups of tea and to deliver printing blocks, layouts, proofs and incoming mail to various departments. During the course of a day I usually visited most departments within the big building. I was happiest when calling on the girls in the typing pool, but less keen to visit the foundry, where metallic dust from the blend of lead, tin and antimony (used for making printing plates) hung in the air from one day to the next. As I was some years younger than most of the people I worked with, I soon learnt a lot about the ways of the world.

I was fascinated by the recollections of the company's uni-formed messenger, an ex-serviceman, then in his seventies. He had taken part in one of the last charges of the Bengal Lancers and had many intriguing tales about his days on India's North-West Frontier. His anecdotes usually set the ball rolling for others on the staff who had recently been demobilised from the services and they chipped in with their lively and revealing tales of battles and brothels.

I enjoyed listening to these reminiscences but as the months went by I grew restless with my unvarying work routine. After a meeting with the manager I was given the chance to serve an apprenticeship as a colour engraver, at that time regarded as the elite of printing production staff. Numerous co-workers assured me that this was the chance of a lifetime, but the prospect of serving a five-year apprenticeship on very low money (even if it led to high wages eventually) had no appeal to me. As ever, my mother was quite prepared to make all sorts of sacrifices to enable me to follow up the offer, but I was certain I didn't want to accept it. I burnt my boats at St. Clement's by deciding not to take the job and, with my mother's approval, left to begin looking for a new employer.

Within a week I had successfully responded to a newspaper advertisement that detailed a vacancy within the media department of Samson Clark and Company, an advertising agency situated near Oxford Circus. It was an old established London firm, with a forbidding bust of its late founder, Samson Clark, grimly surveying the entrance hall. The company's chief clients were Aspro (a leading brand of analgesic) and Ilford (the photographic specialists) with sundry other accounts ranging from banana importers to aeroplane manufacturers. Advertisements for these clients were booked by the media department, whose task was to make the maximum impact on the client's potential customers while remaining within a budget – the agency made its money by collecting commission from the publications in which it had booked space. I quickly learnt to type and gradually gained a broad knowledge of many periodicals and newspapers, all of whom were keen to attract advertisers.

My love of jazz was as strong as ever, but I was disappointed that I hadn't linked up with any fellow enthusiasts. This changed on the day I heard a junior staff member whistling a melody that I instantly recognised. I didn't know the fellow but I went straight up to him and said, 'That's "Jazz Me Blues".' He confirmed that I was right and we were instantly in accord and talking collectors' jargon about various records we both owned. He went on to say that one of the young printers not only collected jazz records but also visited jazz clubs to hear the music played live. Jazz venues flourished in London cellars and in provincial pubs, but I was too young to visit those that were held in licensed premises. However the young printer pointed out that the London Jazz Club at 100 Oxford Street was not then licensed so there would be no problems about gaining admission. He introduced me to that celebrated basement where one could either listen or dance; I chose the former pleasure and sat entranced as I soaked up the sounds of live jazz. Soon afterwards, when I reached sixteen, I visited the Cook's Ferry Inn in north London. I became a regular at both clubs and caught the last train home with exciting music ringing in my ears. I greatly admired Humphrey Lyttelton's trumpet playing (his band appeared regularly at the London Jazz Club) and watched his fingers closely as he played so that I could ascertain which key the band was in. When I told Humph about this years later he remarked in typically droll fashion, 'In those days the speed of my fingering would have allowed you plenty of time.'

I joined a local youth club in Kenton and, between playing table tennis and learning to dance, I did my best to propagate the jazz gospel by trying to get the members interested in Bessie Smith's recordings. This led to one youth saying he had a clarinet that he was attempting to play; a keen pianist joined the conversation and said he knew a drummer, and before many minutes had elapsed we had formed the basis of a band, soon to be augmented by the inclusion of a talented girl alto saxophonist. By January 1949 we were struggling our way through arrangements of 'Ballin' the Jack' and 'A Slow Boat to China'. My colleagues were more interested in dance music than traditional jazz but the mutual keenness smoothed over any dissension. After some months of diligent rehearsal we played our first engagement (as the Swingtette) at a youth club dance; by this time I was playing trumpet and not cornet. We hadn't given a thought to timing our programme so by the time the interval came we had used up our entire repertoire. The group had no leader, so, at the start of the second half I was pushed forward to announce that we had been asked to repeat the first half of our programme for the benefit of latecomers. The kind audience allowed us to get away with this transparent ploy and even forgave our muddled improvisations on numbers like 'At The Jazz Band Ball'. Amazingly, we built up a small coterie of devotees and during that year a party of us went to the London Palladium to hear the great American clarinettist, Benny Goodman. My interest in jazz was burning as brightly as ever and I devoured every mention of it and every moment its sounds were broadcast.

During my lunch-hour I hurried from Samson Clark's to Bron's Orchestral Service in Oxford Street and pored over their huge stock of band arrangements, frustrated that I could only afford to buy one a week. I furthered my deep interest in Jelly Roll Morton's music by buying *Volume One* of his compositions. Then, after staying up all night copying the themes out (these were pre-photocopying days), I went back next day and said I had bought the wrong volume. They kindly allowed me to swap it for *Volume Two*. When I wasn't at Bron's I was visiting Imhof's, a big record store in New Oxford Street. In those days most record shops allowed potential customers a trial hearing of a 78 rpm recording. Nevertheless the assistants at Imhof's must have groaned when they saw me. I bought one record per visit but managed to listen to at least ten sides before I made up my mind.

I continued to list in my diary every jazz record I heard – with a single-mindedness that made my pals chuckle. The girlfriends I had were invariably daunted by the sweaty atmosphere of jazz clubs. Some half-pretended to like the music but were happier going to big, perfumed dance halls – invariably we soon parted company. I remember being total- ly carried away by my first hearing of records featuring the combined talents of Sidney Bechet and Wild Bill Davison. When the radio programme that featured these scorching items ended I came out of my trance and realised that I should have been two miles away, at the Kingsbury Odeon, meeting a girl that I really liked. She waited for my arrival but left as soon as she had given me a well-deserved dressing- down for my selfishness.

Not long after that incident I linked up with someone who was interested in, and tolerant about, my obsession with jazz. Mary, an attractive receptionist at Samson Clark's, was three years older than me. I had seen her every day since I began working there, but soon after she broke off an engage- ment we started going out together regularly and were soon spending every spare minute with one another, much of the time listening to jazz.

The only shadow that loomed was National Service. Like other young men of eighteen I was due to be called up. I passed the compulsory medical examination and applied to join the Royal Air Force; I was told to expect my call-up within three months. My employers at Samson Clark's were used to having their young male staff drafted into the forces and duly outlined their obligation to employ me for at least six months after I had completed my two years service. Joining up meant leaving an affectionate home atmosphere, shared with my mother and brother Ron (who had completed his National Service in the army). I was also unhappy at the prospect of being away from Mary for a long period. I got no joy from being told by several ex-servicemen I worked with (most of whom had served for at least five years during World War Two) that two years would pass quickly.

On 9th November 1950 I followed the instructions sent to me by post and got aboard a train leaving London for Padgate, near Liverpool, an RAF arrival centre for new recruits. Five forlorn young men sat in the carriage making it obvious that the journey north had no appeal. The sixth occupant was by contrast very bright and breezy, an instantly friendly person who was soon asking each of us that we did for a living, where we came from, had we ever been away from our families before? He introduced himself as Arnold Wesker, but said he was more generally known as 'Wizzy'. He was a memorably pleasant fellow who later shaped his RAF experiences into a wonderful play, *Chips With Everything*, one of his numerous dramatic successes.

We got off the train at Warrington and marched, or rather shuffled through the wintry streets to Padgate where we were split into 'flights' consisting of twenty-four new recruits. We were allocated bed space in cold huts that soon became stiflingly hot when the furnace-like coke stoves in the centre of the hut were lit. After a week, during which we were kitted out in uniforms, overcoats and boots, we were put aboard a train that took us to RAF Hednesford, a bleak unit situated near Cannock Chase in the Midlands. There we did six weeks of square-bashing: marching, clambering over assault courses, firing rifles, bayoneting effigies and learning to put a glassy shine on our stout boots. A good spirit developed within the flight as Geordies, Welshmen, Yorkshiremen and Cockneys gradually began to understand accents that they had never encountered before. When the

square-bashing ended we all went in different directions
to practise the trade we had been allocated: I became a
clerk-typist. All of us waited anxiously to see to where we
had been posted. Rumours, virulent in every branch of every
service, kept sweeping through the ranks, one of them outlining a mass posting to Korea, then a war zone for British
forces. This proved false and instead I found myself bound
for RAF Creden Hill, near Hereford, where I was to learn
RAF administration and how to speed up my typewriting.
Despite whistling a wide selection of jazz tunes, in the hope
that someone would home in on the signal, I failed to uncov-
er a single jazz fan at Creden Hill, so I devoted myself to
playing football for the station team. As a result I witnessed
an amazing sight.

One wet afternoon we were playing another service team
on a pitch that was close to a steep Herefordshire hill.
Suddenly the sun came out and with it a resplendent rainbow
which, to our intense surprise, settled its end on the football
pitch. We were all so flabbergasted we stopped playing; it
was a fantastic sight, one that disappeared after about thirty
seconds. We resumed the match but everyone on the pitch,
including the referee, moved about aimlessly, overwhelmed
by what we had seen. An onlooker said we played a second
half lasting only twenty-five minutes instead of forty-five. If
we did, nobody cared. Our biggest problem was convincing
people who had not been at the match of what we had seen.

After six weeks' training we were all on the move again,
this time to our permanent postings – the journey took
me to RAF Mildenhall in Suffolk. There I became part of a
unit that numbered about two hundred, co-existing alongside two thousand American servicemen. Mildenhall was
virtually a United States Air Force base, the home for many

huge aircraft, all of them on standby to fly eastwards to Russia (the Cold War was then at its iciest) loaded with atomic bombs. Being attached to an American base had its advantages, allowing us to use all the entertainments facilities, including seeing various touring shows flown direct from the USA. We could also use their really fine library, and (via American friends) shop at the PX store, buying commodities that were not being imported for the UK market.

At this stage of my life I foolishly thought that every American was a jazz devotee, but after striking up conversations on this subject with the US personnel at Mildenhall I soon became convinced otherwise. Even the African-American servicemen weren't interested, and when I met several airmen from New Orleans who didn't recognise any of the illustrious names of various jazz giants from Louisiana, I realised that the average American didn't regard jazz with much affection or interest. Various shows that crossed the Atlantic to entertain the servicemen naturally got a good reception but, of all the acts I saw at Mildenhall, the one that produced the wildest acclaim was a British one. Because of flight delays an American troupe had failed to arrive on time so a British 'variety bill' was hastily assembled to take their place. The various artistes did their best but the GIs couldn't hide their boredom, but one unlikely act proved to be an absolute sensation.

It consisted of two burly men, both past their physical prime, one clad in a leopard skin, the other in a dark military uniform topped off with a Prussian spiked steel helmet. The leopard-man proceeded to lift a gigantic wooden cartwheel before hurling it across the stage where his partner skilfully manoeuvred his head and caught the wheel on his helmet spike. It was a brave act because the wheel was huge and

heavy and it whirled through the air at high speed. The audience, previously unmoved by a succession of Britishers imitating American performers, were transformed – they had
never seen anything like it. A roar of appreciation developed
into loud calls for an encore. The small British contingent in
the audience, having seen similar strong-men acts on the
music halls, simply clapped politely. The two performers,
their faces flushed, came back on-stage and, in line with the
response, repeated their energetic feat. The audience react-
ed frantically yelling for yet another encore. The two performers exchanged confused glances and one could see that
the wheel-catcher's knees were buckling in the manner of an
outclassed boxer. Nevertheless hysteria won the day and
after the highest throw yet, the wheel hit the helmet with an
enormous clunk. But the triple routine proved too much for
the catcher and he sank to his knees, dribbling and groaning.
Three other members of the show ran on-stage and carried
the valiant one into the wings while the compere spun some
ancient jokes. Happily the catcher soon recovered and tottered on-stage with his sidekick to take a wobbly bow. I have
never heard such applause, even tough master sergeants, well
battle-hardened cheered the groggy stalwart. I am certain
that the act never had a better reception.

One bonus at Mildenhall had nothing to do with the
Americans. Most of the twenty or so RAF officers stationed
there were pilots who had been reclassified as office personnel. However, if they flew a plane for so many hours a month
they could still qualify for certain aircrew allowances. When
they left their desks to take part in these flights they often
offered us National Servicemen the chance of accompanying
them. It made a thrilling break from office routines suddenly to be called from one's typewriter to fly to an air base on

the other side of the country. My first ever flight was on one of these jaunts in a small one-engined plane that banked and turned with a grace that I always missed on later flights aboard giant airliners.

On most weekends the British airmen at Mildenhall were granted brief leave, usually a thirty-six or forty-eight hour pass, but as there was no convenient rail link with London most of us hitch-hiked there via Newmarket and Baldock. There was a great deal of jockeying for position and sometimes it was advantageous to thumb a lift in the opposite direction (away from London) in an attempt to be first in the queue. On one journey two of us felt lucky because we picked up a lift just outside the camp gates. The driver had been delivering meat to the service kitchens. He explained to us that the only space available for us was in the back of the refrigerated van – company rules forbade the carrying of passengers in the driver's cabin.

As we only wanted to get on to the main road (a journey of a few minutes) we readily agreed to his offer and climbed into the back of the van which the driver locked from the outside. After a couple of minutes the vehicle halted and we waited expectantly to be released from the frosty enclosure, but there was no sign of the driver and tiny icicles began to form on the rough serge of our uniforms. We soon began to feel very cold indeed and started banging on the metal doors, shouting as loudly as we could, but there was no response and the temperature continued to drop. We were close to panicking when the metal locking-rods were emphatically drawn back. The doors opened and the driver's worried face peered in, I think he expected to see two carcasses decked out in RAF uniform. He apologised profusely, saying that he had stopped to buy some chocolate and then decided to have a cup of tea, totally forgetting about his cargo. He was shaking with fright and we were shaking with hypothermia. We tumbled out of the freezing van into warm sunshine. The driver promised he would get us to the main road in three minutes but we unhesitatingly turned him down and began a stiff-legged walk towards the highway.

This experience made me reluctant to thumb any commercial vehicles but I carried on hitch-hiking until the day I saw a big, luxurious car climbing over the crest of a hill, moving steadily towards me. It looked a good prospect as only one figure was silhouetted through the wide glass windows. I thumbed enthusiastically and continued to do so until the vehicle drew level with me. I then realised that there were two occupants, but one of them was in a coffin, I had been thumbing a hearse. The driver looked daggers at me and I realised that it was time for me to start wearing spectacles.

Two of my fellow airmen at Mildenhall were devoted jazz fans, and both played instruments. One was a banjoist, the other a trumpeter named Terry Marsh who later became a Hollywood producer. The three of us brought our instruments back to camp and enjoyed taking part in jam sessions held in an echoey outhouse. This impromptu music-making paid dividends as somehow word of these get-togethers reached a personnel officer at the very time that RAF Ruislip, close to London, wanted to add musicians to a newly formed marching band. The unit also needed clerk-typists so I was posted to Ruislip. It was a lucky break because National Servicemen were rarely given the chance to play in RAF bands. Usually the personnel consisted of airmen who had signed on for at least three years but in my case a compromise was reached by my being a part-time member of the station band and a part-time clerk-typist.

4

Fleet Street to Swing Street

At RAF Ruislip I reported as instructed to the sergeant in charge of the newly formed band. I duly gave my name and service number and explained why I was there. He asked me what instrument I played and when I told him it was the trumpet he let out a hollow laugh and said, 'I think you're too late, lots of trumpeters have already arrived.' Seeing how crestfallen I was, he said by way of consolation, 'I've got a good idea. There's a vacancy for a trombonist, you could fill that.' I told him quite truthfully that I could not play the trombone, but he cheerfully brushed this information aside. 'Well, have a try. I'll arrange for you to draw one from the instrument store and while you're learning you can be a reserve trumpeter, on standby in case of illness.' This seemed to be a ridiculously impractical solution but as I had set my heart on the posting I went along with his idea and borrowed an RAF trombone.

I took it home to Kenton (only a few miles from Ruislip) and attempted to blow scales and exercises when I went there at weekends. It was no use. The more I blew the trombone the worse I played the trumpet, the difference in mouthpiece sizes played havoc with my embouchure. I despaired, but my old school chum, Boz Marsden, said he had always wanted to play trombone so I loaned the instrument to him and was pleased to observe his rapid progress (he eventually became a professional musician). Whenever the sergeant asked me how I was getting on I simply gave him the thumbs-up sign and this seemed to satisfy him. When I was eventually posted from Ruislip I handed the trombone back to him reflecting that he had never heard me play a note on it.

I was occasionally called on to deputise in the band but most of my time was spent working as a typist in the Medical Statistics Section. This involved transferring service doctors' notes on to large index cards, all the while learning dozens of medical terms and boggling at the bizarre nature of some of the cases. None was odder than that of a young pilot officer who was convinced that no matter how often he bathed he continually gave off a disgusting body odour that was stifling him. The examining doctor could not detect anything offensive about the man's perspiration, a view shared by a second doctor and two nurses. Nevertheless, the patient gradually became increasingly distraught and finally ended his life by jumping in front of a bus.

Deep in the recesses of the Air Ministry someone decided that the Medical Statistics Section was overstaffed. As a result, various of my colleagues there were posted to other units, and when it was ascertained that I had not actually joined the band on a regular basis I knew I would soon be on the move. As I waited with some trepidation for news of an unwelcome posting I received a 'Dear John' letter from Mary, explaining that she had found someone new and wanted to end our relationship. The sudden cessation of my first love

affair left me despondent, and no sooner had I read the letter than I received news that I had been posted to a tiny
RAF unit on the outskirts of Norwich. I was being sent
there to assist a veteran wing commander in the setting up
of an RAF recruiting office. But despite the wing commander's lectures at colleges and youth clubs and various press
advertisements, never once did anyone even pop a head
round the door to ask for details of a service career. As a
result I had very little to do and, with the officer's permission, I sat and read, or went over to the NAAFI hut and
tried to improve my limited piano technique.

The wing commander was a capable classical pianist and
liked to discuss music; he felt sympathetic that I had been
posted to a unit where my trumpet playing was not being
used and promised that he would try to do something about
this. He must have had influence with old pals because within a month I was posted to RAF Kenley in Surrey where I
took on the newly created post of ceremonial trumpeter for
Number Three Group (which covered a good deal of South-
East England). I was also to work as a part-time clerk typist
in the group physical fitness office, which was housed in a
big mansion on the edge of the airfield. The group physical
fitness officer was also the station physical fitness officer,
which meant he had to send memos to himself. I had to suppress a grin when, as sometimes happened, he wrote to himself asking, 'Do you agree?' and then responded with a 'No.'
As at Mildenhall, there were lots of opportunities to fly as
passenger with officers getting in 'airtime'.

As a ceremonial trumpeter I was allowed to wear a musical lyre on my sleeve just below my senior aircraftsman
badge. I was also issued with regalia consisting of tassels and
braid, to be worn on special occasions; but, because the post

was a new one, no one seemed interested in establishing a working schedule. However, my daily task was to play some set calls on the parade ground as the flag was hoisted in the morning. Happily, nobody mentioned playing for the lowering of the flag at night and most importantly (for me) I did not have to sound reveille. My main job was to play bugle-like calls welcoming various visiting dignitaries.

Carrying out this function led me to an embarrassing moment when an eminent air marshal flew into RAF Kenley. Together with a large number of airmen, who formed the guard of honour, I had spent hours rehearsing on the airfield, with everything timed to the second. I was placed some fifteen yards ahead of the guard of honour, and, as the high-ranking officer stepped down from the aircraft, my task was to begin blowing an appropriate salute which would be the signal for them to present arms. It was a bright winter's day but an icy breeze made me shiver and I began to feel ill at ease. My agitation trebled when, out of the corner of my eye, I saw the visitor's plane flying in to land. It seemed to be coming straight at me – I reasoned that because I was so far in front of the guard of honour the pilot hadn't seen me. I was terrified but knew that I would probably be court-martialled if I abandoned my position. The panic was over in a few seconds, the plane landed at least thirty yards from where I stood, the aeroplane's door opened and steps were lowered for the great man to climb down.

A figure emerged into bright sunlight and began descending the steps. Despite still feeling uneasy I hit my note loud and clear and immediately all of the armed personnel present smacked their hands against the butts of their rifles in perfect unison. It was then that I realised that the emerging figure was not the air marshal; it was in fact a humble airman in denims, who was making extra sure that the steps were securely in place. He looked absolutely startled by the spectacular welcome. To his credit the big chief hurried forward and was soon only a couple of paces behind the airman. Even so, all those present were acutely aware that there had been a cock-up. The air marshal strode over to inspect the guard of honour. Then, changing his mind, he walked over to where I stood and gave me the broadest of winks. Somehow I escaped a reprimand.

At RAF Kenley the barrack block I lived in housed a cross-section of airmen whose trades ranged from cooks to armourers and from clerks to cleaners. One lad was an admin-orderly whose job was to make sure the officers were supplied with refreshments throughout the day and to run errands for them. One of these officers was a squadron leader who was the group psychiatrist. In a session of shared barrack-room gossip the orderly remarked that this officer's daily routine was to fill his blotting-paper pad with dozens of drawings of banjos. Most of us were only marginally interested in this tale of random doodlings but our curiosity moved up several notches when the lad told us of a new development. Just as he entered the squadron leader's office a window had slammed, breaking the glass. The officer hurriedly crossed the room to examine the damage and in doing so he didn't have time to finish the drawings on his blotting pad. The orderly put the cup of tea on the desk, not before noticing that all of the drawings were of male genitalia – the psychiatrist had not had time to add the strings and tuning keys of a banjo.

Because Kenley was so close to London I was able to keep in touch with various musicians I had known in Kenton and we decided to throw caution to wind and form an out-and-out jazz band, which in a burst of unashamed corniness we named the Sportstown Syncopators (we all lived near Wembley Stadium). I did not have time to get to Kenton and back before 'lights out' so we rehearsed in the King's Cross area.

At about this time I successfully applied for an RAF grant to attend the Central School of Dance Music (near Charing Cross Road). There I studied with an ex-Ambrose star, the Canadian trumpeter Alfie Noakes. He was a fine player and a pleasant man but the teaching system at this school used assembly line methods: every pupil jumped through the same hoops in the same order. Later I benefited more by studying independently with Freddy Staff.

The officers at RAF Kenley were helpful in allowing me to take time off to attend classes, but I saw one instance where an officer was abominably cruel and spiteful to a veteran airman who was in the final stages of twenty-one years service. This man proudly boasted that during his entire stay in the RAF he had never been charged (or even reprimanded) for a misdemeanour. If he told us this once, he told us a thousand times and eventually everyone on the station including the officers got to hear of this remarkable achievement. He was not the brightest of fellows but he had memorised the King's Regulations (the book of service rules) and lived by them, also demonstrating his perpetual keenness by avidly polishing his buttons and boots as well as blancoing his webbing every day. He was within days of his release when a sadistic officer put him on a charge for having hair that was too long – despite the fact that the airman always sported a crew cut, winter or summer. The poor fellow, then in his early forties, broke down and wept as he was given chores in the cookhouse as punishment. A week later he left the RAF and, despite our genuine sympathy, he went without saying goodbye to any of us. He was heartbroken. His departure set off a behavioural change in another long-term regular, a proud but rather shy Scotsman called John.

One morning, everyone in the barrack-room arose as usual – all except John. He lay as if sleeping and despite being called by his pals he made no effort to get out of bed. An inspection was due that morning so it was important that he was soon up and about. A close mate cheerfully lifted John but he simply sat silently on his bed, appearing perplexed when anything was said to him. Finally he spoke a simple sentence in French, 'Je m'appelle Jean.' To our amazement he repeated this over and over again, accompanying his pronouncement by a shrugging of his shoulders, Gallic fashion. The inspecting officer duly arrived and John continued to enunciate his short message. The young flying officer then called on the orderly sergeant to take John to the medical officer, who in turn couldn't get any sense out of the francophone airman. He returned to the barrack-room and went on airing his simple phrase for the next month, during which time he went before one medical board after another. No one could crack the carapace that John had put around himself and eventually he was discharged from the RAF. None of us expected to see him again but a year later I was playing a gig in London at the Nuffield Centre in Adelaide Street (an establishment that catered mostly for ex-servicemen) and there I saw the 'Frenchman'. He immediately addressed me in a broad Scottish accent, explaining, 'I didn't like what they did to yon fellow so I thought I'd be on my way.' I never saw him again but remain impressed by the way he 'worked his ticket' and sidestepped a further five years service by temporarily changing nationality.

On the morning of my last day of two years' National
Service I blew up the flag for the final time, but instead of
the usual martial phrases I played a brief excerpt from Louis
Armstrong's solo on 'Potato Head Blues' – and lived to tell
the tale.

It was now time for me to take advantage of my re-
employment rights and return to Samson Clark's advertising
agency. I didn't rejoin the media department, but instead
became a personal assistant to one of the directors, a sour
middle-aged woman whose principal task was to placate the
manufacturers of Aspro. The slightest frown on the face of
any of that product's executives caused pandemonium in
Miss Thomas' office and a great deal of kowtowing took
place. When customers wrote in and praised Aspro they
were immediately rewarded with a large box of free samples
of the product. One of my jobs was to open the incoming
mail and I soon came to the conclusion that some of these
testimonials were fakes, written to get the gift packets. One
letter-writer said that he was an ordinary snooker player
before he took Aspro and now he was the club champion.
Naturally he was rewarded, as was the man who said he
always had to wear two overcoats in winter but since taking
Aspro he only needed one. When I suggested that people
were taking advantage of the company's generosity my comments were taken as high treason, causing a rift that soon
widened between me and Miss Thomas.

Mary, my former girlfriend, was still the firm's receptionist and although we never resumed a close relationship she
always took a keen interest in my musical progress and
encouraged me to think about playing music for a living. But
becoming full-time was easier said than done because most
jazz bands were, in the early 1950s, semi-professional, their

members holding down day jobs. One might be able to find full-time work in palais dance bands, in night club groups or touring with big bands, but I was still primarily interested in improvising jazz rather than in being part of more formal ensembles. Meanwhile, I became increasingly dissatisfied about working at the agency and successfully answered an advertisement to fill a vacancy at the *Daily Telegraph* (then in Fleet Street).

My new job was to help Bill Nichol, a veteran of the company, to ascertain who wrote every word that appeared in each issue of the *Daily Telegraph*. Every morning I collected a satchel containing all the copy used in that day's issue, then, by liaising with the news editor, the foreign editor, the women's page editor, the sports editor, and so on, we were able to mark up an issue with the names of everyone who had contributed to it, including staff reporters and freelance writers. If any reader had a query we could soon locate the relevant piece of copy to see if a mistake had been made. We kept each day's copy separately in huge manilla folders, the contents of which were thrown away after a year. I still regret that I did not retain various proofs that were hand-corrected by famous contributors, ranging from authors to actors and politicians. I'll never forget filing Sir Winston Churchill's handwritten amendments to an article he wrote for the leader page in the mid–1950s. It had originally been typed on handmade paper and then corrected by the author. Had I taken the Churchill item home after a year had passed it would not have been destroyed. At the time I thought it would have been dishonest to do so but I've regretted ever since my failure to preserve it.

When I joined the *Telegraph* there were still a few ex-members of the *Morning Post* on the staff (the two newspapers had amalgamated in 1937). Most of them were reporters of the 'old school', still dressed in the same manner as they were on the day of the takeover. Nevertheless they had a fund of anecdotes from yesteryear which, because of the climate of the time, were never published. One concerned the great African-American boxer Jack Johnson who, on emerging from the swing doors at the riverside exit of the Savoy Hotel, took one look at the large assembly of reporters (many of whom had been highly critical of his previous conduct) and bellowed, 'Out of my way white trash!' A path cleared for him immediately. The story reminded me of a small adventure involving my brother Tom who, as a schoolboy, waited at the same spot for hours to get an autograph from the film star cowboy, Tom Mix. Finally the great man emerged to be confronted by my brother, autograph book in hand, but all he got was a drawled couple of sentences from the Hollywood hero who said, 'Can't help you son. I'm in a powerful hurry.'

Once a week we collected a batch of advance proofs for the crossword puzzles that would soon appear in the paper. We filed them immediately, knowing that there was rarely a query about their contents, but Bill Nichol occasionally fished one out so that he could play a practical joke on his fellow commuters travelling to work in London. He would copy out the crossword answers for the next day's puzzle and learn them by heart. Next morning he would take his seat on the London train, then open up his copy of the *Telegraph* and proceed to complete the crossword puzzle in under two minutes, filling in the squares with a flourish that caused his fellow passengers to look on in wonderment. A few weeks later he would try the same stunt in a different carriage.

One perk that came my way (via Frank Coles, the sports

editor) was a set of tickets for the 1954 World Cup soccer games held in Switzerland. One match I went to was in Basle, between Scotland and Uruguay, a poorly attended fixture held on a warm evening: Scotland were walloped seven goals to nil. By this time I had been to many football internationals but never one where the crowd was so sparse that it was possible to hear the losing players swearing like dyspeptic sea captains. Despite the result, all the attending Scots fans remained cheerful and non-belligerent. In fact, throughout that whole tournament every visitor from Britain remained good-tempered and friendly towards rival fans – the age of the soccer yob was a long way off. The only violence I saw was during an Austria versus Switzerland match when savage fighting broke out in the stand.

In those days the *Telegraph* did not devote much space to jazz and what there was was usually written by Sid Gillingham, an experienced journalist who also played guitar. Sid kindly took me to any press receptions that involved jazz and thus I was able to meet Louis Armstrong for the first time in May 1956. To converse with the musician I admired more than any other in the world, and to find him affable and ready to answer questions in detail was a supreme pleasure. This wiry, small man was undoubtedly a genius, but he was also remarkably friendly. He talked to me about the scars on his lips (created by years of intense pressure from his mouthpiece), then held out his hands and said, 'I've also got corns on my fingers and thumbs through gripping the trumpet hard for these past forty-five years.' And so he had, at every point where his hands came into contact with the trumpet. Despite his extraordinary patience with people who sometimes asked him naive questions about jazz, he could be forthright if he was the target of thoughtlessness, as when a journalist said, 'I understand you go to the dentist every two weeks, Mr Armstrong.' Louis stared at the man and barked, 'No I don't. I go the same as other folk, about every six months.'

I was to meet Louis on various occasions during the coming years and happily had the honour of being one of his biographers. My first impression never altered – he was a great human being as well as a supremely talented musician.

I was still as eager as ever to propagate the jazz gospel so I was delighted when it was suggested that I do some record reviews for the *Telegraph*. It was nice to see one's name in print, and to get extra payment for something that I would willingly have done for nothing. I continued to play trumpet regularly and formed a band (under my own name) which played in the Wembley area, where I still lived with my mother, brother Ron having married Doreen and settled elsewhere. All the members of the band were devoted to jazz so we made sure that the music of our heroes formed the basis of our performances. We rehearsed conscientiously once a week at the home of an old, retired actor, Cecil Wayne, who had a large house in Wembley that boasted a splendid grand piano.

Cecil loved the company of musicians and provided a feast of sandwiches, cakes and tea so that we took a long break from rehearsing which allowed him plenty of time to regale us with ribald tales of yesteryear's theatreland. He never made a pass at anyone in our ensemble but one did not have to be Sherlock Holmes to deduce his sexual preference. Cecil had never achieved stardom but had worked regularly through the 1920s and 1930s, including a long stint as a slave in the record-breaking musical *Chu Chin Chow*. We asked if he got bored playing the same role in the same show for year after year. 'Certainly not,' he said, going on to explain that something new was always happening backstage. For one exciting period, every night as he waited to go on-stage a hand glided around the backstage drapes, slid under his loin cloth and then proceeded to give him sexual stimulation. Cecil could have pulled back the curtain and discovered who the phantom groper was, but instead he memorised every detail of the mysterious hand and then sleuthed his way around the cast and the backstage staff in an attempt to solve the riddle. He never did find out and after two weeks the practice ended as suddenly as it had begun. 'So you see,' he explained, 'one could never get bored when treats like that came out of the blue.'

Gradually the band I was leading extended its area of activity but I was able to combine these gigs with my work at the *Telegraph*. However, I was getting restless because several of my contemporaries had become professional musicians. Jazz, mainly through the growing popularity of the traditional style, was gradually gaining followers and this encouraged a steady stream of players to take it up full-time. I delayed taking this big step because I was involved in an intense affair with a young woman on the staff of the newspaper, even though there was no future in the romance because she was soon to emigrate to Canada. Subsequently I convinced myself that working at the *Telegraph* without her would be unbearable so I decided to give up day work in order to make a career of music (I had already joined the Musicians Union). I had saved enough to live on for six months (albeit in a frugal way) and, as ever, my mother was totally supportive and encouraged me to take the chance. So, in October 1957, just as my girlfriend was crossing the

Atlantic, I jumped into a large, congested pool of freelance musicians.

In order to make my decision effective I had to improve my ability as a trumpeter. I had been playing since I was twelve years old but had never adopted the sort of intense practice regime that is necessary to build up a good technique. By giving up day work I now had the time to practise for long periods but, living in a small flat surrounded by sensitive neighbours, I had to find somewhere to blow without having to deal with complaints. The answer was to book a tiny room at Dinely Rehearsal Studios near Baker Street and to travel there each day to practise for hours on end. When I was not blowing the trumpet I devoted regular time to learning how to arrange music and to this end studied with the American orchestrator, Bill Russo.

I temporarily stopped leading a band, reasoning that if I worked for other leaders I should be tested by playing material that was outside my normal repertoire, and the challenge would also improve my sight-reading. I put a classified advertisement in *Melody Maker* offering my services as a trumpeter and, as a result, began playing gigs of all sorts in musical line-ups ranging from Latin American bands to big swing orchestras and lively Irish show bands. Through a trumpeter I met at the Dinely Studios I also worked in a West African band, Mister Kofi and his Rhythm, a challenging and fascinating experience. I also played in a band that specialised in providing music for bar mitzvahs and another that played only on American service camps. The strategy worked and I gradually improved and became more versatile but playing a pot-pourri of gigs soon strengthened my belief that I only wanted to play jazz.

5

From Butlin's
to a Jump Band

Through the musicians' grapevine I learnt that Butlin's were looking for small jazz groups for their holiday camps. The company had employed commercial dance bands for years but had recently decided to cater for youngsters who wanted to jive to lively music instead of going through the formal routines of ballroom dancing. I quickly rustled up a five-piece line-up consisting of two long-time pals, Sid Taylor (on reeds) and Boz Marsden (who had successfully switched from trombone to double bass) plus two players who had impressed me on various gigs that we had shared, namely John Armatage on drums and Don Shearman on piano. We successfully auditioned for Butlin's and accepted a three-month season at Skegness (a camp that Billy Butlin had opened in the 1930s). The motto above the entrance was, 'Our true intent is all for your delight.'

We did our best to live up to Shakespeare's slogan by playing our jazz as spiritedly as we could throughout the summer of 1958. This was just before the advent of beat groups, but rock and roll bands were flourishing in most British cities so playing for young dancers was something of a challenge for a jazz group. Happily, however, all went well.

At Butlin's Skegness musicians were not allowed to live on the camp. As the bandleader I could have done so, but I didn't want to be separated from my colleagues so we all lived in various caravans on a nearby site. Our working routine usually involved playing from two until four in the afternoon and from eight until eleven in the evening. On sunny afternoons even the keenest of young dancers absented themselves from the ballroom and this gave us time to rehearse new numbers or to listen to the tales of Benny, a senior redcoat and our master of ceremonies.

Benny, who had worked in just about every branch of show business, had an abundance of anecdotes about his travels and loved sharing them during our quiet afternoons. One of his jaunts had been a long tour of Ireland in a company of travelling actors. The troupe's manager always went ahead to discover which film had recently been a hit at the local cinema. He would then hastily sketch out a play based on a sequel to the successful movie, allowing the young actors and actresses space to improvise. Thus the company created dramas such as *The Countess of Monte Christo* and *Dr. Jekyll's Mad Brother*. This strategy pulled in the unsophisticated rural folk who were eager to see more of what had recently pleased them. But things went horribly wrong for *Napoleon's Revenge*, which involved cannon fire. The manager, in a dangerously wild enterprise, stole some railway fog-warning signals and proceeded to mix the explosive material they contained into canisters which he planned to detonate at the appropriate moment in the drama. Unfortunately he misjudged the strength of his blend and created an explosion that blew every window out of the hall and almost caused the proscenium arch to disintegrate. The audience fled in terror but the only person badly hurt was the manager himself, who had to remain in a local hospital for weeks. In a way he was fortunate: if he had been able to walk away from the scene of the explosion he would probably have been lynched.

Another of the staff comedians was a young Irish redcoat named Dave Allen, who was already showing signs of the artistry that was to make him a star. Dave, who liked to relax by singing close harmonies with anyone he could corral into recreating numbers made famous by the Hi-Lo's, usually hung out with musicians. He would try out gags on us, knowing that if we cynical jazzers laughed he was on to a winner. After the season ended, I went with Dave to see a Marx Brothers' film at the Classic Cinema, Baker Street. He was a bit down in the dumps because the right work was scarce. He thought that the answer might be to try his luck in Australia. There his fortune changed dramatically and when he returned to England he was well on his way to becoming internationally famous.

There were several resident bands at Butlin's Skegness, including an 'olde tyme orchestra', a smooth lounge-trio, two big bands and a sing-along group. Most of the musicians got on well with each other and with the redcoats, who worked long hours for very little money, keeping the campers happy. Being a redcoat was good grounding for any youngsters who wanted to become professional entertainers: they learnt how to hold an audience and to appear cheerful at all times. A season as a redcoat was also a way for ex-show business pro's to keep in touch with their calling. Few of the regular staff at Butlin's became romantically involved with the campers; it was somehow considered to be infra-dig to have a fling with a visitor when there were hundreds of attractive people on the staff. Many partnerships formed between those who worked at the camp throughout the summer, but it was generally understood that such affairs were only for the duration of the season. I enjoyed a happy friendship with one of the female redcoats who lived on the camp. After having to clomp through the muddy caravan site night after night I decided to move into the chalet that had been offered me at the beginning of the season.

One night as I strolled back to my new home after finishing work I linked up with my redcoat friend and immediately realised that she was bursting to tell me something. Her news concerned a séance that a group of redcoats, male and female, were holding in one of the chalets. She had declined to attend, but wanted me to join her in listening at the window to the gathering's initial foray into the world of spiritualism. We tiptoed into position and heard a trembling voice ask, 'Is there anybody there?' My friend, who possessed a lively, mischievous streak whispered to me that we could have some fun by moaning an answer. I decided to go a stage further. If one presses the valves of a trumpet halfway down while blowing forcibly into the instrument a very eerie sound emerges. This ghostly gurgling seemed to be just the right tone colour for the spectral occasion. The desperate enquiry, 'Is there anybody there?' was again heard, at which point my friend let out a banshee-like wail at exactly the moment I created my special effect. The eerie combination of sounds unnerved everyone within the chalet and they tumbled out into the night air shivering and shrieking.

We made no effort to run away so they immediately saw we were the cause of their fright, but so too did two of the camp's security guards who had dashed to the scene of the hullabaloo. Next morning, together with my redcoat friend,

I was hauled up in front of Frank Mansell, the entertainments manager, for a reprimand that could have resulted in both of us being sacked. He formally read out the terms of our contract: 'During the period of employment you will conform to such regulations as are laid down by the management as to conduct on the camp. Any breach of such regulations will render the offender liable to instant dismissal.' Then, more gently, he pointed out that séances, although no part of Billy Butlin's entertainment schedule, were not punishable; however making a din in the chalet lines after midnight was. Nevertheless, he said, he would waive the rules about dismissal by putting us on probation for the rest of the season. We were very relieved and made sure we toed the line for the remainder of our stay, but when those weeks had passed we parted and never saw one another again.

Saturday lunchtime at Butlin's was always relaxed and peaceful, because all eight thousand campers from the previous week had left and the newcomers had yet to arrive. Most of the musicians made it a ritual to meet in the Ingoldmells Hotel, which was situated just outside the camp gates. Word spread about these convivial gatherings and we were soon joined by various of the camp's staff including, on one occasion, the keeper of the camp's resident elephant, Saucy. This creature had been featured at the London Palladium in 1912 doing clever tricks, but now she was relegated to carrying children on joy rides. The keeper was not physically cruel to the animal but often cursed her under his breath for walking too slowly or for stopping to pick up morsels of food.

The keeper joined us at the hotel at the very time he should have been taking Saucy for her daily plunge in the nearby sea. Someone asked him about this neglect of duty and the keeper (having swallowed several drinks) said that

the sea was much too far away. Instead he would take the elephant for her dip in the large swimming pool which was just
inside the camp. We all trouped out to see this unusual sight,
one that would certainly have incurred the wrath of the
camp's health inspector. At first Saucy didn't seem keen on
the idea but after much pushing and shoving by the keeper
she walked sedately down the steps of the pool and into the
shallow end. The keeper had no intention of joining her but
by shouts and threats he got the creature to move into the
deep end. Saucy then decided to commemorate her first visit
to the pool by releasing a series of huge buns of excrement.
The keeper turned purple with rage and commanded Saucy
to stop, but a profusion of mighty turds continued to tumble
out of the pachyderm. We had no wish to offend Saucy's dignity but we couldn't stop laughing at the keeper who ran
around the pool shouting, 'Stop it, you bastard. Stop it.' He
then begged us to help him retrieve the evidence that could
cost him his job. Meanwhile Saucy had moved to the shallow
end of the pool and was ascending the steps looking relieved
and relaxed. A musician ran off and returned with a butter-
fly net. Clutching this, the keeper, stripped to his under-
pants, entered the water and began laboriously netting the
floating buns. We could not suppress our laughter and the
keeper never forgave us; nor did he ever again attend our
Saturday get-togethers.

One of my extracurricular tasks was to be on the judging
panel for an ancient ritual – the weekly 'holiday princess'
beauty contest. The most interesting aspect of this was in
trying to ascertain which of the entrants were professional
beauty queens (who spent the entire summer going from one
contest to another) as opposed to various attractive holidaymakers who entered the competition for fun. We did our

best to give the award and the prizes to genuine campers but we were regularly fooled. Often the professionals managed to win substantial prizes of cash or goods before moving on swiftly to the next contest. It was fascinating to observe a contestant's demure personality take on a flinty edge as soon the results were declared.

Being away on a summer season deprived me of paying regular visits to jazz clubs and jazz concerts. I managed to keep my files on jazz musicians up to date, but I missed hearing my record collection; the main consolation was in being able to listen to the American Forces' Network which broadcast (from Germany) a varied selection of jazz recordings throughout the night. Listening to these sessions was always an excuse to drink steadily until dawn and it was at Butlin's Skegness that I first got into the daily habit of suffering a hangover.

In general there were few outbreaks of violence at Butlin's. Families were able to relax there, enjoying ample facilities at a cost they could comfortably afford. The regular tannoy announcements irked some people but by way of consolation there were wonderful flower gardens offering peace and quiet. Only once during our season did serious trouble erupt, which produced some unbridled savagery from two gangs of youths: one from London, the other from Birmingham. Unfortunately the site they chose for their battle was the ballroom where we worked. The first inkling that something was brewing came one Friday when all of the lavatory chains from the men's toilets went missing – we later saw them used as improvised knuckledusters. That evening we were in the middle of playing a tune called 'Perdido' when I noticed a group of hooligans gathering on the left hand side of the ballroom and grimacing at a large gathering of young men who had entered the right hand section. Before the first blows were struck an air of impending violence surged through the hall. The dancers sensed this and hurried off the floor to watch events from the back of the ballroom. The leader of the Birmingham pack let out a loud yell, urging his mates forward, each of them displaying fists bound in the missing chains. The leader himself was more lethally armed; he carried a huge nail in his left hand and a big hammer in his right. Charging up to the leader of the London gang he held the nail against the youth's arm and hammered it into his opponent's flesh and bone. Both gangs (each about twenty-strong) shrieked and shouted as they locked in hand-to-hand combat.

As some sort of gesture to the Chicago jazz groups, who, according to legend, continued to play during gangster battles, we kept blowing until common sense came to our rescue and we made a quick exit into the dressing room. Blood was everywhere by the time a formidable number of security guards had restored order by frogmarching the hooligans out of the camp gates. The police were not called so no details of this carnage found its way into newspapers, national or local. The offenders were banned from reentering the camp for what would have been the last few hours of their holiday and their luggage was unceremoniously dumped outside the gates. Fortunately no bystanders were injured. The rest of the season passed smoothly and then it was time to return to London and begin a search for jobs. I could not get any work for the band so we all resumed freelancing. Having had a long spell of playing small group jazz I vowed I would follow that line – come what may. A lucky break was just around the corner.

I had kept in touch with various pals at the *Daily Telegraph* and often went with them (as a freeloader) to various press conferences and launches, and particularly to anything organised to publicise any aspect of jazz. One such event was the launch of a jazz book. As I wandered around the gathering I came face to face with saxophonist Bruce Turner, one of my favourite British jazz musicians, who had recently left Humphrey Lyttelton's band to form his own group. Terry Brown had been featured on trumpet with this new outfit, but he didn't want to tour so Bruce was looking for a replacement. I had only recently heard about this development and planned to try to locate Bruce as soon as possible to audition for the vacancy. Lo and behold, here he was in front of me. I introduced myself, whereupon Bruce pulled out his wallet and extracted a tiny piece of paper, no larger than a postage stamp, on which my name was written. 'Dad,' he said, using the word he most often used when addressing anyone, male or female, 'I've been trying to find out where you live.' Apparently, I'd been recommended to Bruce by a couple of people, but had we not met at the book launch we might never have linked up. The minimal detective work involved in finding out a telephone number or an address could well have been too daunting a task for an oddball like Bruce.

I didn't undergo a formal audition by playing numbers with the rest of the band. Instead, late the next afternoon, I caught a bus to Bruce's home in Dulwich, where I stood shoulder-to-shoulder with him as we played along with various jazz records. It was certainly a novel, even bizarre, way of applying for a job. To test my ability to read music Bruce pulled out some scraps of paper on which he had jotted the themes of some obscure jazz tunes. Over the years I got to know that Bruce did not like buying manuscript paper.

Instead, when he conceived an idea for a tune or an arrangement he used whatever was close at hand. Frequently it was the grey cardboard that formed the inside of a cereal packet, which made it very difficult to read the notes.

I wasn't sure how I was faring but when Bruce asked if I was available to meet the rest of the band that night I felt more assured. We travelled into the West End of London by bus and then walked to the Institute of Contemporary Arts in Dover Street. I assumed that Bruce had booked a rehearsal room there, but I soon realised otherwise when he led me into the main hall. We ascended the stage where he introduced me to the band. They were all set up and in position to play a concert, but before we could play a note together an official asked us to clear the stage as the people were about to come in. So the first phrases I ever blew with this band were in front of a concert audience. This was an introduction to the way that Bruce worked – much was left to chance. He hadn't told me about the concert in case I got alarmed and fled. He hated confrontations and negotiations and was prepared to gamble on the musical results of pushing me in at the deep end. As the concert progressed we gradually achieved musical rapport and within minutes of the final number I was offered the job, which I accepted with alacrity, eager to work with a musical hero of mine, who despite numerous foibles was a very likeable eccentric who devoutly loved jazz.

Although I had played many one-night stands in the Home Counties, I had not worked with touring bands. With Bruce I was suddenly pitchforked into the travelling life. A few days after the ICA concert I did my first broadcast with the band and soon after that we set out on a tour of Scotland and the north of England. Travelling in comfort was out of the question, with six of us plus a double bass and a drum kit (plus lots of personal luggage) packed into a small transit van, whose age prevented it reaching even moderately high speeds.

The first gig of our tour was at a dance hall in Hexham, up near the Scottish border, an engagement that our agent, Jim Godbolt, had booked with the legendary Scottish promoter, 'Drunken Duncan' McKinnon. Bruce had lost the date-sheet detailing the duration of the gig and the starting time so, as the new boy, I was sent to find out these details. I asked one of the ballroom staff where I could find Mr McKinnon and he pointed grimly to a flight of stairs that led to the ballroom manager's office-cum-flat. I entered the living room to find a tuxedoed figure (the manager) pacing up and down, exuding irritation. When I asked for Mr McKinnon he pointed to the top of a sideboard where, with his head resting against a bowl of waxed fruit (and snoring lustily), the inebriated Scot was living up to his reputation. He was still clad in his overcoat, and despite the warmth of the room he hadn't taken his gloves off. He was out for the count and remained so for the rest of the evening. The manager wrote down the times of the band's sets and said with resignation, 'You'll get no sense out of him tonight,' which proved to be true.

Duncan was responsible for organising several of the Scottish dates on that tour, during which a pattern emerged. In the early evening he was charm and wisdom personified, fond of quoting Rabbie Burns and talking about jazz history, but once Duncan entered into combat with John Barleycorn he soon succumbed to a knockout blow, usually just before we began our first set. I don't think that Duncan heard a note we played throughout the tour, but when it ended he paid up with a smile, saying to Bruce, 'Next time you come

to Scotland you must take a drink with me.' Bruce, a devout
teetotaller, said without conviction, 'Great idea, Dad. Great
idea.'

At the time of that tour (late 1958) traditional jazz was
rapidly gaining widespread popularity and achieving high
record sales. Kenny Ball, Chris Barber and Acker Bilk were
becoming household names – all three of them were accom-
plished jazz musicians, but many other 'trad' bands sounded
like a parody of the great traditional jazz bands of the past.
The trad style was loosely based on a blending of dixieland
and New Orleans jazz, with a heavy over emphasis on the
banjo, an excessive amount of clapping on the off-beat and
the wearing of preposterous band uniforms, musicians being
clad as Mississippi gamblers, Confederate soldiers or colo-
nial explorers. It was absolutely *de rigueur* to feature a front-
line consisting of trumpet, trombone and clarinet: the use of
the saxophone was deplored.

Bruce Turner's sextet was positively not a trad band, specialising as it did in the music recorded by Harlem-based
bands in the 1930s, mixed with the repertoire of Duke
Ellington's small groups and sounds made famous by Benny
Goodman's sextet and Artie Shaw's Gramercy Five. A few
other bands ploughed similar lonely furrows, playing what
was dubbed 'mainstream', shunning lucrative offers to play
trad. We didn't quite adopt a hair-shirt outlook, but we felt
proud that we were doing our best to keep alive interest in
the wonderful jazz of the 1920s, 1930s and 1940s, albeit to a
minority of fans and for poor financial rewards. We enjoyed
the devoted support of a small, hardy bunch of record collectors; we also had followers who played in various trad bands,
earning a lucrative wage playing in a style they said they did
not enjoy.

Bruce underlined our policy by naming his group Bruce Turner's Jump Band, which denoted a style that was midway between traditional and modern jazz (then known as bebop). Bruce could play modern jazz with ease and authority but chose not to. One night a young 'mod' kept asking Bruce to play 'Bernie's Tune' despite already having been told that it wasn't in our repertoire. 'Oh, I see,' said the persistent one. 'You're one of those geezers who think that jazz stopped in 1939.' 'Certainly not,' said Bruce. Then, after an effective pause, '. . . 1929.'

One incident at a gig in a jazz club in coastal Hampshire seemed to highlight the absurd way that jazz had become compartmentalised. Filling in for a trad band that had pulled out of the booking, it seemed we were the only jazz group available at such short notice. Eager to play, we arrived in plenty of time, in fact so early that we decided to fill in time, before the audience came in, by playing each other's instruments, a procedure that was certain to result in cacophony. Bruce played the trombone, I tried the clarinet, the drummer played piano, etc. The sound was abysmal and, just as it was at its most robust, in walked the promoter. 'Thank God you're trad,' he said. 'I'd heard you were mainstream.'

On tour we got paid £3 a night with 15 shillings (75 pence) as an accommodation allowance. On this budget we were usually restricted to scruffy boarding houses, with peeling walls and damp, grey sheets. We fared better in Scotland where prices were generally lower. In Dundee I totally misinterpreted a situation when a young, attractive landlady let Bruce and me back into our 'digs' after midnight and said to me, 'You'll be alright, the pig's in bed.' I took this to be a disparaging remark about her husband and immediately began looking forward to her company. Fortunately Bruce was close at hand to let me know that in this part of Scotland a stone hot-water bottle is known as a 'pig'. At one hostelry in Leicester a large hole in the roof allowed us to see part of a December sky. I sat down to breakfast there and encountered a fried egg that had many pieces of grit on its yolk. I was so hungry I decided to shut my eyes and eat but then realised that the only piece of cutlery on the table was a soup spoon. I called the woman who had delivered the greasy plate and pointed out that it was nearly impossible to eat a fried egg with a soup spoon and she wailed back, 'How can I be expected to remember everything?'

The only thing that bothered me about working in Bruce's band was the underlying tension created by the pianist and drummer. They were old lags of the music business, for whom every bandleader (even a congenial and talented one like Bruce Turner) was an automatic enemy whose choice of tempo and tunes were always wrong. These two veterans did their best to make Bruce's life a misery by complaining about every aspect of life on the road. Happily they were eased out in January 1959 and replaced by the Australian pianist Collin Bates and drummer Johnny Armatage (who had worked in my band at Butlin's). Collin, nicknamed 'Tucker' because of his formidable appetite, was a wonderful musician who instantly added to the band's collective sense of humour by bringing with him a fund of splendid anecdotes and various Antipodean sayings. Johnny, the drummer, was very even-tempered and usually led the chuckling. The other members of the sextet were Bruce on alto sax and clarinet, myself, Toni Goffe (who later became a highly successful commercial artist) on double bass and John Mumford (who was musically the most broad-minded member of the band) on trombone.

Despite the improvements brought about by the changes in personnel there was no flood of well-paid jobs. However a number of loyal promoters and club owners booked us regularly, including Jim Ireland who ran the Mardi Gras in Liverpool; Bill Kinnell, organiser of jazz events at the Dancing Slipper in Nottingham; and the committee of the Anlaby Road Jazz Club in Hull.

The Hull venue was not licensed to serve alcohol so during our intervals we dashed off to the nearest pub for refreshments. There we encountered an absolutely charmless young man who, in demanding tones, wanted to hear a complete run-down of jazz happenings in London. Always in wait for us whenever we visited the pub, he would take in the news then swagger over to his mates to spout what he had just heard. Somehow, he had sensed that I was a repository for jazz information so it was always my sleeve he tugged first. I tried to be helpful but he became progressively more arrogant on each successive visit so I devised a way of making his persistence bearable by inventing a name or two. 'It seems that Don Rendell is still the king of the tenor sax,' he asserted. 'Don is a great player,' I said, 'but these days he takes second place to Boots Boot.' The interrogator scuttled back to his pals to extol the merits of the non-existent Boots Boot. On our next visit the eager beaver began by saying, 'I hear Boots Boot is playing well.' I pulled a vinegary face and shook my head, hesitating so as to allow myself enough time to improvise a new name, 'Boots has lost it. His confidence went out of the window when Snubby Taylor caught up with him in a jam session.' The bore hurried over to his pals to share this startling news. The rest of the band, in on the joke, managed to suppress their laughter until we were on our way back to the gig – on later visits to Hull we found a different pub to relax in.

The Hull pest's attitude typified the one-upmanship that has riddled jazz appreciation for decades, resulting in an absurd belief that if you didn't know who played second trombone on an obscure 1929 recording you couldn't be considered to be a true jazz fan. My good friend Michael Brooks (who knows an enormous amount about jazz) abhors this situation and decided to expose the folly of those jazz and blues fans who automatically equated merit with rarity, thereby ignoring the fact that many recordings are rare because no one liked them enough to buy them when they were first issued. Mike mischievously advertised a test-pressing by someone he called 'The Big Sunflower'. The Big S. didn't exist, but he was soon kitted out with a biography and a photograph (which my wife Teresa had taken of a West Indian busker in Portobello Market). A ring of authenticity was established encouraging collectors (without a grain of evidence) to add a series of biographical details that gathered on The Big Sunflower's c.v. like barnacles on an old boat. The legend grew and fans clamoured fruitlessly for samples of his work – to this day the search goes on.

One of our favourite venues was the Grimsby Jazz Club, a place that was organised and patronised by jazz enthusiasts whose reactions inspired visiting musicians. On our first visit to the club we misjudged how long it would take to get there from London and as a result we had hardly any time to sort out accommodation. In most travelling bands such details are organised well in advance but that was not Bruce's way of doing things so we arrived in Grimsby minutes before the gig was due to start – without any place to sleep. Collin Bates (as the newcomer) was given the task of finding digs. Luckily he spotted a 'Bed and Breakfast' sign on a building we passed. He leapt out of the band bus and hastily booked us into the lodging house. 'What's it like?' we asked anxiously. 'Couldn't see much,' said Collin, 'but at least we've all got individual rooms: 4, 5, 6, 7, 8 and 9.'

Happy in the knowledge that we were going to enjoy the rare luxury of separate rooms we launched into what turned out to be a very enjoyable gig that left us feeling elated. Our spirits fell when we saw the interior of the lodging house. We were shown by torchlight to a long mildewed dormitory – over each of twenty beds was a number marked in phosphorescent paint; the suites we dreamt of turned out to be beds four to nine inclusive. The only illumination was a tiny night-light, so we had no idea what the other occupants looked like. All we knew was that several of our fellow lodgers snored and farted relentlessly, others called out during troubled dreams and one glugged away noisily at what I discerned in silhouette to be a quart bottle of stout.

The occupant of bed three was close enough to give Bruce's bed a friendly kick by way of attracting attention. 'What time do you get up for work, mate?' asked the old dosser. Bruce, by nature reticent, cleared his throat and said, 'Er. We don't get up for work.' 'That's right,' said his new friend. 'Fuck 'em.' The charge of ten shillings a night at this flop house included breakfast, but in order to eat it one had to take a raffle ticket and present it at a café that was about a half a mile down the road. On this occasion we all skipped the first meal of the day.

6

Life on a Liner

Bruce's band seemed to be well-received wherever we played, but we still couldn't achieve a breakthrough. In order to make a living, Bruce sometimes had to work as a guest star with various bands in Britain and in Scandinavia. This meant that the rest of us had to scuffle for work, earning money from jazz gigs as and where we could. During this period Bruce kindly got me a place in the unusual group that recorded the music for Ewan MacColl and Charles Parker's radio ballad 'Song of a Road'. The line-up that gathered under Peggy Seeger's musical direction to create a highly unusual blend of tone colours consisted of me on trumpet, Bruce on clarinet, Bobby Mickleburgh on trombone, Jim Bray on double bass and John Armatage on drums, plus concertina, uilleann pipes, guitar, banjo and autoharp. It was a fascinating endeavour, combining folk music and jazz. Later Ewan MacColl's composition 'The First Time Ever I Saw Your Face' brought him worldwide success.

I was still in touch with a clique of musicians I had worked with in earlier years, including bassist Boz Marsden, Sid Taylor on reeds, drummer Chuck Smith and pianist

Ronnie Smith. They were now part of a pool of players who were doing jazz gigs in a shady west London drinking club, a venue where hard-faced characters gathered to avoid the restrictions of the usual licensing hours imposed during the afternoons and after eleven at night. Supposedly such an establishment was for members only, but no membership cards were ever seen. The most common sight was the flashing of large wads of bank notes by various dubious-looking drinkers. The owners of the club were proud men and in a move that placed them a cut above all their local rivals (who had juke boxes in their clubs) they decided to feature live jazz throughout a good deal of the day and night. In order to maintain this schedule they hired a pool of musicians who permutated into quartets and trios from about 2 pm until 1 am. I became part of this set-up which was flexible in that it allowed one to swap 'shifts' if a more important gig came in.

It cannot be said that the clientele at this club was made up of discerning listeners, but as long as the jazz was reasonably melodic and not too loud we were all paid handsomely for our musical duties, which included backing striptease acts. The strippers were all booked on a freelance basis and drawn from a huge coterie of willing young ladies, many of whom were, it seemed to the accompanying musicians, totally devoid of any previous experience in this line of work. They were impossibly vague as to what sort of number they felt should accompany their gyrations, and many were much too swift in disrobing, to the point where even the politest members of the audience were likely to groan. The girls seemed totally unaware of Gypsy Rose Lee's maxim, 'The tease is more important than the strip.'

The musicians usually did four-hour 'shifts' and to add variety tried to work with everyone in the pool during the

course of a week. The owners didn't mind how we lined up
as long as the music flowed and, in fact, they were kind and
considerate with us. Veteran American jazzmen in their reminiscences all say that the hoodlums they worked for had an
inviolable rule that musicians were never harmed or threat-
ened, and the west London club maintained a similar code of
conduct. The atmosphere there was not homicidal but it did
get seriously violent one night when I was elsewhere playing
another gig. A row broke out between two men who were
thought of as close friends, leading to one of them going to
the boot of his car and returning with a large object wrapped
in a blanket. It was a shotgun and, without further ado, he
fired it at the legs of his pal. Some of the pellets hit their target but others riddled a drum-case that was stacked on the
side of the stage. The stage itself was empty, all of the terrified musicians having dived behind the piano the moment
they saw the shotgun being unwrapped. There was no question of anyone calling the police; whatever happened within
the club was subject only to the laws of that establishment,
and no one was likely to do any informing. Fortunately the
victim was not badly hurt and was soon patched up by a
friendly doctor. Amazingly within a couple of weeks the
marksman and his target were again sitting together at the
bar sharing laughs and lagers.

This incident was not the prime reason for several of us
musicians moving on, but it may have influenced us to
accept the offer of another season at Butlin's, this time at
Clacton, Essex, with pianist Ronnie Smith as the leader.
Before I made my decision I had a meeting with Bruce
Turner, who urged me to take the offer of a summer's work
because he had very few band jobs in his engagement book.
All he asked was that I made myself available for a series of

daytime radio broadcasts, which I could do easily by coming up to London by train. He also said that when the June to September stint was over I would be welcome to rejoin the Jump Band. I half expected the owners of the drinking club to object to our migration but they were charm itself, accepting without a flicker of bad feeling that a new pool of players, recommended by us, would fill the vacancies. The bosses gave us a farewell party during which they issued a promise that if any of us ever needed help we only had to ask.

The season at Butlin's was hugely enjoyable. The summer of 1959 seemed to pass without a cloud crossing the sky, the weather was wonderful and our working schedule allowed us to enjoy it. Pianist Ronnie Smith led the quintet, with Sid Taylor on reeds, Chuck Smith on drums, Vernon Bown on double bass and me on trumpet. We all knew one another well so a happy atmosphere prevailed. As before, our task was to play for those holidaymakers who wanted to 'jive' (a new word for jitterbugging) rather than cavort to the smoother sounds of the camp's two big bands, but musically times were changing and jazz was not what the youngsters who came to the jive ballroom wanted. Rock and roll was spawning a British version of beat music, what we had to offer was not hit parade oriented, and the only time the dancers were enthusiastic was when we heavily emphasised the off-beat on a medium tempo blues. However, a few jazz fans from Clacton came in on guest passes and they cheered us on. We were allowed to get free admission tickets for visitors provided we applied for them two hours before the time of their visit.

One Friday night we were taken by surprise on being told by the security staff that three visitors had arrived at the main entrance saying they were our guests. The security guard said he could not alter the rules: no pass, no entry, but as we were due to finish playing in twenty minutes he would let the visitors sit in a waiting room. We made our way there, pondering who the guests could be. Our curiosity was satisfied the moment we saw three of the regulars from the west London club we had recently forsaken and they asked if we could go somewhere quiet to talk. The only suitable place seemed to be our digs – we stayed at a nearby guest house (run by Les Bennett, the ex-Tottenham Hotspur football star). All eight of us made our way into the largest bedroom, where some squatted on the beds while others utilised various chairs. After an exchange of stilted pleasantries and some everyday meteorological observations the senior of the visitors said in a quiet voice, 'We were wondering, are you fellows paid by cash or by cheque?' We instantly saw where the question was leading and replied as one: 'By cheque,' (which wasn't true). 'Well how about the catering staff, the redcoats and the cleaners?' We all shrugged our shoulders and mumbled. The visitors could see that we were not going to cooperate, so they rose, smiled and firmly shook our hands before beginning their journey back to London. Their farewell words were a reiteration of the promise of help should we ever need it.

Because of our lack of cooperation we took that offer with a pinch of salt, but we later learnt it was genuine. A pianist who had worked at the club subsequently played at a night spot near Paddington; he was booked for a fortnight and told that he would be paid on the last night of each week. Seven days came and went without a sign of the money, and nothing was forthcoming after a fortnight had passed. When he queried this with the owner he was told, 'You came here as an audition, and frankly you're not what we wanted, so best if you say ta-ta.' It was a con trick, the owner had got the pianist's services for nothing and was probably to repeat the strategy with another musician. Remembering the offer of help the pianist called our west London friends. Within half-an-hour two heavies had entered the club and were praising the owner's huge mirror, which stretched for the length of the extensive bar. The owner nervously accepted their flow of compliments, but the visitors continued talking: 'My goodness you must be coining it to be able to afford such a mirror and pay top wages to such a good pianist. If we had a mirror like that we'd always be worried that some nutter was going to break it.' The owner opened his wallet, called the pianist over and paid him. The musician left with his two saviours, thanking them profusely for their help and for living up to their promise.

When the Clacton season ended I rejoined Bruce Turner's Jump Band and met up with the group's new bassist, Jim Bray, a good musician and a witty companion who was also the band's chauffeur, impressing us all with his speedy but always safe approach to driving. Jim had a good eye for vintage cars and bought (for a song) a Rolls Royce that had belonged to King Zog of Albania, with the royal crest still intact. Jim was never a model of sartorial elegance but he had enough presence to wave regally when various commissionaires and doormen saluted as he passed the more sumptuous of London's top hotels. He later sold this mobile treasure to an American collector.

Bookings for Bruce's band seemed to ebb and flow and while Bruce was still guesting with overseas bands in order to make a living, the rest of us scuffled, and I was finding it increasingly difficult to keep up with the hire purchase payments on a new trumpet. I took to going to London's Archer Street, near Piccadilly Circus, which was then an open-air musicians' labour exchange, Monday afternoons being the time that most of the transactions and offering of gigs took place.

A clique of us formed an audition band, ready to play as a unit for erstwhile bandleaders who had the chance to gain a contract for a long booking provided they had an organised band. Often these would-be maestros didn't have their own line-up and relied on rustling up a group with enough polish to pass the crucial audition; once the contract had been signed they set about assembling their own personnels. As part of the duplicity we acted the part of a regular band and were paid a couple of quid each for our efforts.

We got used to the techniques of playing for auditions and this proved very useful when pianist Don Shearman took me, Sid Taylor, John Richards on double bass and Rodney Crump on drums, to an audition for an engagement that involved five months' work. Everything went satisfactorily and the agent fixing the job called Don over to ask if we were all available to sail within the week on SS *Iberia*, a P & O liner leaving for a five-month world cruise. I had some forthcoming gigs with Bruce, but once again he was extremely cooperative and encouraged me to take the long trip, though I made it clear to him that I would quite understand if he found a permanent replacement for me. Sid Taylor had the toughest decision; he had only just got married, but he too decided to make the trip. Before we sailed we were medically examined, fingerprinted and inoculated. We were given the rank of deck officer and accordingly had to buy white linen uniforms before we sailed from Tilbury in December 1959. Unfortunately the drummer who had taken part in the audition had to drop out and he was replaced by a white South African who didn't blend in with us. The rest of us got on well. I shared a cabin in the passenger section with Sid Taylor; we had our own cabin steward and ate our meals with the passengers. The treatment suited us fine. This was apparently the first time that P & O had taken a jazz-oriented quintet on a world cruise. We played in the first class lounge for an hour in the morning, in the tourist section for an hour at tea time and finished the day by playing for dancing each evening, a session that provoked a lively response from many of the teachers aboard, who were on their way to Australia as part of an exchange deal with that country's education authorities.

We had the best of both worlds. Not only were we allowed to use all of the passengers' facilities, but we were also given crew discount on any drinks we bought, including bottles of gin at 40 pence each. The drink accumulated faster than we could swallow it and soon the chest of drawers in our cabin had buckled under the weight. In the end a hammer and chisel were needed for us to get at the unopened grog. We were also bought ample drinks by the passengers for playing requests. We had been told by various stewards that we would be able to live off our tips, without drawing wages, but this proved false. At the end of our five-month journey there was only ten pounds in the kitty, to share between five of us. Our steward, Mr Colaco (from Goa), was a very pleasant man whose family had served the P & O company for generations. Following tradition we tipped him for carrying out various jobs for us, one of which was blancoing our white canvas shoes. We stressed that we were perfectly capable of doing this ourselves, but he proudly insisted that it was part of his day's work. One day after he handed me back my shoes

I did the usual thing and put a two shilling piece in his hand. It was Christmas Eve and I left him immediately to take part in the ship's annual ritual whereby deck officers and their equivalents served the crew with their pre-Christmas dinner. Several hundred of the staff were seated at tables in the tourist dining room, so it was a huge coincidence that I found I was waiting on Mr Colaco, who sat with great dignity offering me the gentlest of smiles. When I had finished inexpertly serving the four courses Mr Colaco beckoned me over and with a graceful gesture surreptitiously slipped into my hand the two shilling piece I had given him an hour earlier. His action made me see what an absurd ritual tipping could be.

The first problem on the trip occurred when we reached the Suez Canal. This was at the end of a time of a continuing rift between Egypt and Britain and, as a result, no one from the *Iberia* was allowed ashore when we docked at Port Said. Scores of angry Egyptians lined the quayside and hurled insults at the liner's closed portholes as we prepared to sail. Sid Taylor and I, after a few drinks, rose to the occasion by going on deck and playing, 'There'll Always be an England'. Amazingly, this rather foolish act of bravado placated the angry mob. I think they would have gone mad with rage if we had played the National Anthem, but somehow the World War Two song charmed them and they bade us farewell by offering friendly waves.

Exotic ports came thick and fast: Aden, where the splendid hat I bought melted after thirty minutes in the sun; Colombo, where I was given a curry so hot I almost fainted; Singapore, a model of liveliness (long before it was sanitised and refurbished); and Hong Kong, where almost everything seemed to be a bargain, and replicas of de luxe goods such as

Parker pens and Rolex watches were copied with such skill that only an expert could detect the fakes. At this time (1960) the international availability of goods from all over the world had not been established and it was still possible to find presents that were only on sale in the country of their origin.

Many of the crew, particularly those who had been sailing on passenger liners for years, often stayed on board, relaxing, while the ship was in port. Amazingly, a good number of passengers, mostly those in the first class section, also stayed on the liner in various ports, even in interesting places such as Hawaii. They had booked their voyage in order to chase the sun and relax, and many of them found it more congenial to play a rubber of bridge on deck rather than traipse about in a hot climate, surrounded by foreigners.

The ship's itinerary allowed us to have a good look at Australia, berthing in Perth, Adelaide, Melbourne and Sydney. Bruce Turner's pianist, Collin Bates, had asked me to look up several of his friends in Sydney so I went to the Australian musicians' union building to locate them. As well as being a centre of administration, the union building also housed a first class club, with an excellent bar, a place to eat, several fruit machines and plenty of armchairs to relax in. Many musicians made it a habit to drop in there when they had finished work. I got there about the time local gigs finished and was told by the receptionist that the fellows I was looking for would soon be in. While I sat waiting a burly guy came and sat next to me, wishing me 'G'day.' After establishing that I was a musician on the *Iberia* he proceeded to rat-a-tat a lot of short, sharp questions: How many hours did I work each day? What were living conditions like? Was the grub good? How much a week did I earn? So as not to appear stand-offish I answered as best I could. Thinking he might welcome an enquiry from me I asked him which instrument he played. 'Mind your own bloody business,' he said defiantly before walking away. It was my introduction to home-based Aussie humour, and over the years I really learnt to enjoy it. I linked up with some of Collin Bates' friends and was told where I could hear live jazz. One of these places, a big pub near the docks, was where I first heard tenor saxist, Merv Acheson, an Australian jazz character whose forthright manner was a legend even in a land where candid comments were never scarce. I struck up a conversation with this veteran during which he said, with some vehemence, 'There's only two great white jazz musicians in the world. Pee Wee Russell... [pause] and me.'

After playing for a holiday cruise to New Zealand and Tasmania we took aboard new passengers and set out for Fiji, Honolulu, the Philippines, Vancouver, San Francisco and Los Angeles. One of those who embarked for the Pacific journey was an American trombonist, Pat Thompson. He brought with him fascinating home movies of his days with famous big bands and joined us in playing jam sessions on deck after midnight. We enjoyed ourselves at almost every port we visited but I was disappointed at not being able to find much live jazz at the stopovers except, of course, in San Francisco and Los Angeles. After North America we set out on the long voyage home via Japan, Hong Kong, Bombay, Aden and Gibraltar.

A letter from Bruce Turner reached me in Japan, offering me my old job back in the Jump Band. 'I'm proffering a plum opportunity,' were the words he used. Although the cruise had been a marvellous experience I greatly missed the jazz life, so I wrote back accepting the offer. I'd also missed listening to my jazz record collection and had tried to ease the ache by buying jazz LPs at almost every port. Throughout the voyage my mother sent *Melody Maker* each week so I was able to keep abreast of events and developments in the jazz world.

Towards the end of the voyage I realised that I had neglected to send postcards to various friends in England, so I bought a stack in Aden, scribbled out a message and put air mail stamps on them, planning to post the cards on board ship where, via a liberty boat, they were despatched by a local post office. This was the usual procedure when leaving a port, but a veteran crew member, seeing me clutching a wad of cards on the quayside, told me that these postal arrangements didn't apply in Aden. I spent two minutes running around trying to find a way of despatching the cards, but I could not locate a post box. Totally frustrated I looked ruefully at the several pounds worth of air mail stamps on the marooned postcards. As I did so an old Arab workman wandered by. He shook his head when I asked if he spoke English, but seemingly understood my gestures indicating that I wanted the cards posted. He took the cards and looked at the mint stamps. I felt certain they were worth a lot more than he received in weekly wages. The least I could do was to give him something for his trouble. I dug into my pockets for cash, but, to my utter shame, I only had a one penny coin, having spent the rest of my money on postcards and stamps. Shamefaced, I passed the coin to him, thinking I might just as well as have thrown the cards into the harbour. He gave me a stern look, then shrugged his shoulders and walked off with the cards and the penny. Back in England I discovered that each and every card had arrived swiftly and safely.

The *Iberia* docked at Tilbury on April 16, 1960. Next day I linked up with the rest of the Jump Band who had arranged a 'welcome-back' gathering including a special showing of one of my favourite films, *Dead of Night*. A few days later I rejoined them formally for a gig at a suburban jazz club. Gradually we began attracting a dedicated following, helped by the fact that our agent, Jim Godbolt, had begun organising sessions at the Six Bells, a cosmopolitan pub in the King's Road, Chelsea, where we played at least once a week.

Among our followers there was an eccentric who often jumped on-stage to conduct us, complete with baton. When he felt we were swinging to his satisfaction he would turn to face the audience, offering them a thin-lipped smile and a bow in the manner of the tuxedoed bandleaders of the 1930s. As he only stayed on-stage for one number, and always bought us a round of drinks, nobody in the band objected to his caper and most of the audience enjoyed the joke. We had no idea of the conductor's background until a couple, who usually came to hear us when we played in the Midlands, visited the Six Bells. They were in London to sort out details of a relative's will and, having spent several hours with a solicitor, they decided to unwind by coming to hear us. They took seats in the front row and beamed and waved but their faces changed dramatically when the conductor jumped up on-stage – he was the solicitor with whom they had spent much of that day. Immediate embarrassment was shared evenly between the three of them, and the result was that none of them ever came to hear the band again – we lost two fans and a conductor.

Bruce Turner was a teetotaller, but he didn't object to his sidemen drinking. The nearest he came to admonition was when he spoke of 'the false camaraderie of the saloon bar'.

Bruce's own weakness was for all things sweet and he regularly put away a prodigious amount of cream cakes, chocolate, sugar buns, puddings and ice creams. He once told me that he was more excited about the launching of a new chocolate bar than he ever was about the release of an outstanding jazz record. A vegetarian who often derided us for what he called 'your intake of toxins', he thought nothing of demolishing two huge pies full of synthetic cream. He believed in fasting if he felt ill and criticised us for foolishly believing in 'the germ theory'. But he remained a very pleasant, amusing character, with a stupendous sense of humour, who was attractive to women of all ages. His political views were firmly on the left, which didn't dismay anyone in the band, and he regularly wrote reviews for the *Daily Worker*. He was frugal in his outlook and careful with money, but conversely he was wildly generous to anyone visiting an ice cream parlour with him, where he would buy double Knickerbocker Glories all round.

We occasionally played private engagements, one of which was to celebrate a by-election result for an ultra-safe Conservative seat. The counting of the votes was a mere formality. When the result was declared all the supporters present gathered in the ballroom where a huge cake was to be cut into many slices, but calamity struck. During the wait someone had taken a large slab of the blue-iced celebratory cake. There was uproar when it was discovered that the centrepiece of the evening's buffet had been pillaged. Bruce was nowhere to be seen and I went into the band's dressing room to look for him. I found him there – wiping his face without quite removing a moustache of blue icing. Before I said a word he began protesting, 'Don't know anything about it, Dad. All a mystery to me.' I pointed to his upper lip and

advised him to wash his face, which he did, dispersing the
evidence. When we returned to the ballroom the gnashing
of Tory teeth could plainly be heard, efforts to find the culprit having failed. For some weeks after that Bruce refused
to talk about it until, in a discussion about cravings, someone
in the band mentioned 'the phantom cake eater'. Bruce
decided it was time to confess, but in doing so he looked for
a mitigating get-out and said with some feeling, 'It was not a
craving – it was a political act.'

7

Living Jazz

Bruce Turner's cravings for sweet things increased with time and eventually led him to visit a doctor for advice. The medic suggested that Bruce try an occasional glass of bitter to stimulate his taste buds. The prospect had no appeal for Bruce but on the next gig (in Leeds) he ordered a pint of bitter and began sipping it with a punished look on his face. He had just about finished the beer when it was time to start playing. Everything set off as normal with Bruce improvising as fluently as ever, then quite suddenly his fingers lost their coordination and he began projecting a series of stuttered, unconnected phrases – a single pint had been too much for him. He was too drunk to finish the set so we carried on as best we could while he tottered into the dressing room to sober up. Someone sent out for a couple of large doughnuts and once they had been consumed Bruce began to feel better and although shaky he managed the second set, albeit in low gear.

But even when he was not in top form Bruce was an outstanding player whose love of jazz permeated every solo he delivered. As if to underline his deep knowledge of the music

he sometimes blew musical impersonations, projecting alto
sax solos in the manner of Johnny Hodges, Benny Carter,
Pete Brown, Charlie Parker and Lee Konitz, and sounding
convincingly like the originals. On clarinet he could create
lifelike sketches of players as diverse as Barney Bigard and
Pee Wee Russell. Some critics took Bruce to task for these
impressions saying he should concentrate on his own individuality, but for those working alongside him it was a
demonstration of the depth of understanding of a wide range
of jazz styles by someone who was one of the best soloists
that Europe has ever produced.

A big change was about to affect the band's working
schedule. In July 1960 we began an eight-week season in
Weymouth, Dorset. Happily, we had Sundays off so we were
also able to play at that year's Beaulieu Jazz Festival. For the
rest of each week we played afternoons and evenings in the
Pavilion Ballroom, supporting Cyril Stapleton's orchestra.
Because we were booked at the last moment to play this season we could not find accommodation in Weymouth so the
six of us rented a cottage a couple of miles out of town. Only
after making the commitment did we discover that there
were no late buses to where we were staying, so after each
evening's performance we had a long uphill walk. Our general fitness soon improved but living cheek by jowl exposed
cracks in the band's previously harmonious existence. As
with most domestic disputes it was the little things that nig-
gled. Bruce (as a vegetarian) was aggrieved to find that someone had cooked bacon for breakfast and then left the frying
pan unwashed, ownership of various foodstuffs in the refrig-
erator was disputed and one of the band regularly woke us all
by banging the front door as he went out for a dawn stroll.

In this atmosphere there was even disagreement about

the records we played in the cottage: too much early jazz, too much bebop, too many big bands, too many small groups. We resolved this issue by temporarily putting an embargo on playing jazz records and instead went to the local markets seeking 78 rpm recordings by obscure comedians of yesteryear – the worse the better. We'd scurry back with the discs and begin analysing with mock scholarly seriousness the fiendish laughter of Will Evans (a pre-World War One favourite), then we would attempt to fathom the odd pauses that peppered shy Tom Foy's act. But the comedic artiste who won hands down that summer was Vivian Foster, who recorded ten double-sided 78s in the twenties and thirties as the Vicar of Mirth. His humour was so obscure that half a dozen listeners might each find a different meaning in his observations. We were only sure that the joke had ended when the comic cleric issued his catchphrase, 'Yes, I think so.' He was a true original, but he sounded very like a real live clergyman, the Reverend Ironmonger, who was often on the radio, and as a result Foster was banned by the BBC. Probably because of this embargo he remained an obscure performer who recorded an annual disc for Columbia and toured the lower division music halls. When our summer season ended, Collin Bates and I shared the cost of an advertisement in the *Stage* which asked for information about this remarkable man and happily his son, Leslie Glenroy (billed in variety as the Long Limbed Laughter Loosener), met us and shared biographical details of his late father.

All of the Jump Band enjoyed a friendship with Cyril Stapleton's orchestra and with the various show people who came to Weymouth to appear at the local variety theatre. Shared parties were regularly held, at which the main drink was a cheap but potent local cider. At one such

gathering, Hattie Jacques (of the *Carry On* films) obviously
wanted something more stimulating: she called me aside and
asked if I had any 'pot'. I was unable to help her – our nightly turn-on was corn flakes with iced milk, consumed after we
had completed the long walk from the gig.

Throughout that season I often played tennis with Bruce
Turner, the loser paying for the hire of the municipal court.
I was not a good player but I regularly took advantage of
Bruce's positional weaknesses. At the end of the last game of
the season, which he lost, Bruce called me to the net and
said, 'I can't understand this, Dad. I've been coached and you
haven't.'

Being temporarily based in Weymouth had another particular advantage for me – it allowed me to make the short
journey up to the Dorchester area where I was able to follow
up my lifelong passion for the writings of Thomas Hardy by
visiting many of the places described in his novels.

Attendance at the Pavilion Ballroom's afternoon sessions
varied. If the weather was hot and sunny we played to four
old men and a dog but, if it rained, the ballroom was packed
with hundreds of people. The quartet of ancients and the
pooch didn't seem to mind what we played, so we blew long,
bold jazz numbers, but the crowds who came in to dodge the
rain needed entertaining. At the manager's suggestion we
added some vocals in an effort to placate the wet weather
influx. This strategy presented something of a problem, in
that no one in the band could honestly be described as a
singer. John Mumford came closest to succeeding. I did my
best, without merit (anyone who thinks that this is mock
modesty should listen to 'Four or Five Times', the only vocal
I ever recorded). I didn't enjoy singing but Bruce saw vocal-
ising as a golden chance for him to project the dramatic skills

that lurked within him. Accordingly, he hammed his way through various show tunes imagining that he was a suave, sophisticated crooner. But our combined warblings counted for nothing – we could plainly see that the audience kept looking desperately out of the windows hoping that a burst of sunshine would release them from their ordeal.

The ballroom manager, being an affable fellow, turned a deaf ear to what was going on, knowing that we had tried to satisfy him. The only time he reprimanded us was when he called all six members of the Jump Band to a special meeting at which he was accompanied by one of the cleaning ladies. Poor woman, her lips were quivering from nervousness as the manager explained that she had been deeply offended to discover a grossly obscene phrase written on a piece of paper she had found on the bandstand after one of our rehearsals. We were totally mystified and eventually someone asked what the disgraceful words were. The cleaner went crimson with embarrassment at the prospect of uttering the lewd cause of the complaint. To relieve her of the ordeal the manager held up the offending piece of paper, which referred to a new Bruce Turner composition that we had been rehearsing. Bruce had given a temporary working title to the theme and it was this that had mortified the middle-aged woman – there on the top of the music were the shameful words 'Pig's Bum'.

In September 1960 we returned from our Weymouth season to the news that we had been offered a brief residency in Norway – at the Metropol Club in Oslo. After a smooth sea crossing we settled down to play to extremely receptive audiences. The craze for trad had bypassed Norway and we loved playing to people who talked open-mindedly about the history of jazz and the great jazz recordings. My earliest belief in the universality of jazz was rekindled. The Metropol was a well-designed club, run by a friendly committee of jazz devotees, most of whom were musicians. Every day we were showered with hospitality while being taken on tourist trips in and around the city.

We returned to London refreshed, bolstered by the Norwegians' reactions to our style of jazz, and our optimism increased when we were told that the Jump Band would be the subject of a documentary film entitled *Living Jazz*. Our spirits soared higher when we learnt that the director was the brilliant Jack Gold, who went on to gain an international reputation. Writer Alan Lovell travelled with us for a few weeks prior to the shooting of the film so that he got the feel of being 'on the road'. He sketched out a sequence of events but didn't burden us with a formal script. All of the band except Bruce felt that our way of life was accurately portrayed in the film. Bruce wanted the band's activities to be more glamorously presented, despite often saying that the world needed more realism and less sentimentality. He felt the life of the Jump Band should be portrayed in the manner of a Hollywood bio-pic of the 1940s, with silhouettes aplenty, white suits for the musicians and an audience whose patent leather shoes tapped almost in time with the beat during the final moments of the movie. Instead, Jack and Alan, with the approval of the film's sponsors, Doug Dobell, Ken Lindsay and Paddy Whanel of the British Film Institute, accurately portrayed us travelling in discomfort, staying at cruddy digs and playing a style of jazz that was not particularly popular.

Bruce's desire to be seen as an actor was the root cause of the disagreements – he became irked to the point where he wouldn't say anything during various key scenes. Years before, he had unsuccessfully auditioned for the prestigious London drama school, RADA. He said he failed because the examining board objected to the way he placed his feet. Problems began on the first day of shooting when Bruce astonished us by saying he could not work without a script. He was eventually persuaded to improvise some lines describing the dire music pumping out of a juke box. He did this very effectively in a way that delighted Jack Gold, but when it was time to film the scene Bruce decided to act out his words in the manner of a thespian from the Edwardian era, holding his hand up to his ear as though he were listening for the phantom huntsman. As a result this cameo was left on the cutting room floor. It was a pity that Bruce adopted this attitude because it meant that little of his eccentric charm found its way into *Living Jazz*.

Despite his wonderful skills on alto saxophone and clarinet, Bruce was not an adept bandleader. Often we would arrive in a town without knowing where we were due to play and this meant buying a local newspaper to find out the whereabouts of our gig. We tried a system of date-sheets detailing future bookings well in advance, but Bruce was embarrassed when he had to distribute a sparse listing of gigs so he filled up the empty spaces with imaginary gigs in places he knew from looking through his atlas (one of his favourite pastimes). Dingle was one of the places he listed but then, a week or two before the engagement was due to take place, Bruce would say, 'Sorry Dads, but the Dingle job has been cancelled.'

Each member of the Jump Band carried the group's complicated repertoire in his head. No music was used on the bandstand, despite the intricacy of the arrangements, written by Bruce, Johnny Armatage and me. The memorising of the arrangements meant a slick presentation, but it was an obstacle if anyone in the band had to miss gigs because of illness. When trombonist John Mumford decided to leave the band in 1961 we envisaged problems, but fortunately his replacement was the brilliant ex-Humphrey Lyttelton band trombonist, John Picard. John had already made plans to become a full-time estate agent but decided to first spend a few months with us on the road. A lively and pleasant companion, he encouraged us to create spontaneous head arrangements during his brief stay with the band. His eventual replacement was Pete Strange. Pete was younger than the rest of us but he was already a formidable trombonist with lots of jazz experience coupled with service as an army musician. He later became an outstanding arranger, but had not yet developed that side of his talents. An even-tempered and generous Londoner (almost a Cockney), he set great store on the merits of a good pint of beer, but rarely got drunk. Later Pete and Bruce worked together in Humphrey Lyttelton's band.

A minority of the people who had been attracted to trad soon tired of the music and began listening to and appreciating other forms of jazz. This obviously helped us and our agent, Jim Godbolt, who handled various bands including Mick Mulligan's Magnolia Jazz Band (with George Melly), Sandy Brown's band, Wally Fawkes' Troglodytes and other jazz groups. As he gradually found himself getting busier and busier, he asked me to work part-time helping him in the agency. I found it interesting to be on the other side of the fence, learning about the laws of contract, the value of publicity and promotion and the art of building a tour in a way that meant musicians didn't have to spend many hours travelling to the next engagement. I continued to work in

Bruce's band and happily the group became progressively busier. Eventually this meant I couldn't do both jobs (playing, and working in the agency) so I left Jim Godbolt in November 1961.

Soon afterwards, the Jump Band took another trip to Scandinavia, this time to Sweden and Lappland. Most of the gigs were in Stockholm and Malmö but a couple of the bookings were in the Arctic Circle, in Malmberget – our trip there was cited in Leonard Feather's *Encyclopedia of Jazz* as being the farthest north that any jazz band had ever appeared. The month was January 1962 and not unexpectedly we encountered colossal snowfalls as we flew from Stockholm to an airport in northern Sweden, where the promoter met us and drove us into Lappland in a huge estate car, travelling for four hours through frozen tundra. Surprisingly, in view of the linguistic proficiency of most Scandinavians, our host spoke very little English. En route he decided to share with us a radio programme featuring Lappland's answer to Bob Hope. I sat next to the driver hearing the comedian issue a string of impenetrable jokes, each one punctuated by a thrust from the driver's elbow. The nudging went on for most of what was one of the most uncomfortable journeys I ever endured.

We arrived in Malmberget in the middle of the afternoon and found the town enveloped in darkness – daylight at that stage of winter only existed briefly each side of midday. The frost was so severe that every droplet of water that lurked within my trumpet froze solid during the short walk between our hotel and the hall we performed in. There we discovered that, due to the language problem, our band suits had been left at the airport. That night we went on-stage dressed as though we had just come off a building site. We

played for a concert and a dance in Malmberget, after which
it was time to bump our way along many miles of icy roads
in order to reach the airport. Fortunately there were no com-
edy programmes on the radio so we all dozed fitfully, dis-
turbed only by the driver's unmusical efforts to acquaint us
with the folk songs of old Lappland.

The *Living Jazz* film, though not a critical or commercial
triumph, gained us lots of useful publicity and some promo-
tional appearances on television. Economically things were
at last stable, but my own domestic life was about to change
dramatically. I had fallen in love with Teresa, the wife of my
good friend, John Kendall, and, as the strong feelings were
reciprocated, the only answer seemed to be to begin living
together. We left our respective homes and moved into a fur-
nished flat in west London where Teresa, who knew as much
about jazz as I did, soon organised what had been an
unkempt record collection. Her divorce came through and
we got married; eventually we moved to an unfurnished flat
near Holland Park where our first child, Jennifer, was born.

My home life was full of joy and contentment but a wave
of dissension washed over the Jump Band. Everyone in the
group seemed to have different ideas on how to capitalise on
the relative success of *Living Jazz*. It seemed to me that the
band was trying too hard to cover too many jazz styles.
Bruce's brief impersonations were one thing but having the
band change its overall sound from number to number did
not get audiences on our side. In trying to prove how versatile we were we split the listeners into different camps. Few
of them liked everything we did. An atmosphere-building
number was followed by one that went down like a cement
balloon. Some of the band felt we should play a more modern repertoire, but I was opposed to this because our swing

and mainstream numbers were always convincingly performed and constituted most of the acclaimed numbers. As
soon as discussions became heated, Bruce eased his way out
of the argument, which was left to fester.

The prevailing mood certainly affected my playing and I
began to feel increasingly jittery on-stage, so it was almost a
relief when Jim Godbolt, taking on a task that Bruce didn't
want to face up to, came to our flat to say it would be best if
I left the band. It was a disastrous time for me to be suddenly deprived of any income, with no savings and a wife and
tiny infant to support, but I felt relieved. I wasn't immediately ejected – we collectively auditioned several trumpet
players for the vacancy before settling on Ray Crane – and in
February 1963 I played my final gig with the Jump Band. I
had no ill feelings toward Bruce and we remained good
friends.

Luckily, I soon picked up some gigs and radio work,
deputising for bandleader Bob Wallis who was undergoing
surgery, but I quickly realised that a steady income was desperately needed, so within weeks of leaving Bruce I started
working for a magazine that dealt with shop equipment. To
say that I was not interested in that particular subject would
be an understatement, but I did my work conscientiously
among pleasant staff – I decided to grin and bear it for a
while hoping that something better would turn up. I did not
have to wait long.

During my touring days with Bruce Turner I had struck
up a friendship with Jim Ireland, who ran the Mardi Gras
club in Liverpool. We played there every few weeks and I
was always impressed by the stylish way Jim ran his club, one
factor being the provision of a comfortable dressing room
for the musicians, complete with a full-size snooker table.

Jim liked jazz and besides presenting it at the Mardi Gras he also promoted Liverpool concerts featuring many visiting American stars including Count Basie and Miles Davis.

Before we worked for Jim at the Mardi Gras we had, like many other jazz groups, played at the Cavern, the dank, steamy tunnel-like Liverpool club that provided a launching pad for various guitar-oriented groups, who originally played during the jazz bands' intervals. The jazz musicians dashed out to a nearby pub during their interval and remained largely unaware of the ecstatic response the local groups were enjoying. However the promoters at the Cavern realised that a musical revolution was at hand and stopped hiring jazz bands, instead offering top spots to what were then known as 'beat groups'. The Beatles began to attract a huge following while we were only too pleased to begin playing in the comparative luxury of the Mardi Gras. Earlier John Lennon had tried to persuade Jim Ireland to book the Beatles into the Mardi Gras, but Jim said he would only be interested if the group added a trumpeter. Years later Jim was present at a big ceremony where the Beatles picked up a prestigious award and as Lennon passed Jim's table he said jokingly, 'We're still not sure about adding that trumpet.'

Bowing to popular demand, Jim gradually introduced beat groups into his club but as he continued to book various jazz groups we were happy to continue playing there. One of the incoming beat groups was the Swinging Blue Jeans, who had enjoyed success at the Cavern playing a blend of skiffle, rock and roll favourites and pop songs. They soon sensed that the Merseybeat explosion was about to reshape the world's concept of popular music: they stopped using a banjo and string bass and began featuring a two guitar, bass guitar and drums line-up, performing contemporary material including their own compositions. Jim Ireland realised that the demand for his home city's new sounds was about to spread far and wide so he signed management deals with the Swinging Blue Jeans and various other local beat groups, including the Escorts.

Jim knew that at that time the heart of the British music scene was in London, so he contacted Jim Godbolt, with whom he had booked various jazz groups, and asked him to be the agent for the newly-signed groups. Jim Ireland also needed someone to handle the groups' publicity, as well as dealing with music publishers and organising fan clubs. He offered me the job and I eagerly accepted. In order to work closely with Jim Godbolt I moved into an office that was part of his Wardour Street agency. None of us had any idea how long the demand for Liverpool groups would last. Jim Ireland offered me a percentage of the groups' earnings or a generous salary, and not having a crystal ball and being so short of ready cash, I foolishly accepted the salary offer. Ireland had various other enterprises in Liverpool, including a considerable share of the earnings from that city's fruit machines. He was as tough as nails but at heart he loved artistic achievement and would have liked to have been a musician or a writer. He was courteous, kind and charming but woe betide anyone who was foolish enough to cross him; he was also an avid gambler who risked huge amounts when playing roulette or chemin de fer.

By 1963 the big record companies couldn't sign Liverpool groups fast enough, even though most of their recording managers were rather sceptical about the musical merits of these signings. In private they were condescending towards the newcomers' vocal and instrumental techniques, though a few (like George Martin) could see the potential of the rich, raw material on offer. The Swinging Blue Jeans were signed by the HMV label. Their recording manager, Wally Ridley, was a pianist and composer of the old school, a thorough professional who had created his fair share of hits, covering a variety of styles. He originally looked on bemusedly at the emergence of the Liverpool groups. Nevertheless, within weeks of making their first recordings the Swinging Blue Jeans were in the lower reaches of the hit parade with 'It's Too Late Now'. As a result Jim Godbolt's telephone never stopped ringing as promoters offered him long strings of engagements for the group, and I was kept busy arranging press interviews, organising photo sessions, setting up a newsletter for fans and going on clothes-buying expeditions for the four young men: Ray Ennis, Ralph Ellis, Norman Kuhlke and Les Braid. Part of my job involved sorting through the demo discs and sheet music that arrived in every post from hopeful composers and songwriters – we listened to everything that reached us but rarely found anything that was even mildly promising. I remember going into the office just after the Christmas 1963 break and finding some sheet music for a piece called 'Yuletide Rock and Roll', with a note from the composer saying, 'You may think I'm late for Christmas, but actually I'm very early for next December 25th.'

By early 1964 the Swinging Blue Jeans had made great progress, with a recording that was either first or second in the charts, depending on which music paper one read. A friend of the group had given drummer Norman Kuhlke an American-issued single by Chan Romero, singing his own composition 'Hippy Hippy Shake'. She suggested it would be an ideal number for the group to record, and so it was. Singer Ray Ennis' spirited, slightly hoarse singing added a layer of zest that the original version lacked. The new recording instantly won over the disc jockeys and the record buyers. One of the group's own songs 'Now I Must Go' was on the B-side, which meant that besides their performers' royalties they also earned money as composers.

At first HMV had been lukewarm about recording 'Hippy Hippy Shake'. Wally Ridley hearing the song for the first time said (out of the group's earshot), 'This sounds like something that Johnny Kidd and the Pirates did years ago.' But he went along with the idea and didn't baulk at the A-side's short duration (under two minutes). Although the Beatles never recorded the number it was part of their early repertoire and they felt that the Swinging Blue Jeans had stolen a march by recording it. Nevertheless, they voted the disc 'a hit' (albeit a trifle reluctantly) when they reviewed it on television's *Juke Box Jury*. On New Year's Eve 1964 Teresa and I were kept awake until dawn by a neighbour (unaware of our connection) playing 'Hippy Hippy Shake' over and over again throughout the night – it was an omen that the record was bound for the top of the hit parade. The fan who passed on the vital original recording was Sue Johnston, later to become the distinguished actress who starred in many television successes, including *The Royle Family* and *Brookside*. The Swinging Blue Jeans' version of 'Hippy Hippy Shake' has stood the test of time and sounded as fresh and appealing as ever when I heard it played in a 2003 edition of *The Simpsons*.

The success of the single meant that I was kept busy thinking up new publicity angles about the Swinging Blue Jeans, and to keep the pot boiling I sometimes improvised or reshaped stories about their escapades. On one occasion I had a sudden brainwave that linked the group with Russia. They had appeared in a short film using a 'Circlorama' process which projected images on to linked screens

designed to surround a standing audience, and there was
some talk that this new process might be exported to
Moscow. I sent out a press release conjecturing that the
Swinging Blue Jeans might go to Russia to help publicise the
film (*Circlorama Cavalcade*), and I suggested that if they did
it would mean that the Soviet authorities were at last indicating a softening of attitude towards western pop music.
Next day every national newspaper carried the story – the
Daily Express even hired a set of Cossack uniforms for a
group photograph. Within hours of the story breaking a
messenger from the Soviet embassy delivered an official note
to me (in Russian) that Tony Cash, a BBC producer, kindly
translated for me. It sternly pointed out that there was no
possibility of a British pop group playing in Soviet Russia.
The arrival of this note revived the embers of the story and
produced a further glow of publicity.

The nearest we got to Russia was Finland, where the
group were consistently mobbed. This was early days for
British groups to work in Finland and the authorities there
were totally unused to scenes of mass hysteria at pop concerts. As a result security was left totally to chance. After
one concert the group, plus Jim Ireland and I, left the concert hall through the stage door and were instantly separated and swept away in different directions by the wildly
enthusiastic crowd. As I was being carried along by an army
of manhandling well-wishers, I was fortunate enough to be
grabbed by two policemen who plucked me out of the mael-
strom to lift me into a cage on the back of a police van. A
worrying hour went by before we were all reunited at the
hotel, bruised and dishevelled.

For publicists, over-embellishment carries a risk, as when
I wrote that Les Braid, the bass guitarist, was learning to

swim in the 'Flunder Pool' near Hamburg's Star Club, only to discover on my first visit to the spot that the pool was little bigger than a drinking fountain.

I went to Hamburg with Jim Ireland to accompany the Swinging Blue Jeans in order to fulfil a contract they had signed on a previous visit. It was for very little money and Jim thought that if we both went over to argue the case we might convince the club owner to pay a more realistic amount, particularly as the group were set to do sell-out business. We finally got into the chief's office, daunted to discover that three burly henchmen had followed us into the dimly lit room. A long silence followed Jim's polite request for improved payment, then a rasping sound began to get louder and louder. The chief, wearing dark glasses, was vigorously rubbing his thumbs on a huge rubber mat that almost filled the top of his desk. This was obviously something he did regularly because his constant tweaking had re-shaped the mat into a series of hills and dales. This eerie sound was soon augmented by a frightening growl that emanated from the chief's throat as though he was attempting to cough up a huge fur ball. The sinister blending of these two sounds was truly frightening and, although Jim Ireland was one of the bravest men I have ever known, we came to a simultaneous conclusion that further negotiations would be fruitless, and we left the room with as much strut as we could muster. The group were held to the signed contract and completed a highly successful residency for a pittance, declining an offer to play a return booking.

The Swinging Blue Jeans tours in Britain were always well received: the group became popular without being idolised. They were basically four nice young Scouse lads whose music pleased people rather than enthralled them. We tried to get them to flaunt the wearing of denim to link in with their name, but they preferred wearing Ivy League suits with shirts and ties, although later they saw the sense of linking image and name and began wearing jeans and jean jackets. Other groups got caught in the suit dilemma, including the Rolling Stones, but they too quickly reverted to an earthier image.

The Swinging Blue Jeans toured briefly with the Rolling Stones which gave me the chance to renew acquaintanceship with drummer Charlie Watts. I had worked with Charlie years earlier when I guested with a jazz band in Kingsbury, north-west London. In those days Charlie was a keen and promising jazz drummer who was not overloaded with funds. This meant he took his drums to and from gigs on a London Transport bus (provided the conductor allowed him to do so). The other member of the Stones who often talked to me about jazz was guitarist Brian Jones. It was something he was very keen on but he preferred discussions on that subject to be clandestine because he didn't want the other members of the group, or eavesdropping journalists, to know how engrossed he was in jazz.

The Blue Jeans never toured with the Beatles, though they appeared together at the Cavern and on a few early radio shows, but even then John, Paul, George and Ringo were moving towards super-stardom. If the Blue Jeans felt any envy in surveying the colossal achievements of the Beatles they never showed it, despite having a similar pedigree in the history of early Liverpool beat groups. If anything they had a huge Liverpudlian sense of pride in fellow Scousers' achievements.

During the following years several of the Swinging Blue Jeans' recordings made the top twenty of the hit parade, including a number three spot for 'You're No Good' (a fine rendition by Ray Ennis of Betty Everett's hit) and a chart placing for a re-make of 'Good Golly Miss Molly'. I wrote a number for them, 'Promise You'll Tell Her', which popped in and out of the charts without causing a stir, and later the group proved their versatility with a moving version of 'Don't Make Me Over'.

Looking back, one realises that the group's weakness was in failing to establish an instantly recognisable individuality – they could recreate other people's recordings skilfully and effectively but they could not find their own sound and style. Gradually record sales dwindled but fortunately the group were always adept at putting on a satisfying stage show so they continued to work regularly over the following decades. It is very difficult, however, to get publicity for a group that is not in the hit parade so eventually, after a three-year stint, we parted company, the best of friends. I kept in touch with Jim Ireland for the rest of his life.

8

Finding Fawkes and Meeting Melly

Throughout the time I worked for Jim Ireland I continued to play gigs, mostly in the London area, leading a quartet which, thanks to owner Roger Horton, played a long residency at his 100 Club in Oxford Street. I also played in, and arranged for, a fine big band that Alex Welsh led in 1963 and over a longer period I was part of a big band led by trumpeter Mike Daniels, a talented and considerate man who had a deep understanding of vintage jazz. Mike generously featured my playing and looked the other way when I had had too much to drink, but he was never afraid to speak his mind. On one gig the comedian Marty Feldman (who played trumpet enthusiastically) climbed on to the stage unasked, clutching a trumpet, ready to blow with us, reasoning, I suppose, that he was famous enough to take such a liberty. Mike knew him of old and said in a stern voice, 'You are not going to sit in. I told you that thirty years ago. I meant it then and I mean it now.'

There was a nice spirit within Mike's big band, but I much preferred working in smaller line-ups, so in 1966 I formed a sextet which was billed as John Chilton's Swing Kings. I used two tenor saxists, John Lee and Frank Brooker (who both doubled on clarinet), Roy Vaughan on piano, Chuck Smith on drums and various bass players. Our intent was to revive compositions of the 1930s and 1940s that had been unjustly neglected. This strategy appealed to several club owners and (with Jim Godbolt as our agent) we played a series of regular bookings in various cities, as well as broadcasting on BBC *Jazz Club* and playing a residency at the Six Bells in Chelsea. To our delight we were also booked to accompany the great ex-Count Basie trumpeter Buck Clayton on a spring 1967 tour. Buck always looked suave on-stage, radiating a formidable presence, his furrowed brow half hiding extraordinary blue-green eyes. He didn't go in for overt showmanship but backstage he was a model of friendliness, likely to bear-hug each of his accompanists. On tour with us Buck played magnificently, perpetually improvising phrases that seemed to glow as they left the bell of his trumpet. Unfortunately in the middle of the tour he collapsed in his hotel room and then spent a week in hospital with blood pressure problems but, happily, first class American stars such as trumpeter Bill Coleman and tenor saxist Ben Webster were on hand to deputise. I regularly learnt more in one night playing alongside these jazz giants than I had by listening to hundreds of hours of recordings.

Bill Coleman, a master of graceful improvising, was a charming man who patiently explained what he wanted but didn't fly off the handle if things went awry. Ben Webster became a friend, though his moods (usually governed by the quantity of alcohol he had taken aboard) were unpredictable. He might rant and rave one minute and weep the next, but my, what a player! His huge tone reminded me of childhood days in the country when the sound of a tractor roaring into

life shattered the silence of a frosty morning. Ben was hugely sentimental and would, on occasion, burst into tears when
saying farewell to someone he was going to see during the
following week.

One day Ben surreptitiously asked me if I knew where he
could buy some nutmeg ('to put on my ice cream'). I surmised that he wanted it for a different usage: Kansas City
musicians of yesteryear used to put a spoonful of the spice
into a bottle of Coca Cola and swallow the bubbling brew
which, it was said, produced a mild hallucinatory 'buzz'. As
we were close to Soho I took Ben into the nearest grocery
store where I treated him to four ounces of the dark dust,
only to hear him say, 'And the same for me please.' I had no
intention of trying out the mixture so Ben went off happily
clutching a half pound of the substance. A year later Ben
re-visited London and we met up again. I thought I'd resume
the easy relationship by asking Ben if he needed any nutmeg,
but he gave me a fierce look and said emphatically, 'You've
got the wrong guy.' If Ben was in a grumpy mood, however,
the surest way of bringing a smile to his face was to get him
talking about stride piano playing, of which he was a highly
competent exponent. Given half a chance he would sit himself at a keyboard and rattle off some lively pieces complete
with the emphatic left hand patterns that are the vital com-
ponents of stride playing.

I had heard about Ben's pianistic skills from other
American jazzmen, but no one ever mentioned that Charlie
Shavers (one of the most technically gifted trumpeters who
ever lived) was also a formidable pianist. I found this out
when my band had the pleasure of accompanying Charlie for
a memorable gig at the 100 Club. The preliminary rehearsal
with him almost didn't take place because on arriving at the

club in the afternoon we found the place padlocked. A run-through was vital because I wanted to try to recreate some of the John Kirby Sextet numbers that featured Charlie. We waited impatiently for a long time, then one of the band got a huge wrench and smashed the padlock, while Charlie looked on with eyes twinkling and said, 'Now, that's what I call keenness.' During the time that elapsed while Chuck Smith was setting up his drums I got out my trumpet and started warming up. Charlie sat at the piano and accom-panied me on some standard tunes; after a few bars I realised that I was being backed by a really top class pianist and Charlie made the point even more obvious by taking a cou-ple of brilliant solos. We in the band were flabbergasted and I asked Charlie why he didn't proclaim these unsung skills. 'I just don't like playing piano in public,' he said. 'I have enough of a battle with the trumpet.' This last comment was pure modesty since Charlie was a brass virtuoso of the highest order as he was to prove on every number he played with us that night before an audience who were transported by his brilliance.

My wife Teresa, who had been a professional photogra-pher, was by now too busy raising our children Jenny and Martin to follow that calling, but she encouraged me to bor-row her Rolleiflex and take shots of visiting American jazz musicians. On one occasion she was not able to fulfil a com-mission to photograph the wonderful pianist Earl Hines so I went instead. Earl was a willing, extrovert sitter, but the problem was that he wore the most ill-fitting wig ever seen: someone said it appeared to have fallen from a tree and stuck where it landed. As I started taking photographs of Earl, he called me aside and said in confidential tones, 'Can

you please make sure you get your angles right because my
hair tends to stick up.'

During this same period I assisted the Jazz Horizons company (jointly run by Jim Godbolt and Jack Higgins) in shep-
herding various American jazz stars to and from their UK
gigs. Jim I had known for years; Jack (then also part of the
Harold Davison Organisation) I knew less well. Later this
situation changed when Jack became the agent for George
Melly and the Feetwarmers. Through my duties for Jazz
Horizons I was able to travel and converse with jazz musicians I had admired for years, including Henry 'Red' Allen,
Dicky Wells, Vic Dickenson, Edmond Hall, Bud Freeman,
Wingy Manone and Rex Stewart. In the hours before and
after a gig these heroes talked revealingly about their careers
and those of various illustrious colleagues, and I was able to
glean many facts that proved extremely useful when I began
writing books about jazz.

Henry Allen was the perfect subject for a biography
because he possessed and was willing to share a remarkable
memory, taking a great pride in being part of jazz history.
But it wasn't only facts gleaned from these great jazzmen
that proved useful. Rex Stewart's daughter, Regina, arrived
unexpectedly in London during her dad's tour and tried
without success to get a room in dozens of London hotels.
Rex asked for my help and somehow I managed to find
a vacancy in a nice, central hotel. Rex was overjoyed and
said, 'John, what can I do to express my thanks? Just say the
word.' I plucked up courage and asked a huge favour in
requesting Rex to show me the secret of his half-valving
technique which had been a much talked-about feature of
his recordings with Duke Ellington. Without a moment's
hesitation, he fixed a time and a date for me to visit him for

a lesson, during which he showed me how to produce the sound effectively. Despite his help and advice I never got anywhere near mastering the effect, but this wasn't through any lack of effort on Rex's part.

Bud Freeman, an anglophile of the first order, was keen to let fans know that he always wore Church's celebrated English shoes but if one could get Bud off the subject of Bud he had many interesting things to say about Chicago in the 1920s. Dicky Wells was friendly enough but was in the grip of alcoholism. Wingy Manone's technique was a little rusty by the time he came to Britain, but his wit was still sharp and his candour rapier-like. He asked me where one could buy the best handmade clothes in London. I said, with some enthusiasm, that they would be found in Savile Row, 'How come you look so shabby then?' he said without missing a beat.

The routine of the Swing Kings often involved travelling hundreds of miles at the weekend to play distant gigs, but gradually we began to wind down the travel and concentrated on working in and around London. This schedule suited a new family enterprise. My mother died in 1967 and left us a few hundred pounds, which was just enough for us to carry out Teresa's dream of opening a bookshop that specialised in jazz: tiny premises, little bigger than a kiosk had become vacant in Great Ormond Street, close to where we lived. We took the lease and began trading as the Bloomsbury Book Shop, specialising in jazz, but also stocking works by Virginia Woolf, Lytton Strachey and other Bloomsburyites as well as general secondhand books. The hours of opening were from 10 am until 3 pm which allowed Teresa to deliver and collect Jenny and Martin from school. This arrangement worked satisfactorily until Teresa gave birth to our third child,

Barnaby, whose arrival meant I temporarily had to take over the running of the bookshop, which, on the whole, I enjoyed. We were tempted to claim the premises as being the world's smallest book shop – it certainly merited the notice we placed in the window which said, 'If you're under 25 stone come in and browse.' This message was sited alongside a placard I devised which read, 'If you think your life is boring you should read some of our books.' At least once a week someone would call in to ask if I was aware that such a message had two meanings. Naturally I said, 'No,' but invariably they bought a book before leaving.

Teresa and I took it in turns to scour various London open-air markets in order to find books to re-stock the shelves, and in doing so we came across a few treasures, Teresa's coup being the purchase of a signed, limited first edition of James Joyce's *Ulysses*. The price: fifty pence. Because we badly needed capital we foolishly sold this rarity soon after it came into our hands whereas we should have raised money on it via a bank and then watched its value grow by hundreds of pounds every year. Another fine item reached us on the very day that Teresa opened the shop. A stranger entered and said, 'I've read this book, take it as a gift.' Thanks would have been in order for a donation of the humblest paperback but this was something special: the rare first edition of John Steinbeck's first book *Cup of Gold*. Teresa leapt to her feet to express gratitude but the amazingly kind donor hurried away without saying a word. Whether he was the patron saint of secondhand book sellers and wanted us to get off to a good start, we never found out because he never called again.

A set of books by Emile Zola also provided a mystery. A browser put a deposit on them and said he would be back the next day to collect them, but tomorrow never came and this made foot-space scarce under our solitary desk. After six months had passed we put the books back on the shelf, and no sooner had we done so than a woman entered the shop and gave a gasp of delight, saying the Zola set was just what she wanted. She said she could not take the books then but would be back within the week, and she insisted on paying a substantial deposit. The plot repeated itself, we never saw the woman again and six months later we contemplated putting the set on display again, but the thought of going through another replay was too much to contemplate. Instead we put the books out one by one and sold them easily.

The dimensions of the Bloomsbury Book Shop meant it was impossible not to be aware of a customer entering. Usually I looked up from whatever I was reading and attempted a smile, but on one particular morning I was so engrossed in a book-trade periodical that I didn't even glance at the newcomer. The article that so intrigued me was by a bookseller who described a frosty encounter he had had with Graham Greene. I finished the piece then glanced at the solitary customer – it was Graham Greene. 'You won't believe this, Mr Greene, but I've just finished reading an account of your visit to a small secondhand book shop. I look up and here you are.' The great man gave a wan smile as I waved the magazine at him. 'Yes,' he said, 'I've read that, but naturally I viewed the incident rather differently.' I was nonplussed. The obscure publication had only arrived that morning yet the famous author had already found time to take in the contents of this small circulation trade journal. He went on to talk about living in Bloomsbury years before; he was revisiting the area to see a friend who was a patient in the nearby Italian Hospital. I pulled a copy of *Our Man in Havana* from the shelf and asked if he would mind signing it for me – he asked my name and wrote a warm inscription. We went on to discuss his days as a film critic and the name of Harold Lloyd cropped up. I commented that Lloyd had named one of his characters Harold Diddlebock only to find the real H. D. demanding an apology. Greene smiled and said, 'I always make a special point of avoiding any name that might be recognised.' We shook hands and he buttoned up his excessively long black overcoat and left. Some while later I read Greene's *The Human Factor* and saw that he had named a character (who appears only once) Chilton.

From the late sixties onwards I did my best to combine two activities: playing the trumpet and writing books about jazz. My first effort at the latter enterprise was in sharing, with Max Jones, authorship of a biography of Louis Armstrong.

My own first book, *Who's Who of Jazz (Storyville to Swing Street)* was published in 1970, with its origins in the compilation of the jazz scrapbook I had started as a twelve-year-old. The facts and figures I collected soon filled the first scrapbook to overflowing and I then began utilising index cards, filling them with the biographical details of hundreds and hundreds of American jazz musicians. Later I was able to interview visiting musicians and I was greatly helped when my Swiss friend, Johnny Simmen, sent me various American musicians' union listings of members and their addresses. This meant I was able to contact many fine players whose career achievements and biographical details had never been published. I gradually came to the conclusion that putting all this information together would form a worthwhile reference book. Teresa and I thought it a risk worth taking to

Parents, Thomas and Eileen Chilton.

Ron, Tom and John Chilton, Northampton, 1942.

The High Society Jazz Band, Harrow, 1952. *Left to right*: Jim Leaper, Sid Taylor, John Chilton, Boz Marsden.

Top: Mr Kofi and his Rhythm including JC, London, March 1958.

Above: Bruce Turner's Jump Band, Paris Studios, London, 1959. *Left to right*: John Mumford, Turner, JC, Stan Greig, John Armatage, Toni Goffe.

Right: With the Swinging Blue Jeans, 1963. *Left to right*: Les Braid, Ralph Ellis, Ray Ennis, Norman Kuhlke, JC (photo by Teresa Chilton).

Left: John Chilton's Swing Kings, London, 1967. *Left to right*: Chuck Smith, Frank Brooker, JC, Keith Howard, Roy Vaughan, John Lee (photo by Reg Peerless).

Left: Buck Clayton and JC, London, 1967 (photo by Reg Peerless).

Below: New Merlin's cave, London, 1972. *Left to right*: JC, Bruce Turner, Matty Matlock, Wally Fawkes (photo by Brian Peerless).

Above: Flip Phillips and JC,
Newport Jazz Festival, 1978
(photo by Mitchell Seidel).

Right: George Melly and the
Feetwarmers, London, 1974.
Left to right: Steve Fagg, Chuck
Smith, Collin Bates, Melly, JC.

Below: A visit to the Laurel and
Hardy Museum in Ulverston, 1981.
Left to right: Barry Dillon, unknown,
George Melly, Bill Cubin, JC,
Bruce Boardman, Chuck Smith.

Left: JC and Teresa Chilton with recording company executive Derek Taylor, London, 1976.

Below: George Melly and the Feetwarmers, at Eddie Condon's Club, W. 54th Street, New York, 1978. *Left to right*: Stan Greig, Barry Dillon, Melly, JC, Chuck Smith (photo by Souvenir Shots).

Above left: Ronnie Scott and George Melly, 1980s (photo by John Chilton).

Above right: A thirsty time in Australia. George Melly, St Kilda, 1983 (photo by John Chilton).

Below: George Melly and the Feetwarmers, 1990. *Left to right*: Ron Rubin, Melly, JC, Eddie Taylor, Ken Baldock (photo by Robert Carpenter Turner).

Left: Melly on a gig at Newmarket race-course, straight from receiving an honorary fellowship from Liverpool John Moores University, July 1990.

Below: George Melly and the Feetwarmers, at Ronnie Scott's Club, Birmingham, 1993. *Left to right*: Eddie Taylor, Jonathan Vinten, JC, Melly, Ken Baldock (photo by Terry Walker).

Above: With Slim Gaillard, 1987.

Right: Gigs afloat with George Melly, Saga Rose cruise, April 2001.

Below: With Teresa and children: Barnaby, Jenny and Martin in Surrey, July 2004 (photo by Jean Convy).

publish it ourselves (as The Bloomsbury Book Shop). To our great relief the book sold well, and by a streak of good luck it achieved good sales in the USA where the Chilton Book Company (no connection) published an American edition. This old-established publisher (which took its name from the first woman to disembark from the *Mayflower*) had suddenly begun to get a spate of orders for '*Who's Who of Jazz* – Chilton'. They quickly came to the conclusion that the book was worth publishing and made contact with us. As a result, contracts were signed and sealed. Later there was a gratifying spin-off when the giant Time-Life Corporation published an edition, as did Macmillan in London.

But, as if to counterbalance this good luck, Max Jones (the *Melody Maker*'s jazz specialist) and I suffered a big disappointment over our book *Louis – The Louis Armstrong Story*. Researching that book was a continual thrill because Louis himself gave us unstinting help, patiently answering dozens of questions in a way that demonstrated his remarkable memory. Earlier Max, Leonard Feather and I had compiled a paperback tribute *Salute to Satchmo* which Louis liked, and this led to him suggesting that Max and I do a full scale biography. The book was favourably reviewed by various critics including Philip Larkin and an American edition went into production – but then came the letdown. A brief item in the City pages of various national newspapers announced that the London-based publishers of the book had suddenly gone out of business. I hurried round to their offices only to find all of the staff making for the exits, the boss, Nicholas Luard, having already departed. Unfortunately, all our royalties and the American advance had been swallowed up by the company's fiscal difficulties.

One morning, as I was taking a parcel of books to a local

post office, I spotted a familiar figure standing astride a bicycle waiting for the traffic lights to change. It was Wally Fawkes, whose passionate clarinet and soprano sax playing had put him a class above most of the musicians on the British jazz scene. Wally was making his way to the *Daily Mail*'s offices where he fulfilled his other working role as 'Trog', one of the world's most celebrated cartoonists. He invited me to go along and sit in with his trio that evening at a pub in Fleet Street, so a few hours later I began sharing some numbers with Wally, Geoff Kemp on double bass and Ray Smith on drums. We got on like a house on fire and I was delighted when Wally asked me to become a regular member of the line-up. Wally's dedication to jazz is total. He is a generous man who can be stubborn but he possesses a remarkable sense of humour which leads him to make the sort of bold observation that others might incubate – for Wally there can be no postponement of an apt comment. In an eightieth birthday tribute he was described as 'a very strong, independent, determined man'. Wally's character and resolute outlook meant he didn't welcome people coming up to the bandstand requesting inappropriate numbers, and his method of refusal left the person requesting the number confused and speechless. If someone asked for 'Cherry Pink', Wally would say, 'Too late I'm afraid, we're already on letter J.' Or if the plea was for 'Tequila', he'd say, 'Sorry but we're not going to get past the M's and N's tonight.'

Pianist Johnny Parker, with whom Wally had worked, led a band for Sunday sessions at New Merlin's Cave, a big pub (with an adjoining dance hall) near London's Mount Pleasant mail sorting office, but ill health meant that Johnny was unable to continue so Wally suggested that we fill the Sunday lunchtime residency. With Wally on clarinet and

soprano sax, me on trumpet, Bill Greenow on alto sax, Les
Handscombe on trombone, Colin Parnell on piano, Steve
Fagg on double bass and my old pal Chuck Smith on drums,
we began playing at New Merlin's Cave in June 1969. Les
Handscombe soon left. Bill Greenow went off to lead his
own band and was replaced by Bruce Turner (who had just
left Acker Bilk). Colin Parnell departed and in his place came
the ex-Jump Band pianist, Collin Bates.

We began what was to be a long stay inauspiciously, playing in the pub's hall to about ten people, but thanks to
publicity gained by the indefatigable organiser, Graham
Tayar (a BBC producer), the crowds started rolling in,
increasing each week: from ten to fifty, from one hundred to
two hundred and then on to three hundred people.
Remuneration was in the shape of whatever coins Graham
and fellow organiser, Duncan Hamilton managed to collect
in pint glasses, but money was incidental. The band was
totally devoted to playing jazz and I never felt as inspired as
when I blew alongside Fawkes and Turner. They created
some wonderful improvisations, each determined not to be
outdone by the other. Wally was a passionate devotee of
Sidney Bechet (whose sound had first attracted me to jazz
in 1944), so it seemed appropriate that we adopted the
name that Bechet used for his band – we became the
Fawkes–Chilton Feetwarmers.

Bertram 'Steve' Stevens, the landlord at New Merlin's, was
a misunderstood man, mainly because he couched most of
his observations in Cockney rhyming slang. Our main bone
of contention with him was the awfulness of the ancient
grand piano on which Collin Bates was expected to perform.
Collin's technique was such that he could make a bad piano
sound good, but the instrument at New Merlin's came close

to defeating him. It was out of tune and lacked several keys as well as having soggy innards, liquidised by countless split drinks. Collin kept asking, 'Please do something about the piano, Steve.' We joined in the nagging without success. Then, one Sunday, Steve announced, with chest-busting pride, 'I've had the Joanna done.' Collin dashed into the hall to test the renovations and we hurried close behind him. Steve certainly had been busy but his efforts were not quite what we wanted – he had painted the piano purple, and that was the sum total of the improvements.

The audiences at Merlin's continued to grow, helped by the fact that, due to an old by-law, parents could bring their children into the pub's hall (where alcoholic drinks could be consumed but not purchased). American jazzmen visiting London got to hear about the place and, as a result, a steady stream of famous jazz musicians came there to play with us (for nothing) including Roy Eldridge, Billy Butterfield, Ruby Braff, Jonah Jones, Bill Coleman, Lloyd Phillips, Ralph Sutton, Eddie Hubble, Benny Morton, Bob Wilber, Matty Matlock and Milt Buckner. Another visitor also caused a stir: he first sang at Merlin's during a benefit night for the ailing Johnny Parker, liked the ambience and started coming on a semi-regular basis. This was George Melly who, at that time, was working with Wally Fawkes (filling the balloons for Wally's *Daily Mail* 'Trog' comic strip) as well as being film critic for the *Observer*. Gradually George became a regular at Merlin's, by which time it was packed for every one of our Sunday lunchtime sessions, with an overflow of people standing outside in Margery Street listening to the music through the open doors.

We started getting national publicity and did a few television and radio shows. Increasingly, we got offers to play for various student unions, some of them at distant universities. The problem about accepting these gigs was the mileage involved. Neither Wally nor Bruce wanted to play long distance gigs so, for engagements out of London, we often worked as a five-piece unit, George Melly singing, backed by me and the rhythm section.

During this period, Derek Taylor, previously the press officer for the Beatles and then working for WEA–Warner Brothers recording company, came to see us in action. At this time, every gig we did had the feel of 'a happening', largely due to our reckless intake of alcohol. Derek liked the music and was intrigued and entertained by the deliberately awful interludes in which George Melly and I revived hoary old routines favoured by unsuccessful double-acts of the 1930s. 'What is Mrs Simpson's favourite toy?' I'd ask, to which George archly replied, 'A Teddy Bear.' We'd then cut through the loud groans of the audience to pile on the corn. John: 'I call my girlfriend Cocoa.' George: 'Why? because she's sweet and hot?' John: 'No, 'cause she's cheap and easy to make.' But despite this absurd tomfoolery we made sure that our missionary zeal for the propagation of jazz was a vital part of each performance, with George telling the audience the background to the numbers in our repertoire originally made famous by Bessie Smith, Louis Armstrong, Duke Ellington, Jelly Roll Morton, and so on. Our devout hope was that some of the listeners would become as hooked on jazz as we were.

This strange mixture of frivolity and a passionate devotion to improvised music put us exactly on Derek's wavelength and within a short time he had changed our lives. Ray Coleman, a former editor of *Melody Maker*, described Derek as 'a theatrical, slightly conspiratorial man'. But for George and the band he was perfect company: witty, generous and perceptive, at his happiest when talking about wartime radio shows, music-hall memories and anecdotes about offbeat characters. He resolved to record George and the band, so, in June 1972, after playing our usual Sunday lunchtime session at Merlin's we made our way to Ronnie Scott's Club in Frith Street in central London to finalise a sound balance prior to making live recordings in front of a specially invited audience.

Warner Brothers spared no expense. All the drinks that the band and the audience supped were free, which, as we had already downed a good quota during our session at Merlin's, was a dangerously generous move. The first half went reasonably well, but by the time the band had done more guzzling during the interval it was a close run thing as to who was the more drunk, the band or the listeners. Those in the audience who were still mobile danced with abandon between the tables while the band tumbled through a batch of lively songs, egged on by Melly's lusty vocals. Later, when we listened to the playbacks of the session in the unfrenzied air of a recording studio we realised that only one number from the entire second half of our performance was issuable. Every wart seemed to be highlighted, including the climactic moment at the conclusion of the recording when George stepped forward (in the tradition of La Scala, Milan) to receive a bouquet but fell into the audience and was too top-heavy with drink to get back on-stage. One afternoon, a few weeks later, we sheepishly crept back into an empty Ronnie Scott's Club and re-recorded enough numbers to make up an album, which was issued under the defiant title *Nuts*. Sounds of an enthusiastic audience were dubbed in so skilfully that none of the reviewers, even those who had been at the original fiasco, realised that rescue tactics had been used.

Our packed sessions continued at Merlin's but we also began to play a Thursday night residency at a pub in Islington, where the band usually operated as a quintet, with Bruce Turner and I making up the front line, George Melly and Wally Fawkes both being busy with their press commitments. The crowds at this new venue began to grow as did the time we spent there after the pub's closing time, rubbing shoulders with professional footballers and off-duty policemen. At one such late night affair a drunk climbed on to a stool and lightly kicked anyone who walked near him, shouting, 'Hurry along, if you please.' Irritatingly, his shoe caught my glass, spilling the contents. There was no hint of an apology which led me to say to the pub's landlord, 'I've a good mind to pull him off that stool.' The landlord, instantly alarmed, said, 'For God's sake don't do that, he's a local chief inspector.' Soon after that incident we accepted an offer to play a Thursday residency at Merlin's (as well as our Sunday session), but not before American singer Susannah McCorkle had gained experience with us at the Islington venue. She had been advised to contact me by the poet Philip Larkin, and as a result I invited her to sing with us. She showed some promise but no one could have forecast the successes both in personal appearances and on record that she later achieved on both sides of the Atlantic.

Out of town gigs for George and the quartet continued to flow in and as a result we played numerous one night stands in places far away from London – after a four hundred mile round journey we got back to London and attempted to do a day's work. George's work as a film critic began early in the mornings and I was helping Teresa run the bookshop and

beginning my next book, on Billie Holiday. Clearly a big
decision was looming: we either played music full-time or
we curtailed our activities. The turning point came in May
1973 when George, myself and Collin Bates played a hugely
enjoyable gig in Oxford – organised by Alyn Shipton (then a
student, later to be a distinguished writer and broadcaster).
My great friend, Brian Peerless, drove us to and from Oxford
and on the return trip, still exhilarated by the pleasures of
the gig, George, Collin and I decided that from the end of
that year we would work together professionally as George
Melly with John Chilton's Feetwarmers. Neither Wally
nor Bruce was interested in becoming part of this full-time
project, but drummer Chuck Smith and bassist Steve Fagg
enthusiastically agreed with our decision.

In the remaining months of 1973 we played a number of
contrasting dates: one night in a pub, the next at a huge rock,
jazz and blues festival. One such big gathering was the
August 1973 Reading Festival. Derek Taylor drove George
and me to that celebrated event but on the way he suggested we drop in on his old friend, the Beatle George Harrison,
who lived near Henley. George and Patti (then his wife)
made us welcome even though they were just about to start
a late, late breakfast. After he had finished eating, George
Harrison suddenly said he would like to go to the festival,
but we had to link up with the rest of the band at Reading so
we couldn't wait for him. Nevertheless, he promised to
follow on. I took this information with a pinch of salt and
didn't even think it worth mentioning to Collin, Chuck
and Steve as we prepared to go on-stage – we were slightly
apprehensive because none of the other attractions on
the bill played jazz. As we strode out to greet the audience
of thirty thousand, I looked behind me and was totally

astonished to see a 'roadie' putting a drum stool in position and then tidying up the stage. It was George Harrison. Nobody in the crowd had recognised him – the thought of seeing a world famous rock star roadieing for a middle-aged jazz group was too improbable for anyone to contemplate.

Despite the increased distances we were covering we kept playing at Merlin's for as long as was practical, a decision that fitted in neatly with a WEA–Warner Brothers' plan to record a follow-up album there, whimsically entitled *Son of Nuts.* This, like its progenitor, was to be recorded live in front of an invited audience in September 1973, and for the occasion WEA hired a magnificent grand piano. The band and George were a little more temperate than at the *Nuts* session, but the old demon grog took over for the last few numbers including a befuddled version of the old music-hall song 'Show Me the Way to Go Home'. George's vocals sounded like a desperate plea for guidance and directions, two things that the incoherent musical support was unable to offer. Some months later I was listening to a BBC2 television announcer closing down the night's transmission and to my utter astonishment he played this track as the sign-off theme. I conjectured that he was leaving the Corporation the next day and had made the selection for a bet. But I had reason to be grateful for the *Son of Nuts* session because it marked the initial recording of my composition 'Good Time George', which became George Melly's signature tune for the next thirty years.

The most important event during the run-in period prior to our return to full-time playing was our first residency at Ronnie Scott's. Our June 1972 recording session there had given the club's owners, Ronnie Scott and Pete King, a chance to observe the drinking capacity of the people who came to hear George Melly. The entrepreneurial sense of both men made them realise that, allowing for the falling about and musical misadventure that marked our performances in those early days, we might bring in a lot of business and our combination of jazz, blues and humour was worth a trial booking. It was something of a bold decision on their part because the music we played was quite different from the club's usual fare, which was mainly modern jazz. However, their hunch paid off. The boozy crowds turned up but so too did a lot of non-drinking youngsters, half-mesmerised by George's personality-filled presentation – he soon became an 'in' figure. We had no sooner finished one residency at Scott's than we were booked for another, setting a pattern that continued for over three decades. The Ronnie Scott Agency, which then had offices above the club, began to get us all sorts of work, and it was agreed that they would become our main representatives when we went back on the road, with Peter 'Chips' Chipperfield looking after our interests in liaison with Derek Taylor, and with John Darnley of Warner Brothers acting as our tour manager.

During our first residencies at Scott's we played opposite American jazz stars Frank Rosolino and Elvin Jones but we soon graduated to being the main attraction, supported by various British quartets and quintets. We gradually got to know Ronnie, and it was his group that appeared with us more often than any other. This gave us a chance not only to hear his fine tenor sax playing but also to appreciate his skills as a stand-up comedian, whose exquisite timing in telling a set repertoire of jokes made them everlastingly funny. Ronnie's business partner, Pete King, was, on the surface, a more serious fellow. Having been a professional saxophonist, he was well aware of the wiles and schemes of jazz musicians.

Pete's impassive face gave little away but over our years at the club we built up a warm friendship with him. During those early days we did our best to belie our middle-aged appearances by proving we had stamina to spare and regularly played other gigs prior to our nightly appearances at the club. A dash from an early evening engagement in Southend to Frith Street was not unusual and on one occasion we played a gig before our two sets at the club and then another job that lasted until dawn.

It was the residencies at Scott's that developed our professionalism. George seemingly had unlimited energy and an abundance of charisma but in the early days his presentation was rather directionless. His ad-lib comments sometimes clicked but often they made him appear much more of a smart arse than he was, and left to his own devices he would sing three very similar songs one after the other. Invariably, he would belt out a long finishing note on each of them that gradually got sharper and sharper until it wandered into another key.

The band needed to be more consistent, with shaped introductions and neater endings. The 'cod' gags were consigned to the deep and were replaced by George telling topical jokes and spicy anecdotes. Cassette recorders were fairly new at the time we first played at Scott's, but bassist Steve Fagg had one, so each night he would record our performance and then pass the cassette to me so that I could play it throughout the following day making notes about what I heard. That night I'd sit down with George and pass on my suggestions, and together we would work out new jokes. George took my advice in the best of spirits, the 'act' steadily improved and throughout our long association he was always willing to receive criticism affably. I sketched out

programmes in which variation played a big part, ensuring
that the tempo of each number contrasted with the previous
number as did the key and the mood of each song. A time-
less blues might follow a humorous cabaret song, a Cole
Porter evergreen could precede a Jelly Roll Morton composition, but the audience was always aware that our crusade
was on behalf of jazz. We made sure that the duration of a
number did not exhaust George or his audience. On the first
few songs of a set George had formerly been prone to jump
all over the stage, eager to impress, but he soon took heed of
the maxim, 'Never open up with a show stopper.' As a result,
he and the audience settled down in a way that satisfied
everyone.

Our management lined up a series of concerts for our
January 1974 debut tour and produced tee-shirts emblazoned
with the words 'Melly Mania'. To boost the tour, we spent
several days at the Granada television studios in Manchester
recording a series of programmes entitled *It's George*, a chat
show hosted by Melly with musical interludes from the
Feetwarmers. The guests were, in the main, friends of
George plus various eccentrics he had met on his travels.
One of these, a Mrs Dennis (who ran a pub in Wales),
exceeded George for ribaldry; so much so, that she had
to come back to re-record a toned-down version of her
anecdotes. Graham Chapman, of the *Monty Python* team,
shone, as did photographer David Bailey, and Tom Driberg
MP, while pre-war cabaret star Douglas Byng was unforgettable. A precocious and sullen Martin Amis came on to plug
his first novel, while critic Kenneth Tynan was laconic and
amusing. These television shows provided an effective
calling card for a group about to go on a national tour.

A London Weekend television programme entitled

Milligan Meets Melly (which featured Spike and George) was also useful. On that one-off show Spike augmented the band by playing trumpet alongside me – what he lacked in technique he made up for in feeling. He invited me out for a meal at the end of the concert (recorded in east London) but, just as we were preparing to leave the hall, the producer, a charming man called Derek Bailey, said to Spike, 'I really enjoyed your trumpet playing.' Spike exploded, 'So you didn't think much of my poetry or my readings, or anything else I did.' With that he picked up his trumpet case, crashed through the bar-locked doors and vanished into the night – meal forgotten. Spike later criticised something George wrote about him and then turned up in heckling mood during one of our stays at Ronnie Scott's. After George commented in print about that visit, Spike turned up at Scott's again, but this time he sat in mummified silence throughout our sets. The television show with Spike marked the night that George changed his method of travelling in London: usually he rode to London gigs on a moped but in making his way home after the Spike concert he took a trip over the handlebars. Thereafter he confined his travel on two wheels to his stays in Wales, where his second home was a converted tower.

In looking back one realises that early 1974 was the worst of times for making a debut tour. The country was in turmoil because of the three-day week, with Prime Minister Edward Heath and the trade unions locked in a bitter dispute. Many street lights were turned off, and power cuts played havoc with amplification equipment.

But there was no turning back for us, and in a burst of alliteration, a headline described us as 'Family Men in their Forties Seeking Fame and Fortune' – others saw the endeavour as both bold and barmy. Steve Fagg was the youngest in the band, George the oldest – the average age was certainly over forty. Our good friend and ex-colleague Wally Fawkes bade us farewell as we set out on our first tour and said, without sarcasm, 'Best of luck, have a good time, and in six months we'll re-form the band.' His forecast was thirty years out.

9

On the Road Again

In January 1974 for our first national tour we hired a band bus, with room for the five of us and our tour manager, John Darnley. John, Chuck and Steve took it in turns to drive while our two roadies travelled in a different vehicle which contained the amplification, double bass, drum kit, etc – a very light load compared to what any rock group carried. In earlier days most jazz bands gave very little thought to amplification; we used whatever the hall provided, which was often a single microphone and a puny amplifier. Rock groups changed all that by making sure that everyone in the audience could hear the performance loud and clear. Sometimes the music was too loud for old ears, but jazz groups were soon made to realise that their audiences also wanted to enjoy the sort of clarity they experienced at home listening to their hi-fi set-ups.

We soon realised that the overheads involved in touring greatly exceeded our estimates. This was a lot to do with the fact that we were determined not to suffer the sort of digs and poor meals we had endured in earlier days, and instead we stayed at the very best hotels and quaffed the

finest wines and victuals on the menu. This carefree spending quickly drained away the fees we received and as a result
we were soon short of money and had to dispense with the
two roadies. The company that we had been advised to form
(Man, Woman & Bulldog Ltd) rarely gathered much into its
coffers. We were often questioned as to how the enigmatic
company name came about. To save embarrassment we
usually said that the three words had been picked out of a
hat, but in truth they were chosen to describe one of George
Melly's more flamboyant capers. I never saw him perform
the exhibition that demonstrated the company name but I
did see a set of photographs of him acting out – Man, where
he boldly stood naked, with arms folded like an old time
wrestler; Woman, a transformation achieved by tucking his
genitalia between his legs and looking coyly ahead; and
Bulldog, which involved him in bending over and pushing his
testicles out rearwards so they protruded grotesquely in the
manner of John Bull's canine.

As to our money shortages, there was no problem in asking Warner Brothers to whisk us anywhere in London by
limousine, but the sight of ready cash was rare. The main
problem was that we were expected to live it up in the manner of rock musicians without benefiting from the huge
royalty advances that they enjoyed. But once we were aboard
the band bus most of our woes disappeared, though saying
goodbye to our wives and children was always a wrench.
Throughout every journey we listened to jazz cassettes and
discussed every aspect of the music. We clapped the best
solos enthusiastically, as though they were being performed
there and then, and applause was also given to an outstanding sunset, a panoramic view or the plump rear of a female
pedestrian. Most journeys were by motorway but after an

hour or two's travelling we would turn off into the country-side to refortify ourselves with a few drinks. We usually allowed ourselves ample time for the vital sound checks: care was needed when balancing the on-stage monitor speakers because of George's hearing problems. His partial deafness meant that his monitor had to be boosted to a level that we found uncomfortable, However, we learned to live with that, encouraged by the warm responses of the crowds who came to our concerts.

Derek Taylor travelled with us when we played some gigs in Scotland. For our Edinburgh dates he settled into the city's most luxurious hotel, and although he didn't play the piano he decided to hire one for his huge suite (at great expense). Huffing and puffing, six brawny Scots carried the instrument in and we then gathered around as Derek sat at the keyboard and with one finger picked out the melody of 'Mighty Like A Rose' (the only tune he could play). That done he said, 'Okay chaps. I've finished. You can take it away.' More puffing and huffing as the six mighty men shift-ed the piano out of the room. We looked on aghast but it was the sort of extravagance that flourished in the rock world. On another occasion, in the same suite, Derek, with-out consulting any of us, telephoned down to the reception desk and asked for 'six black hookers to be sent up as soon as possible.' The stern male receptionist said in a clipped Morningside accent, 'We do not offer such facilities in this hotel.' 'Okay,' said Derek, 'We'll have a pot of tea for six and some toast instead.'

From our first tour I began a habit that lasted throughout my days on the road, namely the visiting of every second-hand bookshop I could find, so that I could help restock the shelves of Teresa's bookshop. It would have been just too easy to while away the hours between gigs in the smoky atmosphere of a bar, so instead I got some exercise and picked up a few bargains. At that time everyone in the band smoked cigarettes, and marijuana played only a tiny part in our lives. The only time we smoked it was during the residencies we occasionally played in Birmingham, where our woe at being there was alleviated by a joint or two. During summer visits I found solace in that Midland city by watching the cricket at Edgbaston. George for his part visited the local art galleries or the nearest zoo.

Derek Taylor concluded his trip to Scotland by coming with us to a gig at the City Hall, Glasgow. Before the concert started we visited a nearby pub where Derek's zaniness again came to the fore. Standing at the bar he noticed a cigarette lighter that a customer was using, depicting a South Sea Island maiden in the section containing the transparent fuel. The design was fairly common at the time but Derek, out of mischief, insisted it was unique and offered the man £15 for it. The Scot was quite bewildered by the offer and patiently explained that Derek could buy a new one at the newsagent next door for thirty pence. 'No sir,' said Derek, 'I happen to know a bit about the history of cigarette lighters. I realise that my offer should have been higher, let's say £25.' The owner scratched his head and said the new offer was much too high. 'Alright,' said Derek, 'let's make it £20... £15... £10...'. He got no further, the loud voice of the barmaid who had been listening to the bartering bellowed, 'Take it, Tommy. Take it!' Tommy accepted the advice and settled for a tenner. Derek held the lighter tenderly and kissed it, but within two hours he'd lost it.

Derek was a pleasure to be with, generous and funny without being spiteful. His hyperactive sense of humour helped him to persuade Warner Brothers that George and the Feetwarmers would be a sensation in the USA. Accordingly, George crossed the Atlantic to discuss the project with record company executives in Los Angeles and, amazingly, they mapped out some dates for our first American tour, but the enterprise almost fell at the first hurdle. Back from Los Angeles, George then re-crossed the Atlantic to do some preliminary interviews in New York prior to our opening at the Bottom Line, a club in Greenwich Village. At that time, however, a strict man-day for man-day exchange had to be approved by both the American and British musicians' unions before the work permits for a tour could be issued by the relevant embassies. George was already in place in New York but to our utter dismay the American embassy in London said they could not issue us with work permits because no confirmation had been received from New York of our exchange with an American group called Blue Oyster Cult. We were advised to return on the following day but on each of, what turned out to be, daily visits the message was frustratingly the same. Meanwhile George and Derek stayed in New York as the date of our opening gig loomed.

After several further journeys to the embassy we were no nearer solving the problem, and the staff seemed to be increasingly detached. They had faced the same situation many times but, for us, the New York gigs were the most important we had ever been involved in. We were saved by the intervention of one of George's dearest friends, Margaret Anne, who knew an influential American senator. The problem was explained to him and, within hours, valid work permits had been stapled into our passports. But, try as we might, we could not catch up lost time and we arrived in New York a few hours after George had played his opening night at the Bottom Line with a pick-up group of American musicians (including the celebrated trumpeter Max Kaminsky). Unfortunately they had no time to rehearse with George, or to discuss his repertoire, and the resultant confusion diminished the launch, which was also the press reception. The only smile to emerge was about our last-minute booking on an airline that pianist Collin Bates wanted to avoid. We asked why and were told that he occasionally played at a drinking club that catered for the flying crews of that company. Collin said he had often seen one particular flyer tumble out of that club absolutely drunk just a matter of hours before taking his place at the controls of a giant passenger plane. He acquainted us with these details just as we settled in our seats, but he was interrupted by a cheery American voice: 'Hi, Collin, great to see you. Welcome aboard.' It was the dawn reveller.

We had a happy reunion with George and Derek in New York. They were staying at the famous Algonquin Hotel on West 44th Street; we were on the other side of the street in a more modern but less splendid hotel. Derek invited us over to his suite to belatedly enjoy a huge celebration cake that had been delivered for our original arrival date. But, as the cake's muslin cover was removed, it revealed an elaborately iced façade that was swarming with mice – reminiscent of Miss Havisham's wedding cake in *Great Expectations*.

The Bottom Line was rated as an 'in' place, and we shared this prestigious booking with the brilliant Argentinian tenor saxist Gato Barbieri. The audience, who had mainly come to see Gato, were friendly but showed no signs of hysteria. The big surprise for us was that 'Nuts' (in Britain the most popular number in our repertoire) got only a modicum of applause. We had not realised that the song was a locker-room ditty that many American youngsters had grown up with. We dropped the number temporarily but reintroduced it as soon as we got back to Britain, where we were gratified to hear each verse creating applause. The reviews of our performances at the Bottom Line were favourable but as we were only there for a few days no real 'buzz' developed.

During our stay in New York we also played a private gig at a launch for some extravagant designer jewellery, and when we had completed our set there an elderly woman came up to George and said, in a thick Southern accent, 'I do declare that you're from my home town, Memphis, Tennessee.' 'No,' said George in his plummiest tones, 'actually Liverpool and London England.' 'Well, sir,' said the old girl, 'I heard you singing and could have sworn you were from Memphis.' I thought for a moment or two that George was about to burst with pride.

Collin Bates and I took our breakfasts in a fast-order bar near our hotel. On our first morning there we were approached by two nuns who asked if we would contribute a dollar or two for a church restoration fund, which we did, but no sooner had we passed over the notes than the arrival of a policeman provided a signal for the two ladies of the cloth to skedaddle at speed. A world weary New Yorker seated near us at the counter said, with a sigh, 'You must be new in town. They're not real nuns.'

George's ultra bold suits caused something of a stir even with the blasé New Yorkers, and the band's pin-striped, double-breasted outfits and two tone shoes made a nice contrast with the Melly garb. George's image also involved wearing wide-brimmed trilby hats. In Britain this proved to be an expensive fashion accessory because so many of them were stolen on gigs and, at £80 each, replacing them involved considerable outlay. People who would not dream of walking off with an £80 briefcase or an expensive shirt showed no hesitation in taking a pricey hat as a souvenir – it didn't seem like stealing to them.

In New York all our hotel expenses were paid for by Warner Brothers, but because we were all buying records, books and presents for our families we soon ran out of money. George kindly agreed to 'sub' us by going to the New York branch of Barclays Bank and drawing out $500, which, split five ways, would be enough to tide us over. Endearingly impractical as ever (and unable to add up), he mistakenly drew out $5,000 in cash and met us for the distribution on the concourse of Grand Central Station where he approached us with the huge wad of money flapping in his hand. In those days New York was more lawless than it is now and a dozen or so likely hustlers and pickpockets looked on in amazement. Normally people then avoided displaying anything more than a ten dollar note but here was this strangely dressed figure waving a small fortune in used bills. A station security guard turned to us as George approached and said, with some feeling, 'Is this mother-fucker crazy?'

A benefit of our New York schedule was that we were granted plenty of free time. After we finished our nightly gig we could visit famous old established jazz clubs such as Eddie Condon's and Jimmy Ryan's, and, by a happy coincidence of timing, we were also able to attend several of the Newport Jazz Festival events. During the daytime I spent every spare moment seeking out and interviewing for my book people who had known Billie Holiday. One of my best friends from London, Michael Brooks, who had emigrated to New York some years earlier and now worked for

Columbia records, was able to let me have cassettes of rare Holiday material and offer advice on people to contact.

Michael's immediate boss was John Hammond, Billie's first recording manager and often her mentor in the early stages of her career. Despite his eminence in the popular music business as a whole, John retained a deep love of jazz. He was also a fountain of background information that amalgamated gossip, scandal and hard fact. Although he was not universally liked by musicians, they respected his power and I always found him charming and helpful. British writer Stanley Dance, then living in New York, had, like John Hammond, been present at many historic events. He too was kind and cooperative, as was *Melody Maker*'s New York correspondent Jeff Atterton (another English friend) whose files were treasure troves of jazz information. Sadly, trumpeter Buck Clayton was in a Jamaica, Long Island, hospital during our visit but he insisted on sitting up in bed and sharing poignant memories of Billie Holiday, who once described Buck as 'the handsomest cat that I ever saw'.

A good source of information was Earle Warren Zaidins, then a judge, who had been Billie's lawyer. He invited me to his home in upstate New York and made me very welcome, allowing me to attend a wedding ceremony he conducted in his parlour. The contrast between the formality that the judge exuded while officiating and his down to earth reminiscences of Billie was remarkable. The lingering feeling I gathered from various of Billie's friends was their regret at not spending more time with her during her last days; however they admitted that, at that stage of her life, they found her to be just too demanding. One of them said, 'You can only take so many late night calls, asking for pastrami sandwiches to be brought to her at 3 am.'

Our next booking was in Massachusetts. We had the chance to fly to Boston but memories of Hollywood films in which bands played jam sessions in the Pullman cars of de luxe trains made us ask if we could go by rail. The travel organiser warned us not to expect too much but we went ahead with the idea and suffered a slow, almost rickety Amtrak journey, which was not in the least conducive to making impromptu jazz. Our destination was a club in Cambridge, where we shared the bill with singer and song-writer Al Stewart. Sadly the attendance figures there were disappointing – despite Stewart's successful records, our combined appeal didn't draw flies. Al moved on fairly quick-ly but we made the most of it, cheered a little by the respon-sive crowds who drifted in to hear us as they waited for ban-joist Earl Scruggs to begin playing in an adjacent hall.

By this time our agent, Chips Chipperfield, was with us, scouring every local newspaper in the hope of finding an angle that would create some much needed publicity. But as our records had failed to reach the local stores we floun-dered. However, Chips spotted one item of news that was dramatically interesting. Under the heading 'Slaying at Cambridge Motel' there was a gruesome account of a homi-cide at the very place we were staying – no one at the motel had considered it worth mentioning to us. On the benefit side I found some first editions at bargain prices in Cambridge, but like the rest of our party I was happy when it was time to move on to Philadelphia, to begin a week's stay at the Bijou cafe on Broad Street. The Bijou didn't specialise in jazz, so we shared the bill there with a company of singers and comedians including saxophonist Tom Shand, who played 'I'm in the Mood for Love' with a stern face while diverting some of his breath into a large balloon that grew out of the bell of his saxophone and blossomed into a huge phallus which burst at the split second he finished playing the melody.

Each day in Philadelphia I was able to explore various avenues of jazz research by linking up with neglected veteran jazz musicians including trumpeter Charlie Gaines, who had been featured with Fats Waller and who had also given Louis Jordan his first big break – years later the material I gleaned proved invaluable when I did a biography of Jordan.

The Philadelphia booking marked the end of our tour. We had all greatly enjoyed playing in the USA but were well aware that we had not made any dramatic impact on the American public. It might have been different if the Feetwarmers had arrived in time to play at the New York press reception, allowing George to perform his best numbers working in close liaison with his accompanists.

The trip gave me the chance to observe George's amazingly durable optimism. Not long before we left for the States we recorded a song from a musical based on *Billy Liar*. Neither the material nor our rendering of it seemed to betoken success and, as I suspected it would, the disc disappeared without a trace soon after it was issued. Nevertheless, while we were in America, George, with beaming face, said, 'I think that single could be in the hit parade by the time we get back home.' His cheerfulness seemed at times quite unreal, but it was endearing, existing as it did within a personality that refused to be daunted by worry.

We flew back to Heathrow and did our first gig back in England that evening at a ball in Cambridge where we were greeted by overwhelming applause, so different from the receptions we had recently experienced in Cambridge, Massachusetts. Throughout the rest of 1974 we were happy to play every sort of London engagement that came our way, ranging from concerts in West End theatres to pub gigs, from fashionable clubs, such as Dingwall's, to 'hooray' parties at which London's smart set hoofed and hollered. Besides this array of local gigs we continued to play dates all over Britain, taking part in what proved to be the final stages of the northern cabaret club scene. Appearing at garish venues that were usually sponsored by big breweries, we were part of a series of acts trying to keep alive the style of yesteryear's music-hall bills. Even Louis Armstrong had played at the Batley Variety Club in Yorkshire, one of the biggest of such places. We existed on a gentler slope, sometimes playing in rather ramshackle clubs, more for fun than for big fees. We all liked the atmosphere of these places, particularly those that existed around the Liverpool area. Occasionally we would play two such clubs on the same evening, dashing from one to the other in high spirits, gleefully refusing to accept a pipe and slippers approach to middle age.

Some of the acts we worked alongside still had hopes of performing at the London Palladium, but most accepted that they would not do more than earn a reasonable living pursuing a profession that they couldn't give up. We enjoyed sharing the backstage camaraderie, and often the same dressing room, with the rest of the cast. I found it fascinating to observe at close hand the way an audience made up its mind about a performer from the moment he or she walked on-stage. I witnessed various examples of this unpredictability during our excursions into the cabaret club world. One comedian, affable and pleasant, well stocked with reasonable jokes, worked with us at a club in the Potteries, and the poor fellow failed to get a single laugh or clap out of the audience. He came back to the communal dressing room sweating profusely, his eyes radiating shock and sadness. 'I don't think the microphone was on,' wailed the disheartened funster. The manager gave him a long hard look and growled, 'They heard every bloody word.'

Despite our failure to gain a toe-hold in America, Warner Brothers allowed us to make another album, one that tied in with our new television show, *It's George*. We decided to make an emphatic change by augmenting the Feetwarmers' personnel on some tracks, expanding temporarily into a ten-piece band featuring top class British jazz musicians (playing my arrangements), including Bruce Turner, John Barnes, Roy Williams and Tommy Whittle. But despite all the planning and effort the recordings were spoilt by my own instrumental efforts, which were execrable. Knowing that it is a poor workman who blames his tools, I was determined not to acknowledge that there was something wrong with my trumpet (at the time I had only one instrument). I struggled through the recordings scarcely able to get air through the horn, never mind creating a decent tone, but as the musicians had been assembled in a big expensive studio I battled on – and lost. I cannot listen to that album without thinking it was a golden chance wasted. When the sessions ended I went to an expert trumpet repairer who soon fixed the problem. The only consolation for me was that the album contained a composition of mine, 'Give Her A Little Drop More', which was taken up by Columbia Pictures and featured in the film *St. Elmo's Fire*, starring Demi Moore, Rob Lowe and Andie MacDowell.

The continued success of *Owning Up*, George Melly's wonderfully evocative memoirs about his early days touring with Mick Mulligan's Magnolia Jazz Band, meant that at every gig we played, people gathered around George asking him to sign copies of the book. Occasionally some of the characters he had written about came forward to reintroduce themselves. The buxom blonde of twenty years earlier was now a grandmother bedevilled by varicose veins; the young stud of yesteryear now had to worry about the capers of his own offspring. A particularly promiscuous girl of early days, known to many a travelling jazz musician, turned up as a demure middle-aged woman. Everyone in the band was amazed at this transformation and someone suggested a photograph be taken as proof of the metamorphosis. Her ancient aunt came and stood next to me in the line-up and, obeying the photographer's instructions for us all to get as close to one another as possible, I put an arm around her waist and pulled her towards me. She misinterpreted my squeeze, explaining without a trace of unpleasantness: 'I don't fook, never have done.'

Every tour we did in those early days ended with a ritual. After completing a series of one-night stands we would travel to London to arrive in the early hours of the morning. We always made for a quiet area of Hampstead where George had lived a few years earlier. His neighbour there had been the television stalwart, Nicholas Parsons, and, somehow or other, Parsons' lifestyle had grated on George. To commemorate George's longlasting irritation everyone in the band was woken up just before we reached Chez Parsons. We would drive slowly past, lower the windows of the band bus and utter the full throated cry, 'Yah Boo! Yah Boo!' A temporary driver whom we used on one occasion muttered 'Childish. Childish,' because he just couldn't comprehend the pleasure our bellowing gave to George. Eventually we came to realise that the noisy ritual was losing us about an hour's sleep on our homeward journeys, so we dropped the joke and the strange noises that Nicholas heard in the middle of the night ceased as mysteriously as they had begun.

George was regularly interviewed on television chat shows, and because he invariably sang a number or two we were involved as his accompanists. As with most television work, this entailed a lot of waiting around, but I never felt the time was wasted. Off-screen, Terry Wogan and Michael Parkinson socialised with the musicians, with 'Parky' ever willing to talk about jazz and sport, but neither of them did elaborate run-throughs with their guests, saving face to face contact for the camera. On the other hand, Derek Nimmo, who had his own chat show in the 1970s, liked to outline his questions during extensive pre-show rehearsals, and he did so on a show we shared with the distinguished journalist, James Cameron. The transmitted programme was unremarkable, but the twenty minutes of exchanges that Cameron shared with Nimmo during the run-throughs were totally fascinating; sadly the two men had used up all their zest before the show began. Off-screen, Cameron confessed that he had a lifelong interest in horoscopes, finding them convincingly accurate. Then, late in life, he saw a copy of his birth certificate and discovered his first name was actually Mark, and that he was born in June 1911, and not July 1911 as he had always supposed. This meant that he was born under a different star from the one he always consulted for his horoscope. He decided not to correct the situation and continued to follow the 'wrong' forecast and to carry on admiring its accuracy.

Probably the most proficient television inquisitor was Dick Cavett, on whose show we appeared in New York. This ex-Yale man utilised researchers but was able to summarise and use the information they gave him in brilliant fashion. Back in Britain, a lesser-known interviewer, Shelley Rohde, who worked for Granada Television, always managed to get interesting revelations out of George, but no matter how we tried we rarely got him to 'plug' his latest album, which was often the very reason we were there. Shyness certainly wasn't the cause for his reluctance; rather, he thought it was more fun camping it up or sharing gossip than adroitly slipping in a sales pitch. I think that George was worried that the public would like him less if he ostentatiously plugged his own record. However, whenever I had a new book published George kindly publicised it for all he was worth.

Over the years we regularly did charity shows. These sometimes produced backstage tensions between artistes, the main cause being that some performers got carried away by a large, responsive audience and wilfully overran their allotted time. This put the running schedule in chaos, forcing acts that followed the culprits to cut their contribution to the show. For my own part I must admit I enjoyed being in touching distance of famous stars. I was particularly impressed at one charity show by Sir John Mills' compering. I saw the organiser hand him a large sheet of paper which detailed our personnel, as well as listing appeals for needy organisations and details of several future events. He read through the list very slowly, gave it back, then walked to the microphone and announced every item word perfect – a remarkable display of memory and training. At this same event Ava Gardner provided George Melly with a marvellous moment when she flamboyantly crossed the floor in order to ask him for a dance.

One problem of taking part in charity concerts was that the musicians usually had the earliest of the rehearsal calls, and this certainly didn't suit the Feetwarmers – hangovers, lack of sleep and obstinate body clocks meant that we were never in the best of humour before noon. We usually took breakfast together but conversation was sparse, except in George's case. He would exude an almost painful amount of cheerfulness at the breakfast table, being quite unable to hear any responses because he made it a habit not to put in his hearing aid until the first meal of the day had been consumed.

In fact, many professional entertainers take a while to cheer up early in the day, and we were reminded of this while staying at the Turk's Head Hotel in Newcastle upon Tyne, where we were astonished to see the entire cast of the television show, *Dad's Army*, then on tour, sitting apart at breakfast. There were apparently some genuine friendships within the troupe but amity was not on show first thing in the morning. The sight of Arthur Lowe sitting alone munching his toast was too much for our pianist, Collin Bates. In an action that was totally out of character, Collin marched across the dining room and with great gusto saluted 'Captain Mainwaring', who responded with a look so disdainful it made his 'Foolish Boy' catch-phrase seem as benevolent as a papal blessing.

To emphasise our dislike of an excess of cheerfulness before noon, I proposed that anyone displaying exuberance during the early morning should be transported far away on an imaginary charabanc. We quickly realised that the coach would soon burst at the seams if all the mindless chucklers we encountered were put on board, so we decided that places were to be allocated one to each profession; thus we had a coach-photographer, a coach-chef, a coach-newsagent, a coach-waiter, etc. We didn't take a formal vote on who was to be included; the merest raising of eyebrows was enough to consign an overly optimistic person to eternal travel aboard what became known as 'the coach for cheerful cunts'. By dusk we were all merry again and midnight was always greeted with a smile.

This nocturnal happiness was rarely upset, but late one night in Southampton, after a long post-gig tipple, we decided it was time to crash out in our hotel and reeled into the hotel's courtyard, only to find that the entrance was locked – we had not been forewarned that this might happen. We began tapping lightly and politely but there was no sign of any response on this frosty night, so our bangings got louder and louder until we were hitting the stout door with all our might. Finally we heard a shout that signified the night porter was close at hand. A key turned in the lock, and we barged past the old fellow and took our places in front of the reception desk. We were still fuming, so the demands for our room keys were decidedly terse. Unfortunately none of us could remember our room numbers and no matter how carefully the night porter pored over a list of the hotel's guests, he couldn't find our names. Our grumblings got louder until suddenly I realised that the staircase was in a different place from where I remembered it when we booked in, and the reception desk had also assumed an entirely new shape. At about the same moment all five of us realised we had come to the wrong hotel. To say we slunk out would not adequately describe our shamefaced retreat along the street to the right hotel.

Gradually the hangovers I suffered from got worse, and at least two of them were the occasion of alarming manifestations. An effective pick-me-up was a particular brand of ice cream sold in London's Tottenham Court Road, near where

I lived. I set out to buy this panacea one morning but was baffled and alarmed to find I was walking in the midst of an army of men and women of notably restricted growth. I feared I was hallucinating. To break the spell I asked one of the little people in a trembling voice what was happening. The answer was mundane; they were all making their way to an audition for the film *Star Wars*. More frightening was an afternoon in London when I decided to sleep off a drink-induced headache in Queen Square. The nap did the trick but as I opened my eyes I saw to my horror that I was surrounded by dozens of very old people, with parchment-like faces, all in nightwear, many of them lying on mattresses. Suspecting that I was in the early stages of the DTs, I jumped to my feet, but then was relieved to see a nurse wending her way among the mattresses. She saw the alarm on my face and explained that the nearby hospital had received a bomb threat, so that all the infirm and bedridden cases had been carried out to lie on the grass of Queen Square until an all clear signal was given.

I was slowly coming to the conclusion that it would only be a matter of time before I became a teetotaller. But a lot of the energy we burnt up doing hectic tours came from alcohol, particularly when we were working abroad.

During our first years 'back on the road' we played several times in Germany without gaining a following, mainly because the audiences had difficulty in following the lyrics and especially the jokes, with which we sometimes courted trouble. This was certainly so on George's *pièce de résistance* 'Frankie and Johnny'. When he sang 'sitting in the electric chair' we shouted 'having a pony', using Cockney rhyming slang, 'pony and trap' meaning crap. This somewhat juvenile interjection usually produced a crop of smiles from a British

audience but, not unreasonably, the Germans could not follow the argot, which, for our own perverse amusement, we
left in. On one occasion, the German promoter asked what
the phrase meant, and when we explained his face suddenly
glowed with excitement as he thought of a Teutonic equiva-
lent. There and then he taught us to sing the German equiv-
alent of the phrase 'shitting in his pants'. We realised straight
away that this aphorism could not be compared to Oscar
Wilde's best but we duly aped the promoter's words and
watched a German audience almost do themselves injuries as
they rocked with uncontrollable laughter. We had found a
German show-stopper.

10

New York, Sydney and Beijing

Our relentless touring schedule continued and took us to many interesting places, but the increased scope of the itinerary meant we saw less and less of our wives and children. Bassist Steve Fagg was the first to call it a day, followed by Collin Bates, who needed to spend more time with his wife and young son. Barry Dillon, an Australian pal of Collin's, came in on double bass, and Collin's place at the keyboard was filled by Scottish pianist Stan Greig.

By this time our Warner Brothers' contract was a thing of the past so we started recording for Pye, beginning with an album of compositions by Hoagy Carmichael, followed by a tribute to Fats Waller. It was the start of a long and happy association with recording manager Terry Brown. I had known Terry for some years, he having preceded me as the trumpeter with Bruce Turner's Jump Band. He was a small neat man with twinkling blue eyes and a Cockney sense of humour, highly intelligent and with a fine musical ear able to detect the faintest wrong note within the swath of sound produced by a big band. George and Terry got on well together even when Terry was devising subtle ways of getting him to sing the correct melody, which in a desire to emote, George sometimes bypassed.

It took a lot of effort to alter one aspect of George's recorded performances: namely, his habit of acting out the message of a song, attempting to illustrate the lyrics with dramatic hand movements and extraordinary facial grimaces, as though he believed that everyone who bought the record was magically able to see his actions. From the inside of a glass recording booth George sang along with the accompaniment but carried on as though he was giving a lecture to young children who had only a slender grasp of the English language. If a telephone was mentioned in the lyric then an imaginary phone was picked up and held to his ear, and any hint of violence in the words produced a workout that Muhammad Ali would have been proud of, with George weaving and ducking in front of the recording microphone. Gradually we got him to think more about the lyrics and he began depicting a song's message without the extravagant gestures.

George, by his own admission, was not an emotional person, though his eyes often filled with tears when the death of his heroine, Bessie Smith, was mentioned. George worshipped Bessie's singing, but sometimes this adoration caused him to try too hard to imitate the 'Empress of the Blues' and the results could come close to parody. Yet when George sang material associated with another of his great favourites, Jelly Roll Morton, he achieved a perfect blend of artistry and feeling. We recorded several Morton numbers on various albums but no recording company encouraged us to make an entire album devoted to Morton's work – a pity because I have always felt that George's interpretations of Jelly Roll's material were absolutely superb. Collectively we had a particular affection for Morton's 'Animule Ball' but, try as we might, we could not get the listening public to share our joy. Applause or no, we greatly enjoyed playing the number. Then came a golden night in Carlisle when a man in the audience shouted out, 'Please play the "Animule Ball".' If we could have spotted where he sat, we would have lifted him shoulder high and promised eternal friendship. But, sad to say, he remained a tribe of one; no one else ever requested the song, or commented on our recording of it, and eventually we had to drop it from our repertoire.

George continued to accept advice and guidance without a qualm and we enjoyed smooth sailing during those early years, except for a mighty row during our one and only visit to Berlin. The contretemps was dubbed 'The Dance of the Old Men' by the rest of the band because both George and I jumped up and down in rage at the fiercest point of the fall-out. The quarrel concerned a visit to the club we were working in by one of Germany's leading television producers. He approached me and said he liked what he had seen and heard and asked me to call George over for a discussion. George, well nourished by a smooth liquor called Persico, was too intent on acting the goat with a group of students, telling a complicated farting joke which involved him blowing raspberries on the back of his hand. I repeated that the producer was keen to talk to us about being featured in a programme but George could not pull himself away from the admiring group and launched into another long joke. The producer left in a huff and bang went our chance of appearing on a widely viewed television show. To say I was annoyed at George would be an understatement; we badly needed exposure in Germany because our tours there were just like treading water. Despite the ferocity of the row there was no lasting rancour, George apologised profusely and we were pals again.

Our next booking was in Munich. As we waited to fly there, a devout German jazz fan who had come to see us off took the opportunity to warn us of the miseries we were sure to encounter in the south: 'Those Bavarians are so stupid, you will be amazed,' adding, 'Vereas ve Berliners are kvik and vitty.' In fact, we enjoyed ourselves in Munich and were pleased to take a re-booking there. While having my breakfast on our first morning, I sat reading an English newspaper in which a gossip columnist revealed that author and jazz fan Kingsley Amis had given up all forms of alcohol and was now a strict teetotaller. My eyes left the page as I pondered this surprising news, and immediately focused on a plump, middle-aged man who sat a few tables away supping a huge stein of lager before tackling his boiled eggs. It was Kingsley Amis.

We made fleeting trips to Belgium and Denmark and also fulfilled several bookings in Holland where the language problem was virtually non-existent. The drawback was that we were not known by the Dutch general public and at one venue we were billed as 'G. Mel Yenco', which should have been 'G. Melly and Co.' But slowly, by playing festivals and hippy clubs (where the marijuana smoke was as thick as the London pea-souper fogs of my childhood), we built up a regular following with the ultra-friendly audiences.

One of the most alarming reactions we ever encountered occurred during a Channel Islands concert in Jersey. At that time we did a routine based on a song about Marie Laveau, a New Orleans voodoo queen, whose speciality was in creating a potion consisting of gunpowder, saffron and dog shit. Usually, when George had finished listing the ingredients I shouted out the name of a locally brewed beer, and this always produced a good belly laugh from the audience. But not in Jersey. As usual, I did my homework and acquainted myself with the name of the local brew so when the moment came I hollered 'St. Anne's'. The good natured mood of the audience changed immediately and for a few uneasy seconds I thought they were going to jump on-stage and attack me. The concert staggered to a close with shouts of derision greeting the final announcement. We never risked using the routine again.

Perhaps the most depressing reaction we ever encountered was at the West Yorkshire Playhouse in Leeds, which had previously been one of our favourite venues. George wanted to be present at his granddaughter's birthday party so he decided to travel by rail instead of coming with us in the band bus. Unfortunately an accident en route meant his train was drastically delayed and he arrived much too late to do the concert. The theatre manager had to inform the sell-out crowd of the cancellation of the show and to give them their money back. We were as disappointed as they were, perhaps more so since we had travelled two hundred miles to play the gig, and we were soon to feel very aggrieved when a good percentage of the audience gathered outside the stage door and hurled abuse at us. We had to run the gauntlet to get into the band bus in order to reach our hotel – try as we did, we couldn't raise a smile when George finally linked up with us at midnight.

In general we were well received and the only on-stage problem continued to be the overwhelmingly loud output from George's monitor speaker. This didn't affect the audience's listening but almost deafened the band and regularly produced sound distortion. George's hearing waned as the years went by but he resisted the idea of wearing a hearing aid on-stage until it became obvious that he was courting disaster by not being able to hear the musical accompaniment.

Off-stage he made light of his disability and good-naturedly approved of the band compiling a list of his 'deafies', some of which produced bizarre misunderstandings. For example, at a sponsor's after-the-show gathering at Wavendon, George cheerfully asked a middle-aged woman if she lived locally. 'Yes,' she said, 'but I spent several years in Uxbridge.' 'Oh you poor soul,' sympathised George. 'My heart goes out to you. To have undergone such terror and tragedy and still be able to smile is remarkable.' The woman was startled by George's words but managed to say, 'It wasn't quite as bad as that.' 'Such bravery,' said George, his voice laden with emotion. It eventually transpired that he thought the woman had said Auschwitz.

Signing records could be disastrous. Many an Elsie got a dedication to Elkie, and a Melanie was perplexed by a 'for him and me'. Audiences were delighted by George's surreal rejoinders to hecklers, but they didn't realise that most of his quips were created without him clearly having heard what was being shouted. A bellowed 'Aren't you embarrassed?' brought the riposte 'I am plainly here and not in Paris.' Worse followed when a fan in the audience shouted exuberant praise: 'You're as great as ever, George,' only to hear George say, quite fiercely, 'I haven't come here to be insulted.'

We tried not to be cruel about George's affliction but as he determinedly made light of the deafies they became part of our touring life, falling thicker and faster as the years went by, so much so that eventually only 'double deafies' were commented on. During a discussion on the merits of saxophonist Coleman Hawkins, George was asked if he liked the 'Hawk'. 'I do very much' he replied, 'but it gives me gout.' 'No, not port – Hawk,' brought the reply, 'I think I like the crackling more than the meat.' On one occasion the thick curtain of deafness proved a blessing. George got himself involved in a row with a lady friend just before we went on-stage. She had taken too many drinks on board and, eager to continue the quarrel, she found her way to the front row of the audience and sat down. At that time I used to announce George in a cod impersonation of a town-crier's proclamation: 'It is now my pleasure to introduce the wisest of the entertainers...' I got no further before 'Hefty', as she was known, yelled, *Oh no, he fucking well isn't*. Fortunately, George was unable to hear his wisdom denied. I tried to ignore the shouts and continued, '... and the most entertaining of the wise men.' Hefty at double her previous volume sallied, *Oh no, he fucking well isn't*. She was then ushered out by two attendants. After a backstage snooze she reverted to her usual affable self and joined us after the show – no one mentioned the incident.

George never relished confrontations, so even if he had heard her emphatic denunciations he wouldn't have dreamt of reprimanding Hefty. Whenever grumpiness erupted around him George remained cheerful and optimistic; asking people to toe the line was just not part of his make-up. We were both supposed to share the task of maintaining what could only loosely be described as discipline but at crunch time George always found a way to duck out, even when a reprimand to one of the musicians was at his suggestion. At one of our occasional band meetings I would mention a grievance that George had raised only to see him cross the room to pat the transgressor on the shoulder, which certainly diminished the effectiveness of my rebuke.

I took consolation from the fact that much of our success was built on George's overwhelming desire to be liked by every audience he encountered. I would cast my mind back to 1950, when I first saw a twenty-four-year-old George in action as part of Mick Mulligan's Magnolia Jazz Band at the Hammersmith Palais Jazz Band Ball. While awaiting his turn to be featured he sat on the side of the bandstand, ceaselessly cadging attention by dramatically lifting his hands above his head in the manner of a hell-fire preacher, grunting and groaning loudly to make sure he was being noticed. As an eighteen-year-old erstwhile jazz musician from a quiet London suburb I felt certain that I was seeing what was then known as a 'dope fiend' in action. Years later George told me that my supposition was totally wrong; in those early days a good supply of Guinness fuelled his performances (later it was to be Irish whiskey).

At Hammersmith his amazingly bold shtick might have turned the audience, many of whom were seeing him for the first time, against him, but they, like my chums and me, were instead won over by his sincere lack of inhibition. He wasn't simply a show-off, he was also an anarchic pioneer of performer freedom, proud of the fact that in the fifties Derby magistrates had banned him from singing Bessie Smith's bold songs, a ban he ignored. One famous British jazz trumpeter said that he thought George acted his way through life from the moment he woke. However, as someone who travelled with George for day after day over many years, I felt that if a strategy of perpetual acting made him such an affable, intelligent and considerate companion then by all means let him carry on with the procedure.

Part of the reason that George beamed at the world was because he had a poor memory for faces, even those he had encountered many times. A secretary who had worked for us for at least six months turned up at a concert a few years later and George greeted her with warmth and attention. But when she had gone he said in utter mystification, 'Who was that?' Similar situations arose on many occasions but the visitor was never the wiser because George would have hated to be thought of as being 'big time' by blanking people. He was always courteous to strangers who asked for his auto- graph or who insisted on sharing a joke with him, and great- ly enjoyed this part of being a celebrity (or as his wife Diana put it, 'of being fat and fairly famous'). George kept smiling, even when an approaching stranger made preposterous observations. On one such occasion a man got within inches of George's face and said, 'Don't tell me... you're J. B. Priestley,' despite the fact that Priestley was at least thirty years older than George at that time. This was not quite as bad as the woman who said, 'I know this isn't a compliment but my friend says you look just like George Melly.'

The question that we of the Feetwarmers were regularly asked concerned George's sexual outlook and preferences. An audacious minority of the public was eager to know if George was still homosexual. We answered to the best of our abilities by saying that in the distant past he had been but he then became bisexual on his way to being a mighty camp heterosexual.

Scarcely a gig went by without someone asking about George's actress sister, Andrée. During our early days Andrée and her husband Oscar often came to gigs in the Home Counties but we rarely saw her after they made their home in Ibiza. George's brother Bill, an ex-officer in the

Royal Navy, often brought his family to hear us. Bill didn't share George's extrovert qualities but he was good company and a fund of humour. George's son, Tom, a charming fellow, regularly saw us in action from his childhood onwards, and he was always welcome, even when, as a lad, he brought his pet mice aboard the band bus. George's stepdaughter, Candy, came to many of our London gigs and kept us in touch with the views of the younger section of our audiences. Diana, George's wife, rarely came to gigs, but she never missed seeing us during our annual seasons at Ronnie Scott's Club. Despite the fact that they had been married for many years, her presence made George nervous. At Scott's I could always tell without looking when Diana was in the audience because of George's fidgety reaction, and the same situation applied when she came to a gig in New York. Whatever the locale she seemed reluctant to applaud George's efforts.

When we were on tour George made good use of his spare time by writing, creating a mass of journalism including regular articles for *Punch* describing his travels (these were eventually collected in book form and published as *Mellymobile*). Other books included new volumes of autobiography (*Rum, Bum and Concertina* about his days in the Royal Navy and *Scouse Mouse*, tales of his early years in Liverpool, to be followed in 2005 by *Slowing Down*). He also wrote successful books on art, artists and fishing. George never thrust his considerable knowledge of modern art on anyone, but if there was interest he would willingly act as an informative guide, delighted to share his knowledge and enthusiasm. His other great interest was trout fishing, a pursuit he had followed passionately since childhood. I think it almost equalled his love of jazz, but he never lamented the one that got away and generously brought samples of his catches on

tour in the hope that an obliging hotelier would cook the
trout for our dinner.

Usually we ate together, the table being the place where
we learned to tolerate George's mania for neatness. An ill-
laid table was anathema to him. Everything had to be just so,
with George unable to stop himself rearranging the cutlery
into symmetrical patterns, despite our unison cries of 'Sit
down, you old queen.' At one time everyone in the band
sported a beard, but if the tiniest crumb lingered in the
whiskers George would be instantly up on his feet attempting to flap away the morsel with a serviette. Backstage,
everything had to be orderly, newspapers neatly folded, all
coins of the same denomination stacked in orderly piles and
all drinking glasses uniformly in place on trays. But a devil-
may-care attitude existed alongside these quirks. On tour
George and I occasionally explored gambling clubs in
provincial cities in order to play roulette. I am not an ultra-
cautious gambler but I like to quit when I'm ahead, whereas
George, even when he had (on occasion) won a lot of money,
would make sure that all his winnings disappeared as his
bets became more and more extravagant, most of them on
number 17 (his birthday being the 17th August).

In the summer of 1978 we made a return trip to the
USA, principally to play a residency at Michael's Pub in New
York. This venue was misnamed, it being an elegant, wood
panelled dining room which happened to feature jazz. The
sophisticated manager, Gil Weist, viewed our antics with a
tolerant smile and re-booked us without blinking. But again
with very little record company support, we failed to establish an effective beachhead. Nevertheless the residency was
fun and various ex-pats turned out to hear us. They included
the gracefully camp Quentin Crisp who arrived with two

muscular companions dressed as pirates, half-stripped for some sort of action, wearing neckerchiefs on their heads and displaying arm muscles bulging under tight copper bands. They gained entrance without any problem but we had to vouch for the BBC's Alan Yentob, whose casual clothes were deemed 'not suitable' for Michael's Pub.

The timing of our stay in New York allowed us to play at the most prestigious event in the American jazz calendar, the Newport Jazz Festival. Our appearance as part of the Festival took place on a delightful sunny afternoon and, in order to arrive in style, we hired a stretch limo and a chauffeur. During our set I was thrilled to look into the audience and see several famous jazz musicians listening to us. As part of this same tour we played a jazz club residency near Salem, Massachusetts, where we stayed in a sombre guest house run by an eccentric landlady. In an interview with a local newspaper, George unguardedly described her as 'barmy', which fortunately got printed as 'balmy', a description that inspired the landlady to do a veiled dance in and out of the dining room, like Blanche du Bois on speed. From there we moved on to Toronto where we ended each evening of a week's club residency playing in a jam session with the Climax Jazz Band, which, like the audiences there, consisted mainly of Europeans who had settled in Canada.

My trips to the USA with George and the band continued to give me the opportunity to do on-the-spot jazz research but, to my disappointment, it looked unlikely that we would ever be booked to play in New Orleans, where the richest seams of information still existed. So, in January 1979, during the band's post-Christmas break, I took the whole family, Teresa, Jenny, Martin and Barney, off to Louisiana for a long stay in New Orleans. The family had a fine time exploring that fascinating city and I was equally absorbed in trawling through archives and interviewing veteran musicians and the relatives of those who were gone.

The trip yielded rich nuggets of information, many of which were very useful for two books I was working on: one, a history of bands led by Bing Crosby's brother Bob; the other, a biography of the jazz virtuoso Sidney Bechet. Several of Bob Crosby's sidemen were from New Orleans, including one of the most underrated of all jazz clarinet players, the late Irving Fazola; I experienced great pleasure in locating his old school friends and former colleagues. Digging for details of Bechet's early years was equally rewarding but one had to be ultra-careful in double checking every fact that came to light, because Bechet's autobiography *Treat It Gentle*, though admirably poetic, was as full of improvisation as his solos. My family returned to London, happier, wiser and heavier, all of us having been totally captivated by the Crescent City.

By the time we entered the 1980s, George and the Feetwarmers were following a similar itinerary year after year. Each December we would play a Christmas season at Ronnie Scott's, usually for a month. Then for the rest of the year we would tour, leaving dates free to play regularly at the 100 Club in Oxford Street and allocating a week in August for engagements in Edinburgh. Our tours embraced universities, municipal halls, some clubs and various jazz festivals. We travelled to gigs in a new band bus, driven by Chuck Smith who managed to combine this arduous duty with his work as a drummer. Chuck was a talkative traveller whereas his front-seat sidekick, bassist Barry Dillon, was often silent throughout an entire long journey. Barry also conscientiously carried out extra duties such as collecting the cheques from the promoters and banking the money we accrued from selling records on the gigs. There was still a good deal of variety in the venues we played but, if we had to pick favourite surroundings, the old Frank Matcham-designed theatres (with a balcony and upper circle), such as the Theatre Royal, Bury St. Edmunds, would have come out top – the acoustics were invariably perfect.

Our regular engagements at Langan's Brasserie in London's Stratton Street were definitely out of the ordinary, due mainly to the behaviour of that restaurant's infamous owner, Peter Langan. When sober, Peter was likeable, generous and interesting, but when alcohol took over he became bellicose and immodest, liable to jump up on-stage to join us in a song he didn't know, or to lower his trousers, creased like a concertina, in what he thought was an amusing cabaret. Peter's behaviour meant that a London gig (at which we were generously wined and dined) was less enjoyable than it should have been, and we found it vexing when customers complained to us about the proprietor's antics. Peter could certainly be very taxing but, like so many others, I was deeply saddened by his death.

In early 1982 George and the band made the first of several visits to Australia. I had been there during my stint aboard the SS *Iberia* and for Barry Dillon it was a return to his home country, but George, Chuck and our new pianist Bruce Boardman were making their first Antipodean trip. We finished our usual Christmas season at Ronnie Scott's during a particularly cold snap then flew off to the warmth of Hong Kong, where a festival booking provided a perfect break in the journey to Australia. We were made very welcome by numerous ex-pats and taken out to view the harbour and coastline on private yachts, combining these jaunts with diligent shopping. On my 1960 visit, there were bargains galore in Hong Kong but, by 1982, inflation and a perpetual influx of tourists meant that only through careful foraging could a visitor find a bargain. The concerts were all sold out. A minority of the audience were local Chinese but the rest were British, many of whom came backstage to reminisce about their early days as carefree 'jivers' almost forty years earlier.

Our first engagement in Australia was at a festival concert in Perth. We then played a batch of one night stands in the very hot northern part of Western Australia, acclimatising ourselves to temperatures of 102° Fahrenheit in Port Hedland, almost 80° above what we had recently experienced in London. One of the band's perpetual sources of amazement concerned George Melly's immunity to heat or cold; despite the high temperatures he continued to wear his thick woollen suits. The band devised names for each of these ensembles, and the three he took to Australia were: Murphy's Mistake, the Deck Chair and the Mad Scottish Comedian. Wearing these outlandish creations in the intense heat produced howls of derision from the off-duty miners who relaxed in the hotel bar clad only in singlets, shorts and sandals. George was unperturbed and waved cheerfully, pleased that he had created a stir.

Our next gig involved flying on to Paraburdoo while all the equipment including bass and drums was transported by road. Unfortunately, a freak storm washed away the highway, leaving the equipment truck stranded. The roadie telephoned us to detail the predicament and the concert organisers made an appeal over the local radio which led to kind people loaning us a bass and a drum kit. The storm had also deprived the area of electricity and, although the concert hall had emergency power, it was only designed to provide minimal stage lighting and enough electricity for one microphone. There was no way of getting it to operate the air conditioning. As the evening temperature was still uncomfortably high, all the hall windows were opened, allowing whatever breeze came off the bush to enter the stifling hall. The stage lights, such as they were, and the open windows provided an irresistible attraction for insects to swarm in just as we began our performance. Dozens of species that were new to me floated up to the stage and settled on us or bunched wherever there was landing space. Huge moths, dragonflies and ladybirds made a few circuits of our heads then did their best to fly into our mouths. I looked down and saw a large creature that I took to be a praying mantis about to climb up the inside of my trouser leg. For the only time in my career I considered dashing off the stage. Happily this alarming creature changed direction and crawled under the drum kit. We managed to splutter our way through the performance, fortified by the audience's sympathetic response.

When the concert ended we hurried back to the motel without changing out of our stage suits, eager to enjoy the air conditioning provided by an in-house generator. I entered my room and threw down the suit bag, only to observe, with utter horror, that a cross-section of all the insects we had encountered that night had decided to travel with me; they tumbled out of the suit bag and scuttled across the floor. I tried my best to mop them up but, for every one that I gathered in, another two made an appearance. I pulled a pillow and a duvet off the bed, shut the bathroom door, put a damp towel down to seal it off and then made a bed in the bath. After a restless night's sleep I plucked up courage and re-entered the bedroom. To my astonishment and relief all of the creatures had disappeared. Where they went to was a total mystery but one that I did not intend to wait around to solve.

We flew on to a warm welcome in Karratha where we were reunited with our equipment. An after-the-show party was held for us, which pleasantly filled in time before we caught the dawn plane to our next destination. The fare at the party was that Australian culinary delight, 'the floater' – a giant meat pie dotted with peas and swimming in thick gravy. I was eager to tuck in but hadn't been given a knife and fork. I waited for a while and then asked, 'Please can I have some cutlery?' One of the guests issued a growled response, 'Well, here's another bloody educated pom.' Earlier that same evening I had experienced another Aussie send-up. As evening came I called out to the rest of the band that I would see them after I'd taken a shower. From out of the darkness came a deep Australian voice: 'It must be Friday, the poms are taking a shower!' There is nothing shy about the Australian sense of humour. Enjoyable but brief stays in Melbourne, Adelaide and Sydney and a week back in Perth at the Festival Club rounded out a tour that was deemed a success by the promoters and we were re-booked to tour Australia a year later.

The week we spent playing at the Perth Festival Club had allowed us plenty of time off during the day. Having had a surfeit of sunbathing, Chuck Smith and I decided to visit Memorial Park where there were seemingly endless rows of specially planted trees, each bearing the name of a soldier killed in World War One, most of them at Gallipoli. To see the names of brothers and their father next to one another was a very moving experience. Peter Weir's epic film *Gallipoli* was showing that week in Perth so we decided to go to an afternoon screening. Without doubt it was my most memorable visit ever to a cinema. The majority of the Aussies who gave their lives in the Gallipoli carnage were from Western Australia and although the magnificent film was not made as a tear-jerker it was possible to hear choked sobs coming from every section of an audience that had lost someone in the long-ago slaughter. At the conclusion of the performance everyone left the cinema in silence, their eyes filled with unstoppable tears.

The break-journeys for our second trip to Australia were at Kuala Lumpur and Singapore. Unfortunately, at that time (February 1983), diplomatic relations between the UK and Malaysia were going through a bad patch, due to Britain cutting the student quota from that part of the world. In retaliation all the workers at the Kuala Lumpur concert hall behaved as awkwardly as they could when we arrived, carrying out what might be called a conscious withdrawal of efficiency. Although we realised it was nothing personal, it was exhausting for us to move sound equipment and a grand piano in the intense heat. We eventually began our sound check but no sooner had we played our first notes than the entire staff of the hall filled the front row of seats and pretended to fall fast asleep, apparently a formidable insult in that part of the world. To their chagrin we were highly amused by the way they acted out their fake slumbers. We were instantly put into a good mood which lasted throughout an enjoyable concert.

For the follow-up tour of Australia we declined the chance to return to the fierce heat of the north and instead played a city circuit, working in Perth, Melbourne and Sydney as well as one-night stands in Adelaide and Canberra and club dates and concerts in Queensland, at Brisbane and Townsville.

George's humour pleased the Australian public and the Feetwarmers' music, with Collin Bates back on piano, got good reviews. After appearing on Mike Walsh's television show in Sydney we flew north to reach Townsville, where we did our best to confirm Nöel Coward's lyrics about Englishmen and the noon day sun. We were only there on a fleeting visit but, eager to see something of the terrain, we took a morning walk and the locals were aghast. They strolled in the shade and rested when the sun was at its hottest. Our explorations didn't take us far but we chanced on one other soul who was not bothered by the high temperature, an aboriginal fishing with a primitive rod. George was naturally delighted to meet a fellow enthusiast and began a carefully enunciated enquiry about fishing prospects. After he had uttered a couple of slowly delivered sentences the fisherman said, 'Didn't I see you on television yesterday?'

On that tour, Chuck Smith's brother, Brian (another drummer), who lived near Melbourne, journeyed to Sydney to see us and we spent a convivial afternoon in a hotel bar which boasted a huge television screen on which we saw bush fires advancing through the state of Victoria. Someone asked Brian if the fires were anywhere near his home and he told us they were many miles distant but, to reassure us more than himself, he telephoned home and was told by his wife that the blazes were indeed a long distance away. We settled down to another bout of reminiscences which were interrupted by a dramatic telephone call from Brian's wife telling him that their entire house had been burnt down – they had lost everything in the swiftly moving inferno. The tragedy gave us a sombre insight into the hazards of living close to the bush. Within a week we were in playing a gig at Geelong

and en route we saw miles and miles of blackened countryside cloaked in thousands of tons of wood ash.

Our gigs in Sydney were in a night club called Kinsella's
which had previously been one of the city's best known
funeral parlours; happily, none of its macabre past was obvious and we loved playing there. Being temporarily based in
Sydney gave me the chance to hear some of the many fine
Australian jazz groups, to meet up with the famous jazz
leader Graeme Bell (whose band made such a big impact during its 1947 visit to Europe) and to hear wonderful soloists
such as trumpeter Bob Barnard and reed player Don
Burrows. During our stay a middle-of-the-night call from
Teresa told me the good news that I had won a 'Best Sleeve
Notes of the Year' Grammy award (relating to a Time-Life
boxed set devoted to Bunny Berigan's work).

On returning to Britain we took on more private engagements. One in July 1985 was to play for a party held in Robert
Maxwell's office celebrating his first year as owner of the
Daily Mirror. For me the most memorable moment of
the evening was observing the dubious look on his wife's
face when, as a surprise, Captain Bob gave her a copy of
every edition of the *Daily Mirror* that had been published
in the year since he took over – all bundled up in packages
tied with horse-string. It was a lively gathering attended by
eminent politicians, including Neil and Glynis Kinnock who
displayed a genuine talent for jitterbugging. On another
occasion I was struck by the extremely rhythmic dancing of
Princess Diana, during a gig at the Guards' barracks in
Chelsea, where her partners were dashing young officers –
there was no sign of Prince Charles, and Diana danced with
absolute abandon. However, Charles was present on the next
occasion that Diana danced to our music, at a charity event

held at Hatfield House in Hertfordshire. We were booked to provide a cabaret spot in the middle of which, to our utter surprise, the royal couple got to their feet and began dancing. The number that George was singing at the time was 'Careless Love'. I couldn't help noticing Diana's careful, measured steps. They made her seem a totally different woman from the flamboyantly spirited creature I had seen at the Guards' barracks. Several couples felt obliged to follow the royal example and they too began dancing which certainly put the kibosh on our cabaret presentation. Later Diana sent a message through the hostess, apologising for the misunderstanding.

The only truly damp squib we ever encountered occurred at a private party we played in an enormous house on the outskirts of London. The preliminaries to the gig began when a middle-aged woman approached George and me in the downstairs bar at Ronnie Scott's to ask if we would play for a special party she was organising. She explained that her marriage was going through an awkward patch but she felt that if she had a surprise birthday party for her husband, featuring George Melly and the Feetwarmers, the event could well build a bridge of reconciliation, but she stressed that the whole thing must be planned in secrecy. Contracts were exchanged and a schedule devised that involved us hiding in the kitchen while the guests assembled. The big moment came, and on her signal we followed the hostess into the ballroom. In a voice quivering with excitement she said to her husband, 'My darling, here to sing at your party is George Melly!' His face bursting with hostility, hubby summoned up an exasperated one-word question: 'Who?' I don't think our presence did anything to mend the matrimonial breach.

In September 1985 we made a round trip of thousands of miles to play a single gig – in Beijing. Apparently the British embassy there wanted to show diplomats from various countries that the British were capable of enjoying themselves, and in an effort to confirm this they booked us to play for an embassy dance. For the only time in the band's history, our agent Jack Higgins travelled with us, as did my son Martin, who filled a spare place as a temporary road manager in the seven-piece travel party. The embassy staff's hospitality could not have been bettered; the Lido Hotel was fine and we were allocated a minibus and a driver to spend four days visiting the Great Wall, Tiananmen Square and various other tourist attractions. It was a hugely enjoyable adventure, the only blemish being that the embassy piano had been tuned a half-tone sharp, making it nearly impossible to play along with, but having travelled halfway round the world we did our best to entertain a multi-national crowd. Although we were delighted to make the trip and demonstrate jollity and jazz to a wide selection of diplomats, I was mystified as to why we had been chosen for this distant mission. Years later I was told that when the British diplomatic staff in China suspected that their conversations were being bugged they put up a blanket of sound by playing our recording, *Nuts*. Perhaps the powers-that-be within the British embassy wanted to see if their inscrutable Chinese guests would crack a smile when flesh and blood musicians were seen creating what they had so often heard as disembodied sounds.

An instance of outstanding hospitality occurred during a gig we played nearer home, at Loughborough Town Hall, where a concert was held to celebrate the birth of a new locally brewed bitter. The evening began with a reception in

the civic parlour hosted by a stern-faced mayor, whose countenance gave no indication that high jinks were to follow.
Throughout our concert the real ale flowed unceasingly for
the civic party, so much so that by the time we arrived at the
post-show gathering it was obvious that the entire council
had misjudged the potency of the new brew; they swayed
and staggered uncontrollably. The mayor, by now a picture
of extreme jollity, insisted on taking off his ermine, his chain
of office and his ceremonial hat, and then commanded
George Melly to put them on. Naturally George entered into
the spirit of the occasion and gave his wide-brimmed fedora
to His Worship. All present, including the Feetwarmers,
cheered loudly before helping the mayor and a costumed
George to climb on a desk where they gave an appropriate
rendering of 'Now is the Hour'. Years later we again played
the Town Hall and met up with people who had been part of
the shenanigans. One woman almost expired with laughter
as she recalled the bacchanalian scene.

But warm civic welcomes were not universal, and one of
our visits to Cornwall produced antagonism from the local
council. Prior to us playing a gig in St. Ives, George made a
jocular comment in a newspaper interview saying that it was
a pity that all the Cornish inhabitants of the place had been
banished to a reservation outside the town in order to make
room for people from other counties. The council failed
to see the funny side of the matter and barred us from
playing within the boundaries of St. Ives. We managed to
play the contracted engagement but only by appearing at a
rugby club that was outside the jurisdiction of the rattled
administrators.

11

The Frith Street
Charm School

It is difficult now, in an era when jazz tastes have broadened, to envisage the general amazement that greeted the 1973 news that George Melly and John Chilton's Feetwarmers were to play a season at Ronnie Scott's Club, long a bastion of modern jazz. No one was quite sure how the club's regular clientele would take our mixture of jazz, blues and jocularity, but happily they enjoyed our efforts with a gusto that led to us playing there regularly throughout the following three decades. Booking us was a bold move by Ronnie Scott and Pete King, particularly as they were well aware that we had no plans to change our repertoire or our approach to performing.

During our initial residencies at the club the Feetwarmers played the opening set of the night without George. I decided to lay down our cards on the first evening by introducing the audience to the oldest piece in our repertoire, a ragtime opus entitled 'Black Cat Rag'. The sounds of this delightfully quaint theme stopped the club's door staff dead in their tracks, but not for long; they soon mockingly began to do an old time dancing routine to our efforts. However, the warmth of the crowd's response settled us down and impressed the staff, all of whom became our firm friends during subsequent residencies. It took a while to appreciate their brusque humour, typified by an incident when a titled friend of George's came to the club and told one of the door staff that she was a guest of George Melly, whereupon he replied, 'What am I supposed to do, jump in the fucking air?' After this I nicknamed them 'The Frith Street Charm School', for which they eventually forgave me. At first we played opposite American stars, but Ronnie and Pete soon realised that it was time for George to become the headline attraction. Not only did we take the top spot, playing hour-long sets at 10.45 pm and at 1.30 am, we also had the duration of our bookings extended from three to four weeks, and then from four to five weeks, usually supported by Ronnie Scott's group.

Playing opposite Ronnie over the years gave us a chance to get to know him – not an easy endeavour. He was more broadminded about jazz than I had previously supposed and spoke admiringly of swing era stars such as Bunny Berigan, and even more surprisingly of earlier players like cornettist Red Nichols. He loved talking about the Hollywood films of the thirties and forties, happy to reel off the names of countless obscure bit-part actors and actresses. To the punters he appeared rather suave and sophisticated, with a wonderful gift for telling jokes, but backstage he often borrowed George's hat and pulled it over his ears to give a realistic impersonation of the grizzled cowboy Gabby Hayes, prior to twisting his face in a way that could have won a gurneying contest. However, Ronnie was the victim of dark moods and depression and some nights he just couldn't bring himself to converse with anyone; a week might go by without Ronnie saying anything more to us than the solitary word, 'Gentlemen,' as he entered the dressing room to indicate it was time for us to go on-stage. But no matter how low Ronnie felt, he was still able to go on-stage and deliver his gags effectively and his mood swings did not stop him from playing the tenor sax magnificently. He was an outstanding jazz musician and I was surprised and disappointed that several obituaries dwelt on his comedic skills and his work as an entrepreneur while virtually ignoring his superb musical abilities.

Ronnie's business partner, Pete King, had given up playing the tenor saxophone to run the club. With Pete, it wasn't a question of poacher turned gamekeeper, but his first-hand knowledge of the guile of musicians made him a formidable negotiator who was always one step ahead when anyone tried to take a liberty. Pete, a burly man, tended to favour rolled up shirt sleeves; Ronnie, soft leather jackets. Both were from London's East End, neither drank heavily and both remained dedicated jazz fans who sometimes booked American jazz attractions whose work they enjoyed, knowing they would lose money. Their pioneering work in bringing solo American musicians to guest with the club's resident rhythm section certainly enriched the listening of British jazz fans. To their eternal credit neither Pete nor Ronnie asked us to alter or tone down any part of our performance; the only reprimand ever delivered concerned an occasion when one of our number attempted fornication on the dressing room floor.

The oddest interlude during our many bookings at the club occurred when George fulfilled his longstanding ambition to perform a set in full drag. A good deal of planning (by his wife, Diana, and his friend, Margaret Anne) went into the selection of the outfit that George was to wear. Having played the first half of our programme we took a long intermission so that George could put on a wig, a frock and high-heeled shoes prior to being expertly made-up. When the transformation was complete I walked on-stage and (as per plan) announced that George was unfortunately indisposed, but luckily his aunt Georgina, who knew all his songs, was valiantly about to fill the gap. Georgina swept on-stage, looking as convincing an old battle-axe as ever drew breath; in fact the disguise was so complete it led the audience to believe that it really was George's aunt, and thus by implication to think that George really had been taken ill. This put something of a damper on proceedings but an even bigger 'downer' concerned the audience's reaction to the songs being sung. George cheekily warbling 'I Want a Hot Dog in my Roll' always received bellows of appreciative laughter, but when Georgina sang the suggestive lyrics they presented a pathetic picture of an old trout begging to be serviced – the crowd were not amused. George might have saved the day if he had suddenly thrown off his wig, as Dustin Hoffman did in the *Tootsie* movie, but the pleasure he was getting from the firm clasp of the huge padded brassiere persuaded him to continue with the ill-fated impersonation. At the end of the set we left the stage to meagre applause, and a minute later two people came up to me and said they sincerely hoped that George would soon be well enough to return to the club.

All this passed without comment from Ronnie and Pete, they were tolerance itself. Ronnie certainly wasn't a tyrant – the only time he became regimental was in the way he organised events each New Year's Eve. Every December 31st at 10 pm Ronnie entered the dressing room and said, without variation, 'Now John we need to finalise the details of what will happen at midnight. At one minute to twelve I'll bring the radio on-stage, tuned to Radio Four. As the chimes of Big Ben start I will place the radio in front of the micro-phone and as I do so I want the drummer to begin playing a roll, gradually getting louder until twelve chimes have been heard. I will then wish everyone a Happy New Year and you will count the band into "Auld Lang Syne".'

Each year Ronnie recited these details without variation. One December 31st, having heard this annual plan of action many times, I started to parrot it word for word along with Ronnie, but he, totally out of character, became quite angry – for him this was a serious business. Imagine the consterna-tion the year the radio broke down just as the chimes were about to begin. Ronnie, the born improviser, was equal to the calamity; he simply leant close the microphone and sang 'Bing, Bong, Bing, Bong.' The band were convulsed with laughter and unable to start playing but one fierce glance from Ronnie soon launched us into the planned number. Twelve months later, on the 31st December at 10 pm, Ronnie entered the dressing room and said, 'Now John we need to finalise the details. . .' You could joke about anything with Ronnie except New Year's Eve.

Ronnie Scott's Club marks the spot where, in August 1982, I became a teetotaller, after being a heavy drinker from my late teens. I went to the club to hear Dizzy Gillespie and augmented my listening pleasure with a lot of drinking, forgetting that I had to deliver a sleeve note to Time-Life Records on the following day. I awoke with a start, late the next morning, suffering the inevitable hangover, and managed to pull myself together enough to write the piece, but only just. It was all so nerve-racking I resolved to quit drinking. This instant abstinence was a big step because I'd always felt a desperate need to have a supply of drinks at my elbow whenever I played a gig. It was beyond social drinking, I could only drink to get drunk. Happily I soon managed to readjust, and went through one decade after another without alcohol. I certainly don't miss the vicious hangovers, nor do I miss the belligerent, troublesome character who used to invade my body every time I got drunk.

Other than Ronnie Scott's, the 100 Club (at 100 Oxford Street) was for years the venue we played most regularly. It held a special place in our affections because George and I, quite independently, had been habitués of the place during the late 1940s and 1950s when it was the London Jazz Club. It was where George had made an early public appearance by jumping on-stage, uninvited, to sing 'Doctor Jazz' with Humphrey Lyttelton's band. Humph didn't know George at this time but had seen him and nicknamed him 'Bunny Bum' on account of his unusual style of dancing. I was too involved in listening to the intoxicating sounds of Humph's band, and particularly his trumpet playing, to consider dancing.

Originally the 100 Club was not licensed to sell alcoholic drinks. In order to buy these, one had to dash out in the intervals to a local pub such as the Blue Posts or the Champion – the club was finally granted a drinks licence in 1965. In all my years there, as punter and performer, I never saw a violent incident. I worked with several different bands besides leading my own quartet for a long residency, and George had played there many times with Mick Mulligan's Magnolia Jazz Band, so every gig was a trip down memory lane. We developed a clique of devoted followers who sat in the same seats every time we played at the club. The most dedicated of these supporters also came to see us whenever we were in action elsewhere in the London area, but none was keener than Hugh, who bestowed on himself the accolade 'Number One Fan'. His involvement often meant he joined us in the record-signing sessions we did after the gig, where he insisted on inking-in his self-awarded title on the sleeve of a disc whether the purchaser wanted it or not. We could tolerate his written embellishments but keeping his behaviour in check was beyond our remit. He insisted that everyone in the audience had to listen as closely to our performance as he did, and if they failed to do so he gave them a public dressing down. Eventually he was barred from almost every venue we played until his only remaining listening spot was the Pizza On The Park, Knightsbridge; but even the doors of that tolerant establishment were closed to him after he forcefully reprimanded someone for talking during our set. He explained, very loudly, that he had a right to demand silence as he was our 'Number One Fan'. The words had scarcely left his mouth when his adversary jumped up and yelled, 'No! I'm the Number One Fan.' Unfortunately the contretemps occurred just as we were playing one of our quietest, most reflective numbers. The two stood eyeball to eyeball mouthing the mantra, 'I'm the Number One Fan,' until Hugh, adjudged the originator of the dispute, was ejected, losing the right to enter what had become his last listening post.

It always seemed to us that the 100 Club audiences were rich in songwriters. We hardly ever appeared there without being offered the lyrics and melody of a piece that the donor had 'specially written with George Melly in mind', but which usually turned out to be a ditty about the antics of someone called 'Sean the Horn' or 'Gorgeous Gavin'. Nevertheless we listened carefully to every song we received including those posted to us or delivered to theatres where we were due to appear, but in thirty years of unhurried listening we never found anything suitable. However, some lyrics given to me by the great novelist, Jean Rhys, formed the basis of the song 'Life With You' which we recorded. Jean gave me a few stanzas of a bitter-sweet poem and asked if I could put a melody to them but unfortunately at that stage there were not enough words to complete a vocal chorus so the plan was shelved. Some while after, I came across the lines she had given me and saw that if I devised lyrics for a middle section there would be enough words for a full vocal chorus. Francis Wyndham, Jean's literary executor, approved of the additional stanzas I had added, so I devised a melody and George recorded the piece (as by Rhys and Chilton). At the time that Jean gave me the lyrics she was staying with George and Diana and regularly came to Ronnie Scott's to hear us. An extremely game eighty-five-year-old, she had an unusually soft voice which meant that George (because of his hearing problem) rarely heard a word she said.

Over the years I wrote numerous songs for George including 'Give Her a Little Drop More', 'Punch Drunk Mama' (a salute to one of George's early girlfriends), 'The Food of Love' (examining the aphrodisiac qualities of organic food), 'I Won't Grow Old' (a defiant look at the ageing process), 'Please Don't Mention your Sign' (outlining George's detestation of horoscopes), 'Oh Chubby – Stay the Way You Are', 'Living on my Own' and 'The Story of Punch and Judy' (which celebrated George's lifelong fascination with the matrimonial woe of these ancient puppets). We also managed to get permission for George to sing various parodies I wrote on the framework of evergreen songs: 'Happy Feet' became 'Crappy Feet' (which allowed George to transmit his detestation of fouled pavements) and 'I Can't Give You Anything but Love' reappeared as 'I Have Really Had my Fill of Love, Baby'. Our most popular parody was a take-off I wrote on 'The Ovaltinies', but the Wander Company (makers of excellent beverages) would not give us permission to record 'The Inbetweenies – Neither Boys nor Girls'.

We occasionally performed the music for advertising jingles. This was money for old rope when a good musical director who could explain what he wanted was in charge of the session, but sometimes an over-ambitious advertising agency executive took it upon himself to issue instructions in musical terms he plainly didn't understand. Under these circumstances the performance of a short, simple piece of music could become very time consuming. Nerves were worn to a frazzle on one occasion when the big chief insisted we play the entire jingle at a much slower tempo but under no circumstances was it to last even a split second longer than the faster version.

The funniest situation I encountered in the world of advertising occurred when I was with Bruce Turner's Jump Band. We were booked to provide the music for a brief film that advertised a well-known brand of shoes. The account executive explained how important it was to capture the raw atmosphere of an early caveman's habitat, and for this reason he chose to record the soundtrack deep in the heart of the Chislehurst Caves, which meant a team of men carrying a piano, a double bass and a set of drums into the subterranean site. The results were horrendous because the sound we made bounced off several walls – not quite simultaneously. After many 'takes' the expensive session was abandoned. During the following week we reassembled in a west London recording studio where the executive again aired his artistic message. A patient sound engineer listened politely before sending us into the studio to play the number, and then simply added echo by turning a control knob. The executive leapt into the air and shrieked 'Eureka' as though he had played a part in creating the rarest of tone colours. We kept our eyes firmly on the ground, knowing that a serious outbreak of the derisive giggles was very close at hand.

During the 1980s we greatly enjoyed doing three series for BBC television entitled *Good Time George*. These featured George and the Feetwarmers working alongside various guests including Slim Gaillard, Ralph Sutton, Madeleine Bell, Memphis Slim, Acker Bilk, Paul Jones, Helen Shapiro, Elaine Delmar, Linda Lewis, Will Gaines and Georgie Fame. The shows radiated a happy atmosphere, with producer Simon Betts always willing to listen to our suggestions. We almost succeeded in getting Jack Lemmon to guest on piano, but all our efforts to feature Ella Fitzgerald were in vain.

However, we did link up with Ella during a brief London residency she did at the Grosvenor Hotel. For these July 1984 dates, George sang a couple of numbers before introducing Nelson Riddle, who then welcomed Ella to the stage. Big occasions usually brought out the best of George, but on the first night he came perilously close to forgetting Nelson Riddle's name. For some reason he was having difficulty in remembering it so he prepared himself with a memory aid by thinking of the great American arranger as Trafalgar Conundrum, but this mnemonic nearly proved George's undoing. Having worked for so long with George, I could see the warning signs of a mental brick wall looming but, after a long, alarming bout of silence, George mercifully plucked the right name out of the air. It was fascinating to watch Ella arrive as an old lady then see her shed thirty years the

moment she heard her introductory music. For me, the
bonus of the week was being able to talk at leisure with Ella's
manager, Norman Granz, who was also the world's most
notable jazz impresario.

George continued to guest on various television and radio
programmes, on most of which he sang and I played either
with the Feetwarmers or with a studio band. On one radio
show we both took part in a brief sketch with Frankie
Howerd. Before the recording began I was given a script
that seemed as flat as a pancake but half an hour later,
when Frankie Howerd began working on it, he had the
studio audience convulsed with laughter. Like many another
comedian Frankie was funnier on-stage than off, but when
we appeared on Ted Rogers' *3–2–1* television quiz show I was
surprised to find that the reverse was true of the host. Off-
stage, Ted was a very amusing man, infinitely funnier in the
dressing room than he was in front of an audience.

We had the dubious pleasure of encountering Bernard
Manning on a couple of occasions, the first of which was in
1973. I was appalled by the subjects covered in his material
but was much impressed by his technique as a comedian.
Four years later we appeared on television with him in the
Wheeltappers and Shunters' Club. Bernard decided to heckle
George from the moment he sang his first note. George
countered by lifting a rejoinder from G. B. Shaw: 'I agree
with you Bernard, but who are we two against so many?' A
series of barbed exchanges ensued, all of which were cut out
of the transmitted programme – a pity because George more
than held his own. However, Bernard wanted the last word.
He followed us into the car park when the filming ended and
continued to harangue George as we climbed into the taxi
that was to take us to Manchester Airport. I waited until he

paused for breath then asked, 'Excuse me, but are you working on New Year's Eve?' using a bring-down phrase which
suggested there was little demand for a rival's services.

My most memorable brush with a comedian occurred
early in my touring days, back in the 1950s, when, as a member of Bruce Turner's Jump Band, I played for the annual
Stockport Press Ball. At this event a young northern comedian had been asked to draw the raffle, and we went on-stage
to play the second half of the gig just as the young man took
the microphone and began calling out the winning numbers,
accompanying his selection of the tickets with a line of
patter that was so funny everyone stopped talking to listen
and laugh. I never saw anyone, including the great American
comedians, take such command of an audience. Almost two
hours later, having long finished drawing the raffle, the
young comedian was still producing streams of zany humour;
the crowd gave no thought to dancing, preferring to bathe in
the cascade of jokes. At midnight the comedian waved good-
night to the audience and we played the obligatory national
anthem, which was all we were called on to do throughout
the entire second half of the evening. The audience
answered the comedian's toothy farewell smile with several
minutes of unrestrained cheering. I had experienced the
genius of Ken Dodd for the first time.

There were no dramatic changes in our presentation during the late 1980s; we still offered a mixture of vintage jazz,
blues and humour, but as George became less and less
mobile his cavorting became more restrained and he began
accompanying every number with a joke or a comic
anecdote. Both of us worked hard to find fresh material and
occasionally jokes we devised went into general circulation.
The main root of George's comedic inspiration was Max

Miller, with traces of such disparate funny men as Robb Wilton, Redd Foxx, Lenny Bruce and Sandy Powell. I was happy to be part of an enterprise that paid homage to the great days of the music hall and was more disappointed if a joke we had devised went wrong than I was if a musical number ran into difficulties. With music one could usually put things right before the number ended but a mistimed joke died there and then. George gradually developed into a fine comedian but at first he was prone to over-egg the pudding by adding huge helpings of dialogue to a joke that was already working effectively. If an audience were slow to laugh George mistakenly thought they would crack if they heard more background information. He would add a hundred words in the belief that to double the length of a joke would double the laughs. However, by trial and error he eventually triumphed, particularly in telling dialect jokes.

When we first went on the road together it seemed to me that George was more popular in the north of England than in the south, but with the passing of thirty years the reactions evened out as conformity and similarity became the hallmarks of British life. Nowhere was this more obvious than in the hotels we stayed in which gradually became similar, even when owned by different chains. After travelling for two hundred miles one was likely to be greeted by curtains, carpets, menus and staff chat that were nearly identical to what had been encountered the night before. However, a level of comfort was assured and after a while the repetition created its own appeal, particularly when one remembered yesteryears' digs. Occasionally we were invited to stay with band followers but generally we declined these offers on the grounds that too much time was lost in gathering up the troupe when we set out for our next destination.

In one north-eastern town, where we had previously had difficulty in finding a suitable hotel, we all accepted an offer to stay at a large farm. The host promised us individual rooms, a late breakfast and snooker throughout the night for those who wanted it. He gave us the address of his farm which was on the outskirts of the town. Chuck Smith was driving the band bus but even his calm temperament was severely tested as we travelled round and round the town looking for the place. Eventually we found a pedestrian who pointed towards the horizon. After a long ride we saw a sign-post indicating that the farm was close by; the building loomed into view and we saw that its size was as promised. Chuck jumped out and entered the farmhouse to announce our arrival. Five minutes passed and he failed to emerge. I asked Collin Bates to go and look for him but, in the manner of an Agatha Christie plot, he too disappeared. Some while later, the two men came back to the band bus to report that there was no sign of the farmer, or anyone else. However, on the dining room table were two untouched lunches gently giving off wisps of steam. Chuck and Collin explored every part of the dwelling, shouting as they did so, but there was no response. We had no option but to drive back into the town where we took the first vacant rooms we could find.

That night, as we were signing records at the end of the concert, the missing farmer approached us looking dishevelled and sporting a black eye. He apologised profusely for letting us down. It seems he hadn't told his wife that we were coming to stay until they were about to eat their lunch. She was decidedly vexed by the news, so much so that she punched him vigorously in the eye and left immediately to stay with her mother. Sitting alone, full of woe and ashamed of his swollen face, he had heard the band bus pull up and decided to run upstairs to hide under a bed, ignoring Collin's and Chuck's shouts. We felt badly let down by the farmer but he was immune to our hostility and said, with some spirit, 'Never mind, we'll make you reet welcome next time you come.'

On tour, Chuck and I made every effort to attend football matches, not only by visiting provincial grounds in England but also by watching various teams abroad including the New York Cosmos and Bayern Munich. Back on-stage, one mildly competitive pastime I shared with Chuck involved detecting wig-wearers in our audience. I don't know what made us start this foolish pursuit. Chuck had a magnificent head of hair and I was as bald as a billiard ball, but for some forgotten reason we devised a 'Spot the Irish' game (Irish jig equals wig in Cockney slang). 'Row 3, seat 16' one of us would whisper during our performance. This utterance would be followed by a nod or a faint shake of the head, and the one claiming the most detections was the winner. During an Australian tour we noted a possible sighting in the front row, but we couldn't make up our minds and even at an after-the-show party which the man attended we remained unsure. Was the thatch genuine or not? We circled the man slowly but had to abandon our scrutiny for fear of causing embarrassment. We flew back to London soon afterwards, both of us feeling defeated – toupee or not toupee. When we resumed touring Britain we became resigned to the possibility of never knowing the answer, but joy was close at hand. We were soon invited to return to Australia and again played in the man's home city. We didn't know his name, so an invite to our concert was out of the question. He failed to attend the show but at an outdoor barbecue next day there was our quarry, his hand outstretched in welcome. Under the bright blue sky we took one glance at the man's head and exchanged beaming nods of agreement. It was a wig, albeit a superior model.

Tours of Australia became a regular part of our schedule in the late eighties, but there seemed no prospect of us returning to the USA. Researching a new book on jazz meant that I had to make special journeys over to the States to gather information. These excursions, taken during band holidays, enabled me to unearth invaluable background details. They also provide happy memories. One absorbing research trip to the USA was to trace the background of the great tenor saxophonist Coleman Hawkins who, like Sidney Bechet, had deliberately created false biographical trails involving his place of birth, date of birth and family history. But Hawkins' efforts to fog the facts made me very determined to establish his background and, after a good deal of sleuthing, I ascertained the truth, which I was able to include in *The Song of the Hawk*, my biography of him. I'm proud to say that my persistence won me an award in America from the Association for Recorded Sound Collections, for writing the best researched jazz book of the year.

One trip to New York was hastily arranged when I found out that there was to be a reunion of Bob Crosby sidemen for a television special. This was very timely because I had just started writing a book about this group of musicians (*Stomp Off, Let's Go*). Sitting at leisure in a New York hotel with these revered veterans provided a glorious opportunity to gather fascinating anecdotes as they reminded each other about shared whoopee making. Through my great pal Brian Peerless, who organises tours by American jazz musicians, I got to know various former Bob Crosby musicians when they were in Europe. There was trumpeter Yank Lawson whose gruff exterior hid a heart of gold, bassist Bob Haggart who, despite earning a fortune from his composing royalties, remained a careful man with a dollar (he was, however, a nice mixture of suavity and humour); and dapper tenor saxist Eddie Miller who never let his years in Hollywood studio bands blunt the joy that filled every solo he played – he was a man whose company was as exhilarating as his jazz playing.

Former Bob Crosby trumpeter Billy Butterfield was equally friendly but, not being an extrovert, he tended to stay on the edge of group conversations, though in one-to-one settings he proved to be knowledgeable on many subjects and always radiated a quiet charm. His ex-colleague Matty Matlock thought that Billy was the 'greatest all round trumpeter in jazz', a view echoed by the brass virtuoso Manny Klein. Billy and Yank Lawson were the twin spearheads of the World's Greatest Jazz Band, but if people asked Billy who he was working with, he was just too modest to say the World's Greatest Jazz Band and invariably said, 'I'm with Yank Lawson and Bob Haggart.'

Yank was a generous man who willingly gave his time to play at a benefit for our ailing bassist Barry Dillon. Besides being one of the most emphatic trumpeters in the business, he was proud of his cooking and got a lot of pleasure out of showing his skills by preparing a splendid meal for a gathering at Brian and Valerie Peerless' house. Yank and Bob Haggart managed to stay friends despite Yank's long standing carp about the composer royalties for 'The March of the Bob Cats'. He had helped to devise this for a recording session that took place while Haggart was away on his honeymoon but somehow the piece was credited to Haggart.

Eventually, late in their lives, some sort of financial settlement was reached.

12

A Jazz Scrapbook
Comes to Life

In my early teens when I began compiling my first jazz scrapbook I could not have imagined that I would get to meet
many of my musical heroes and be lucky enough to establish
friendships with some of them. Not that every encounter
was filled with bonhomie: Count Basie was positively the
most difficult interviewee that I ever encountered. I first
met him in London in April 1957, and well remember my first
question to him, 'Have you seen Lester Young lately?' His
terse reply was: 'Buster is just fine.' There was no further
embellishment. I had done a lot of research into Basie's early
days in Kansas City so I followed up with some questions
about this period of his career.

He had left his New Jersey home to tour widely with a
theatrical troupe but contracted meningitis in Kansas City
and stayed there throughout a long convalescent period.
While recuperating, Basie is said to have found inspiration
in the economical piano style of a young local favourite,
'Sleepy' Hickcox. Basie subordinated his considerable skills
as a stride pianist to develop his own version of this sparse
approach to the keyboard. No details of these important

events in Basie's life had ever been published so I was determined to put my enquiries directly to him. But I was soon
made aware that Basie had no intention of sharing his
memories. He wasn't belligerent, just totally unhelpful; his
countenance suggested that I might have been talking to
him in an ancient Aztec dialect.

Eventually I halted my enquiries but tried again on a later
occasion with a new set of questions – Basie's response was
similar. I had begun to think it was something personal but
people who knew Basie said he was generally affable except
when anyone tried to question him about his life and his
career. My good friend Dan Morgenstern called the Count
'a notoriously difficult interview subject', a sentiment I
heartily endorsed. Over a long period I made a couple more
attempts, then called it a day. Happily for jazz lovers, Basie
finally decided to tell his story to Albert Murray and their
collaboration *Good Morning Blues* was published in 1985.
Sadly, however, Basie died before the book came out.

My relationship with Benny Carter almost got off to a
bumpy start. I was interviewing him at the Strand Palace
Hotel in London and everything was going smoothly. Benny,
who had a reputation for polite reticence, was being surprisingly candid. I had tried to do my homework in selecting
questions that might open him up and one involved an interview that he had given to a British publication, *Swing Music*,
in 1936, in which he revealed that the celebrated clarinet
player Darnell Howard was his cousin. I commented on this
family relationship only to see the expression on Benny's
face change dramatically, 'How did you know he was my
cousin?' I told him about the 1936 article. 'Impossible,' said
Benny querulously, 'I've only recently found out that we are
cousins.' I certainly wasn't going to dig my heels in and show

him a magazine article from thirty years before, so I said I was mistaken and that I must have heard it lately from a visiting American musician. This placated him and all our subsequent conversations were warm and friendly, though I never did find out why he had been so touchy about a family link. I kept in touch with Benny for the rest of his long life, and an annual August pleasure was the telephone conversation I had with him on his birthday. He was always bright and sharp and never seemed to age; his urbanity and wisdom were remarkable.

Even the briefest meetings could provide insight into a great jazzman's personality. The wonderful trombonist, Jack Teagarden, seemed to epitomise a Texan blend of confidence and charm. I have never forgotten his reply to a question about his son Jack Junior's trombone playing: 'Well he does-n't do too much of that these days. Trouble was, everyone used to say, "You ain't never gonna be as good as your Pappy." And of course they were right.' Singer Victoria Spivey had a penchant for lopping years off her age, so, in answer to my question about the recordings she made with Louis Armstrong in 1929, she suddenly acted sweet sixteen and said, 'I was just an itty-bitty little girl when I made those sides.' In contrast, tenor saxist Don Byas was willing to date every move in his career. I was able to glean a lot of informa-tion when we both stayed at the Standard Hotel in Oslo, because each evening we had dinner together before going off to our respective gigs. On the final night there, we had an involved conversation about Don playing baritone sax in various territory bands but the clock ended this discussion and it was to be five years before we met again, this time in a Wardour Street pub. I wondered if Don would remember me but he waved and crossed the bar to say, 'The problem was getting baritone reeds when one was on tour', picking up the conversation at exactly the point we had left it years earlier. He could be a problem when he was drunk, and trumpeter Bill Coleman was amazed and appalled when Byas (on a concert they shared) suddenly dropped his trousers. Don also needed no encouragement to recite aloud a long erotic poem he carried with him.

Bill Coleman was a different kettle of fish, charming and engagingly shy. Because he spent so much of his life playing in Europe he never gained a big reputation back home in the USA, but numerous musicians appreciated Bill's melodically imaginative jazz and his quicksilver technique. One admirer was Louis Armstrong who, to Bill's everlasting joy, warmly congratulated Bill when they met in New York in 1940 on various recordings he made in France during the 1930s. I have never forgotten the masterful way that Bill played when he guested with my Swing Kings at a Wimbledon gig. The occasion was made doubly memorable because we had the superfine bassist Dave Holland in our line-up.

Trumpeter Jonah Jones was universally popular with his brass-playing colleagues. His affability and openness were remarkable and I have never heard anyone say a bad word about him. When Roy Eldridge (who was not noted for praising his rivals) commented on Jonah's worldwide recording successes, he said, 'It could not have happened to a nicer guy and if people think I'm using a stock phrase to praise Jonah – well, let them find out where I've ever said it about anyone else.' I first met Jonah in 1971 when he and his wife, Elizabeth, were on vacation in London. He had been given my telephone number by a mutual friend and called me with an invitation to visit him at his hotel. This was the start of a long friendship, as he made me very welcome and we were soon in relaxed conversation. Jonah had a wonderful store of anecdotes and a remarkable ability to create thumbnail sketches of his colleagues. He was a jazz historian's dream because it seemed as if he could remember every gig he had ever played, when it took place and who shared it with him. When I asked him about his first trip to New York, he willingly gave me all the background details. After playing in various big bands during the early 1930s, Jonah began a highly productive musical partnership in Buffalo with the jazziest of all violinists, Stuff Smith. Stuff's sextet was soon talent-spotted and offered a booking at the Onyx Club in New York but Jonah was apprehensive about making the trip.

'All of us except Stuff were sceptical about going to New York but he was very eager and knowing we were doubtful he went ahead and started fixing a new line-up consisting of New York-based musicians, but word of this reached the New York bookers and they came down hard and said, "We want the regular band from Buffalo." Next thing I know a tough-looking little guy calls on me. I'd never seen him before and I've never seen him since. He looked straight at me and said, "It would be very good for you to go and play in New York, and very, very bad for you to stay here in Buffalo." It was a threat but I wasn't worried, I thought I'll go down to the musicians' union and they'll sort all this out. So in all innocence I went to the Union in Buffalo and said, "Some guy is pressurising me into going to New York." The union guy looks at me and gives a sickly sort of smile and says, "I think you better do what the man says." It was like a bad movie. It was all sewn up that I was going to New York, so I did.'

Stuff Smith was unpredictable on and off the bandstand. Jonah said, 'He'd do anything that came into his head. One night he got a pistol and ran into a bakery shouting, "Okay, this is a stick-up, give me all the dough you've got." It was a dangerous joke, he could easily have got a kitchen knife in his belly. But his improvisations on that violin were fantastic; when he backed you it was like having a whole saxophone section riffing behind you, he had so much rhythm. Everyone got to know about us at the Onyx. There was a sort of infectious madness in that club, we used to get drunk on whisky and high on pot for months on end. I began to feel that things weren't right with my health. The doctor gave me a thorough check-up and said, "If you carry on drinking and smoking like you're doing you won't last a year." I took his advice and quit, and I guess that saved my life.' Jonah lived to see his ninetieth birthday.

I was delighted when Jonah accepted my invitation to come and blow with the Feetwarmers at New Merlin's Cave. He played splendidly and was surrounded by well-wishers when the session ended. He was deluged with questions and, as ever, didn't shirk any replies. The subject of Louis Armstrong (Jonah's all-time favourite) came up and Jonah responded by singing one after another of Louis' greatest solos – it was a touching moment. During various later meetings we had in London, New York, New Orleans and The Hague, Jonah was always ready to give straight answers. Typical was his re-living of the last part of his association with Stuff Smith, four years after they had blazed into New York.

'Stuff's band finally folded in the fall of 1940. Before that we tried augmenting by having Ben Webster join us for a while but that didn't last. We were playing a residency

at a club in New Jersey that was run by some very tough
operators. We finished playing at around one in the morning
and decided to have a game of cards: Ben Webster, me,
drummer Cozy Cole and pianist Sam Price. It seemed as
though nothing could go wrong for me that night and I was
soon $85 up. There was a bit of tension at the table so I
bought everyone doubles. The more the time passed the
more I won and Ben in particular got saltier and saltier. Stuff
came over and broke up the game by saying, "Quit now,
because I want a rehearsal tomorrow at one o'clock in the
afternoon." Something snapped in Ben. He picked up a
chromium bar stool and smashed Stuff to the ground. Stuff
was frail in comparison to Ben who was built like a barrel.
We knew instantly that this meant Ben was out of the band,
but next day he turned up as sheepish as could be, bringing
Benny Carter with him, who had the job of apologising for
Ben. But it didn't work, one of the club's owners saw Ben
coming into the club and he walked right in his path and
said, "You're real lucky, mister. If I had been here when you
attacked a smaller man with a bar stool I would have shot
you dead there and then." Ben wasn't ready for that sort of
hardness. He went out of the door and never came back.'

After leaving Stuff Smith, Jonah spent over ten years
being featured with Cab Calloway's band before settling in
to a New York theatre orchestra. He began toying with the
idea of taking a day job but, encouraged by agent Sam Berk,
he formed his own quartet which was soon making huge-sell-
ing recordings – marketed as 'Muted Jazz'. Despite his fame
Jonah was still always ready to shed light on any jazz event he
had been part of. He was as friendly, generous and candid as
ever. The last conversation we had took place in the spring
of 2000, not long before he died. Trumpeter Jimmy Owens

was at the hospital bedside when I telephoned. He had previously warned me about the parlous state of Jonah's health, but even so Jonah recognised my voice and began to marshal a series of reminiscences about his activities seventy years earlier in riverboat bands. He was an ace trumpeter and an ace human being.

Trombonist Dicky Wells was from the same Louisville, Kentucky background as Jonah Jones but, whereas Jonah gave up hard drinking in 1940, Dicky fought a long battle with the demon grog and during his 1965 solo tour of Britain it was obvious that he was still locked in combat with his old enemy. The saddest part was that Dicky was a secret drinker, insisting to everyone that he never touched a drop. One felt compassion but, with cunning of the highest order, he would secrete small bottles of spirits in dozens of places so that he could swig one down in an instant. Keeping him sober for his gigs was a difficult task that three of us shared: the tour agent Jim Godbolt, his assistant Don Kingswell and me. Despite all the problems Dicky caused us, he could be a charming man, and modest too, considering that he had once been one of the most brilliant, innovative trombonists in the history of jazz. But somewhere something went wrong after his glory years with Count Basie and he became an alcoholic, causing his long-time wife a good deal of woe.

On one of the nights off during his tour Dicky and Jim Godbolt came to spend the evening with Teresa and me. By this time we were well aware of Dicky's craving for alcohol. To make matters worse Dicky said with a chuckle, 'I haven't had a drink for some years,' despite the fact that on the previous night he had been unable to put the slide back into his trombone, causing the promoter of the gig, Derrick Stewart-Baxter (a Sussex jazz devotee), to say almost tearfully to the

audience, 'It seems as though our hero has feet of clay.'
Things got no better on subsequent gigs and the tour had to
be curtailed. Dicky flew back to New York and I thought we
would never see or hear him again, but within a week he had
written to each of us, sending small gifts and saying how
sorry he was that a bout of pneumonia had caused his 'wonderful' tour to be cancelled. I exchanged letters with him for
a while and was saddened to learn he had been mugged.

Later, during a residency in New York, we had a night off
which happily coincided with a one-off appearance by Count
Basie's band at the Roseland Ballroom. As I stood at the
back of the hall listening to the formidable sound of the
band I saw Dicky wandering around the edge of the crowd.
I went over to say 'hello' and we began a conversation in
which he said he couldn't miss turning out for 'the old gang',
but I could tell his mind was on other matters. His eyes had
that thirsty look I had seen before. Off he went and I lost
sight of him in the crowd. We never met again.

Tenor saxist Lawrence 'Bud' Freeman was always punctu-
al and sober and played consistently well on all of his gigs,
but travelling as his guide was less enjoyable than it should
have been. Bud's brother, Arnie, was a successful actor and
Bud did his best to follow in his thespian footsteps. Getting
ready for a gig, Bud would speak to me as though he were
addressing a valet, 'Should I wear the blue shirt or the
striped one?' 'Should I wear the brogues or the suede casu-
als?' And finally, 'Shall I wear the grey overcoat or the her-
ringbone tweed one?' All these enquiries delivered in a crisp
but over-the-top English accent. On one occasion, after he
had spent about four minutes admiring himself in the mirror,
I said, 'Take it from me Bud, you look like a Duke.' Bud
beamed with satisfaction and said, 'I was thinking along

those lines myself, John'. One could hardly believe that this man had seen the rough side of many escapades in his home city of Chicago. With effort, it was possible to get him talking on the subject of jazz, and then he spoke with authority and considerable intelligence. He was, after all, a true jazz original and I was always an admirer of his playing. A schoolfriend's father possessed only one jazz record, Bud's 'Muskrat Ramble', and I often walked a mile out of my way returning from school so that I could hear this stimulating example of tenor sax playing. But Bud in person was less enjoyable.

One day I was in the basement of Doug Dobell's record shop when I heard the unmistakeable sound of Bud's adopted accent as he descended the steps. Escape was the only answer. I managed to squeeze into a store cupboard before he made his entrance, where I had the long, cramped experience of listening to Bud in full conversational flow for at least ten minutes. I had time to think back to the thrill of hearing 'Muskrat Ramble' and I felt thoroughly ashamed that I was hiding from a man of such talent. Thereafter I was more tolerant of Bud's idiosyncrasies, but I remember Ruby Braff laying down his fork on the dinner table when someone spoke glowingly about Bud. 'I'd travel a long way to hear Bud Freeman play,' he said, 'but not if I also had to talk to him.'

Ruby was invariably outspoken. He could be an affable companion or an extremely argumentative little man, bristling with bad temper, but fortunately his variable moods never diminished his artistry. He was one of the jazz sensations of the fifties, when he mostly played trumpet. Later, however, he switched exclusively to cornet, a change that brought even more flexibility to an already remarkable

technique. He could move from high to low registers as easily as a great racing driver changes gear, and his sonorous
bottom notes had a beautiful cello-like quality. His powers of
improvising were formidable and his technique speedy
enough to transmit any ideas he conceived. With such skills
at his fingertips it was hard to understand why he was riddled with discontent.

I first heard Ruby live at a concert in Paris. This was in
1961, in the era when the exchange of musicians between
America and Britain was sporadic due to the rulings of the
musicians' unions. Pee Wee Russell was on the bill with
Ruby, and as neither had visited Britain it seemed to Bruce
Turner and me that we must go over and hear them play a
double concert in the Paris Olympia. When we were on tour
in Britain we regularly played Ruby's recordings in our leisure
time but one live example was rather blemished for us
because a near-maniacal laugh kept surfacing on the record.
We went backstage to meet Ruby who let out a loud chuckle on being told we had flown over from London to hear the
concerts – we realised instantly that it was Ruby's laugh that
had addled the disc for us. Because we had journeyed a long
way to see him, Ruby was friendly towards us, and remained
so ever after – he never lost his temper with me. However, I
was to see the other side of him. When he made his first tour
of Britain he was very downcast, saying he was unhappy with
the musicians who were accompanying him and he was
thinking of going home. The next night he was delighted
with them; another twenty-four hours passed and they were
next to useless, and so on. Ruby was not above stage-whis-
pering quite savage criticisms of his backing musicians and
his audible comments to pianist Lennie Felix during one tour
were nothing less than cruel.

Ruby came to New Merlin's Cave to sit in with us and was soon at loggerheads with the implacable side of Wally Fawkes' personality, turning his nose up at any tune that Wally suggested. It began with Wally affably selecting 'When You and I Were Young, Maggie', one of Ruby's recorded triumphs. 'Oh, has that got here?' asked Ruby sarcastically. After the session he began looking for an argument by denigrating Art Tatum and calling Lionel Hampton 'a moron'. We could hardly believe that someone who had played so beautifully could be so antagonistic. Yet Ruby was capable of kindness and came to our first two nights at a New York booking saying, 'You guys turn out to hear me in London so I'm going to support you now you're here.' He was also capable of writing friendly, warm-hearted letters. The nearest that he came to barking at me occurred when I gave him a copy of my biography of Sidney Bechet. He looked at it with utter disdain and said with some venom, 'Don't you know I hate his playing?'

Ruby's final years were plagued by various respiratory problems, all of which he maintained were soothed by a steady intake of marijuana. During the early 2000s he made annual trips to Britain, principally to play at the Pizza on the Park, and used a wheelchair while touring. I must say he always welcomed me warmly, and it was fascinating to hear him reminisce and a fulfilling experience to hear him play. Fortunately, he made many recordings during his last years, the merits of which led me to pluck up courage and say to him that I thought his jazz playing was better than ever. The shortage of breath made him less inclined, and less able, to fly all over the instrument continually filling every gap. Instead, he relied on majestic phrasing, elegant ideas, a superb tone and an abundance of feeling. Even those to whom Ruby had been misanthropic could never belittle his musicianship. He died in February 2003.

My 1961 trip to Paris with Bruce Turner also produced a brief meeting with Duke Ellington's long-time associate, Billy Strayhorn, who was socializing in the French capital. Bruce had always been interested in the extent of their musical collaborations and was delighted to have the opportunity to ask Strayhorn about various numbers he had co-composed with the Duke. Strayhorn's eyes twinkled as he gave Bruce the gentlest of verbal cuffs, saying, 'Don't worry your head about such things, baby, just listen to the music.' The elucidation went no further – he had been asked the same question too many times.

The repetition factor also affected violinist Joe Venuti's willingness to answer questions, but Joe had made a rod for his own back by mischievously giving various locations for his place of birth. When tackled about this he would tersely reply: 'It's all in the books. It's all in the books.' Practical joking had been Venuti's prime pleasure in earlier years, his most famous stunt being his telephoned offer of work (using a disguised voice) to dozens of bass players, all of whom were given instructions to meet on a certain street corner for what turned out to be a non-existent gig. But Joe wasn't only a prankster out for laughs. He also had a violent side to his nature and, during their days with Paul Whiteman's orchestra, he punched Jack Teagarden with force enough to knock out two of the trombonist's teeth. By the time I met Venuti he looked for all the world like a retired headwaiter. Gone was the hard drinking and his strongest tipple was ginger ale, but he could still play astonishing phrases on the violin.

I was present when another famous jazz violinist, Stéphane Grappelli, was being asked (for the millionth

time) what it was like working with guitarist Django
Reinhardt. Stéphane made a hand gesture that signified
absolute pleasure, then added, 'Mon dieu, he was marvellous,
but, oh, the smell of his feet was terrible.'

Over the years I have encountered several musicians who
have lied about their age. One such was the trombonist
Herb Flemming who, in communications to me over a span
of twenty years, not only changed his date of birth, but also
supplied me with three different places of birth and the
same number of surnames. Bandleader Sam Wooding did his
best to fool the world by altering all the dates on his early
press cuttings, making it appear that he was a true pioneer in
bringing African-American jazz to Europe. Clarinettist
Edmond Hall was selective about his answers. He was always
friendly and courteous, as well as proud of his Louisiana her-
itage, but he had answered the same questions about New
Orleans so many times that he preferred to steer the conversation on to the merits of Jaguar cars or politics, a subject on
which he held well-informed views.

Some of the musicians who stayed behind in New Orleans
in the 1920s and 1930s felt that players who left the city to
earn their living elsewhere were akin to deserters. I experienced an example of this reaction when, invited by trombonist Preston Jackson, I journeyed on a bus with a New Orleans
band visiting Britain. Preston left New Orleans for Chicago
in 1917 and only moved back late in his life. While travelling,
I happened to ask him about a Crescent City character
called Beansy Fauria but he replied that he didn't know anything about him. Out of the darkness of the band bus a voice
heavy with contempt said loudly, 'Says he's from New
Orleans and don't even know Beansy Fauria.' Preston bris-
tled but, although the animosity in the bus was palpable, not

a trace of it could be felt on the bandstand as the musicians forgot their differences by creating joyous music.

One New Orleans musician who never moved back to his home city was the white trumpeter, Joseph 'Wingy' Manone, who as a child lost his right arm in a streetcar accident. He gripped the trumpet with a false arm, fingered the valves with his left hand – and blew emphatically. Wingy had a salty but humorous outlook on life. My involvement with his first visit to Britain in 1966 was to help co-ordinate his tour and Wingy asked me to make a list of his recordings that had been issued in Britain. I did so, he perused it for a few minutes and then exclaimed, 'Jesus, I've forgotten all of these.' His accompanists were Alan Elsdon's band and together they quickly worked out a programme of standards featuring Wingy's playing and singing. At the end of the first rehearsal Wingy said, 'If we run out of tunes I can play the blues all night and each one will sound different.' With that he picked up his trumpet and blew two exquisite blues choruses, revealing a sensitivity that had been difficult to detect in the robust character who had joshed and cajoled the band throughout the rehearsal.

It was hard to get Wingy to talk about jazz history. He spoke colourfully about his early days and adventures in Hollywood but if a specific question was asked he would go off at a tangent. Facts flew out of the window when he gave his version of jazz events, none more preposterous than when he claimed that King Oliver had sent for both Louis Armstrong and him to audition for the post of second trumpeter in the Creole Jazz Band. 'But Oliver didn't know I was white until I turned up so I didn't get the job and Louis did.' A young jazz tyro solemnly wrote down this amazing fib. Wingy got great pleasure in citing the many bounties that were available in Las Vegas, which had been his home city for some years. Nothing in England could compare with Vegas, a comment he repeated to members of Alan Elsdon's band throughout that tour. While visiting picturesque Cheshire Wingy said, 'This looks a dump, what has it got to offer?' Alan said, 'They make marvellous cheese here, why don't you try some?' Wingy did so, but later, finishing the last crumb, he growled, 'Well I guess they export the best of it to the States.' When I asked Wingy why he had moved from rural California, his answer was, 'Well, the mountains look great but you can't put ketchup on them.'

Lively though Wingy was, his personality was eclipsed by that of Slim Gaillard, a multi-instrumentalist who invented his own 'hip' language. He composed dozens of intriguing novelty songs including 'Dunkin' Bagels', 'Cement Mixer' and 'Matzoh Balls'. Slim, who had moved to London in 1982 and joined the British Musicians Union, was usually on hand on the rare occasions that George Melly was too ill to perform, and he was certainly a lively deputy. Slim was a born improviser who was prone to alter everything that had been rehearsed, suddenly pitchforking everyone into a highly unusual key, a new tempo or a totally different routine. These ploys, more often than not, proved inspirational and I can never forget the way he played on the run-throughs we did for a television show recorded at London's Theatre Royal, Stratford East. On that occasion Slim played guitar (he could also perform skilfully on piano and vibraphone), and he was fantastic during the rehearsals, playing the most complex of musical ideas but imbuing them all with an amazing swing. Alas, after swallowing a few pints of 'brew' (his name for draught lager), his phrases lost their edge. He still managed to perform admirably for the actual television

show, but not up to the standard of his playing during the
run-throughs.

Slim was great company, possessing a fund of anecdotes
which were as delightful as they were improbable. The sight
of a photograph of Jack Dempsey in my home unleashed
tales of Slim's boxing adventures which, so he said, included
being Joe Louis' sparring partner in Detroit. An aeroplane
flying overhead brought forth Slim's memories of his
wartime service as General Douglas MacArthur's personal
pilot. Slim's imagination was up and away after the flimsiest
stimulation, but adventures in the air didn't quite tie in with
the fact that Slim was terrified of heights – even the
prospect of staying in a first floor hotel room could induce
obvious agitation. In Belfast, not long after Slim first arrived
in Europe, he was allocated just such a room, which he
(thinking as an American) thought was on the ground floor.
'No sir,' said the receptionist, 'your room is up that single
flight of stairs.' The prospect of ascending that far was too
much for Slim and he slept the night in the ground floor ballroom. On another occasion we played a gig in East Anglia
where the promoter had laid on some nice rooms in a country pub but, to Slim's horror, his room was upstairs. Nothing
could make him attempt the climb and at his own expense
he hired the only ground floor room the pub had, namely the
bridal suite. With all this in mind I just couldn't believe that
Slim was an air ace, and years later I researched his service
career in the US air force and discovered he was a radio
mechanic. I didn't publish this information at the time
because it seemed like snitching on a friend: a great guy
whose powers of romanticising were Olympian.

Louis Armstrong's long-time trombonist, James 'Trummy'
Young, was one of the most charming of all jazz musicians. I

first met him in 1956, during the early part of his twelve-year stay with Louis. I was struck by his youthful appearance which he put down to eating half a dozen hardboiled eggs every day. He later changed this regime but this quaint diet got him past the threescore years and ten barrier. I shall never forget the amazement in Trummy's voice when, during a gig at Ronnie Scott's, he said, 'John, I never thought I would ever make the big seven-oh.'

He had been something of a raver and, knowing this, Jimmie Lunceford, whose approach to his musicians was that of a headmaster, decided to lecture Trummy before introducing him into his band in 1937. Lunceford stressed that he didn't approve of his musicians swearing, whereupon Trummy retorted, 'If anyone calls me a mother-fucker I'm gonna call him a mother-fucker back.' Lunceford, well aware of Trummy's instrumental and vocal talents, accepted this philosophy, and Trummy went on to become one of the band's stars.

Seventy came and went for Trummy, who had left Louis to move back to Hawaii. He used this as his home base for touring but also led his own small group at the Sheraton Waikiki Hotel in Honolulu. He became, in the later stages of his life, very religious, but did not inflict his beliefs on others. He continued to play splendidly, mixing powerful shouting phrases with subtle, whispered musical asides, and his singing retained the same debonair quality that had been a feature of his original recordings. Louis Armstrong thought the world of him and he worshipped Louis.

Over the years I made it my business to meet up with as many of Louis Armstrong's ex-sidemen as possible, and each and every one of them regarded Louis as a genius. The most extraordinary of my link-ups with these veterans provided

me with a very topsy-turvy night. For some while I had been
in sporadic correspondence with tenor saxist Al
Washington, a star of Louis' 1931–32 big band, who had
retired, after working as a school teacher, to Guadalajara,
Mexico. After a long silence a letter arrived from Al saying
he was planning to come to Europe to look for band work
(he was then eighty-five years old). He asked what the
prospects were of him gaining regular musical employment
in Britain. I wrote back explaining the exchange restrictions
enforced by the Musicians Union and pointed out how strin-
gent the airport authorities were about allowing foreign
musicians to enter Britain without a work permit. I heard no
more for a long while. Then, in the summer of 1987, I got an
out-of-the-blue telephone call from Al. He had arrived
in London and was staying at a hotel a few hundred yards
from where I lived. I was flabbergasted to learn that he
had escaped scrutiny by bringing his soprano sax in a large,
long cardboard box. He said he'd had a nice time guesting
with bands in Paris and although he only had a day in
London he would like to sit in with a band. By coincidence a
group led by American trumpeter Freddie Hubbard was in
London playing a 'Tribute to Louis Armstrong'. I immediately thought this would be the perfect showcase for Al, providing a chance for the audience to see and hear a former star
sideman.

I picked him up from his hotel and we took a taxi to
the Pizza Express in Dean Street where the tribute was taking place. There I explained to Freddie Hubbard that Al
would like to sit in on soprano sax. Freddie, not being too
well aware of Al's former eminence, was semi-reluctant. I
could see his point, in that the band's presentation was based
on a strict running order, with features for each individual

musician. However, he agreed that Al could play one number with them. Al was asked by Freddie to select a standard tune and set the tempo and the key – he chose Louis Armstrong's old favourite 'Ain't Misbehavin''. I don't know what came over Al but he tapped it in so slowly that it was almost impossible to guess the tune and there was a long pause between each and every note of the melody. A dirge would have seemed brisk by comparison. The piece seemed to last forever and when it finally ended the audience could only offer some hesitant applause. Freddie Hubbard looked at me with a jaundiced eye and offered Al weary thanks.

It was a very depressing moment. I felt responsible for leading Al into a highly embarrassing situation. He was too good a musician not to realise that his one number with the band had been a fiasco. We caught a taxi back to his hotel, with me carrying an already split cardboard box. The night was still fairly young and I asked him if I might buy him a drink. He declined the offer but said he didn't want to go to bed, he would sooner sit and talk. He went to his room briefly and returned with a clutch of handwritten notes which proved to be an account of his stay in New York during the early 1930s. I soon discovered that they were among the most fascinating jazz memoirs I had ever encountered.

The chapter he read to me concerned his late-night meeting with a drunken woman sitting on a Harlem sidewalk. At second glance he recognised her as Mamie Smith, the first nationally popular black singer, whose 1922 'Crazy Blues' had made her instantly famous. Ten years later she was almost down and out. Al offered to help her and they began a friendship in which Mamie told Al the background to her first recording deal and about her dealings with the Okeh

Recording Company's manager Fred Hager and the coast-to-coast theatre tours she pioneered.

My mood changed from dejection to exhilaration as I listened to these revelations about historical events in early jazz. I stressed to Al that he must put these invaluable memoirs into book form. Next day he left for Mexico and to my regret I never heard from him again. A few years later I was saddened to see his brief obituary – I never found out whether he finished his book.

One encounter with an American jazz musician proved to be decidedly less fruitful than hoped for. This was a recording session, which was also filmed, with pianist Art Hodes. Art was in London in June 1977 and was invited by Dave Bennett to do this daytime session at Pizza on the Park with Bruce Turner on alto sax, Peter Ind on double bass, Lennie Hastings on drums and me on trumpet.

Unfortunately, Bruce was at his most Turnerish – he arrived at the correct address but looked no further than the restaurant above the night club, thought he had gone to the wrong place, left in confusion and drove back home. We waited and waited for him, with Art Hodes getting increasingly exasperated. After many attempts I eventually got through to Bruce, by now back home in Luton (some thirty-five miles away). He simply said, 'Full of waiters, Dad. Thought I must be in the wrong place.' When I relayed this information to Art Hodes he was furious. We attempted a few numbers but the atmosphere was laden with irritability, not helped by the fact that I casually picked up, and looked at, a listing of Art's repertoire. It was as though I had stolen the secret plans for a new sort of submarine – he was truly piqued. Things got no better and it was agreed we would try again the following day.

Lennie Hastings couldn't make this follow-up so his place at the drums was taken by Johnny Richardson. Bruce Turner was there with time to spare but there was no sign of Art Hodes. We waited about for several hours; then, very late in the evening, Art appeared in company with singer Eric Lister, who had taken him to the Houses of Parliament. The atmosphere was definitely cool and time was precious but we did manage to get some jittery numbers recorded and filmed. However, a long version of 'Black and Blue' was not captured on film because the cameraman thought we were rehearsing. The session stumbled to a disgruntled close – it was never released. I was given a sound cassette of our efforts but was so scarred by the experience that it took me twenty-five years to get around to playing it.

13

Pals and Personalities

Our 1990 tour of the Antipodes was an important landmark
in the saga of the Feetwarmers because two founder members decided to remain in Australia when the tour ended:
Collin Bates returned to the land of his birth (with his New
Zealand-born wife, Claudia) and Chuck Smith, together with
his wife Sylvia, decided to emigrate. Because both men had
thoughtfully given us plenty of notice, we were able to fix
their replacements (Eddie Taylor on drums and Ron Rubin
on piano) to be ready to join us on our return from a tour
that took in Australia, New Zealand and Hong Kong. Sadly,
Collin died just over a year after he and Claudia had settled
in Sydney, but Chuck became a member of the New
Melbourne Jazz Band, recording and touring the USA with
them before deciding to move back to England.

Considering that the Feetwarmers were on the road for
thirty years, changes in personnel were few and far between.
In 1974 the group had started out as a quartet to back
George Melly, with myself on trumpet, Collin Bates on
piano, Steve Fagg on bass and Chuck Smith on drums, but
Steve, who was recently married, did not stay long. He had

worked in aeronautical engineering before turning professional with us and, whereas the rest of us had toured a lot in
years gone by, the tribulations of one-night stands were new
to Steve, who was a good deal younger than we were.
However, he was a solid and consistent player and his recorded work with us gives no cause for complaint. The parting
was amicable and Steve brought his growing family along to
our gigs during the following decades. His replacement was
Collin Bates' old chum from Sydney, bassist Barry Dillon. I
had met Barry but knew little of him, and ten years later,
having spent many, many hours in his company, the position
had scarcely changed. He was (as far as George and I were
concerned) a secretive fellow. Not that there was anything
unpleasant about him. He was a thoroughly decent family
man, with a wife and a daughter, but he would sit in silence
throughout a two hundred mile journey, never attempting
to pick up the threads offered by the band's multi-subject
conversations. However, he fulfilled his playing duties
efficiently. Though we were never sure, we felt he was often
anxious about his health. In 1987 he was diagnosed as suffering from cancer and after that he became a model of bravery
throughout five years of suffering.

During Barry's long illness Ron Rubin acted as his replacement, on the understanding that when Barry was well
enough he would rejoin the band. But that was not to be. We
had all known Ron for years and he had worked for us briefly
both on piano and bass. Tall and craggy, he was a gentle man
who detested excessive noise. Renowned for his limericks,
he has enjoyed considerable success in literary competitions
organised by the *Spectator* and the *New Statesman*. His Jewish
upbringing in Liverpool endowed him with a double helping
of humour from both Scouse and Yiddish sources, although

he wasn't flippant. He approached every tour as though it was an expedition up an uncharted South American river, bringing a sturdy case full of every type of pill and potion to combat any misfortune that we might encounter. He played bass with us for a while but when Collin Bates left in 1990 Ron took over the piano chair, allowing bassist Ken Baldock to join the band for what turned out to be a long stay.

Chuck Smith, the drummer, was a gentle giant. Well over six feet tall and powerfully built, he loved all sorts of jazz and enjoyed being part of a touring group. His pleasure at being recognised by the general public was touchingly obvious. Although he seemed a model of boldness he had a fetching streak of shyness. He possessed a marvellous dress sense and even though he didn't spend a huge amount on clothes he always exuded style. On tour he comforted himself by buying countless flamboyant tee-shirts. Chuck's mighty arms and his enthusiasm (held on a very loose rein) for drumming sometimes led to him overwhelming us all with his sound and eventually, at my request, he only played with brushes. He never developed a formidable technique but he could swing effectively when he was relaxed. For a while he did all the driving on tour. He also expertly set up the sound system and, on arrival at a hotel, he would casually pick up four of the band's suitcases in one haul and carry them with ease. He was patient and affable, an easy travelling companion whose charm only sagged when he attempted to tell anecdotes in regional accents, all of which emerged in plain west London dialect.

In 1977, when pianist Collin Bates completed his first stay with the band, his replacement was the vastly experienced Stan Greig. Stan, who came from Edinburgh, had been a member of Humphrey Lyttelton's and Acker Bilk's bands and I had worked with him in Bruce Turner's Jump Band. I had always been good pals with Stan and happy in his company, but the relationship was less smooth in the Feetwarmers, mainly because I sometimes had to lay down the law. At this time we were still a cooperative band and Stan hated it when money had to be spent on publicity and advertising – he almost had apoplexy when we voted to hire a stretch-limo to make a spectacular arrival at the 1978 Newport Jazz Festival. He was well liked by our audiences who admired his powerful boogie woogie and blues playing. He stayed with the band for three years and eventually, although we never had any dramatic quarrels, his decision to leave was a relief to him and to me.

In 1980 his place was taken by Bruce Boardman, then in his twenties and half our average age. Bruce was a good musician and looking back we should perhaps have been more tolerant about his lack of experience. But he was stubborn about taking advice, and easily got under our skins by hinting that his musical ambitions were on a loftier plane than ours. One of our American tours coincided with the New York run of *One Mo' Time*, a splendid recreation of African-American theatre life of earlier days. We were thrilled at the prospect of seeing the show but Bruce said he would not be going because 'it would be too much like a busman's holiday.' This greatly vexed George, who even found the fact that Bruce came from Watford unforgivable. I suppose we were partly to blame for the lack of social cohesion that affected Bruce's stay. Travelling for years as a tightly-knit unit we had adopted single-word descriptions for a variety of situations as well as our own catch-phrases. These were not devised to exclude newcomers from the conversation but created to save time and energy, and in retrospect we should have given Bruce more time to catch on. Bruce and Barry Dillon occasionally went to classical music concerts together. But, apart from a shared visit to the West Australian Cricket Ground, he and I didn't spend off-duty time together. George and Bruce certainly didn't socialise. Early in 1983 we heard on the grapevine that Collin Bates was hankering to rejoin us, so we parted company with Bruce and reintroduced Collin to the band.

Collin, known as 'Tucker', was highly intelligent, with a superfine memory that stored thousands of tunes embracing all styles. Remarkably, he could play a startling version of an obscure bebop theme and, with the same ease, rattle off a charming old music-hall song complete with the words and music of chorus and verse. He had an expansive sense of humour and loved to hear or tell a good anecdote. Recollections of his early days in Sydney were always a delight.

Tucker loved cats, good suits and bold ties. He was very well read, with a specialist knowledge of detective fiction. Off-stage he was not a graceful person but once he sat behind a keyboard he was poise itself. We had worked together for so long with George Melly (and with Bruce Turner) regularly playing hugely enjoyable musical duets, each of us trying to top the other's phrases. But, although we shared many situations and saw many lands together, something prevented us from becoming bosom pals. Nevertheless, I miss him a lot and writing his obituary was a very sad task.

Without doubt the most eccentric Feetwarmer of all was bassist Ken Baldock, who was with the group for sixteen years. Ken is an extremely skilful musician whose vast experience encompasses hundreds of recordings, often in top class company. He also accompanied many world famous American and Canadian musicians, including Oscar Peterson. Ken could be, and often was, very amusing. We were both from working class London families and as a result shared many verbal expressions learnt from our mothers, with which the rest of the band were unfamiliar. He had many likeable qualities but he could be exasperating.

He was a dedicated and inspirational player who gave his best no matter what the circumstances, but his striving for excellence meant that he spent an inordinate length of time getting exactly the right timbre for his double bass at the band's sound checks. He would check and re-check his amplified volume dozens of times, seemingly oblivious to the fact that George was on-stage twiddling his thumbs waiting for the ritual we called 'balancing the bass' to conclude. Even signing hotel registers brought problems. Ken suspected that the staff of big hotels were in league with the burglars of London, informing them of his comings and goings. To combat this he wouldn't give his home address but gave George's instead. Mischievously, to counter this, our roadie, Andrew 'Pep' Peppiatt, always entered Ken's address instead of his own in the hotel register.

George and Ken regularly argued over which of them was fatter, and eventually they decided to go on a competitive diet. Ken, being slightly taller, was challenged to lose two and a half stone in three months, while George had to shed two stone in the same period. Ken was doubtful about taking part in the contest so we gave him incentives. If he completed his weight loss in the allotted time pianist Ron Rubin would dye his hair bright red, roadie 'Pep' promised to have his shoulder length hair cropped, I was to wear any wig of Ken's choosing for a whole day and Eddie Taylor vowed he would play an entire gig wearing a green dress. These promises persuaded Ken to go to his task with a vengeance, even after George dropped out. We became genuinely worried when we learnt that Ken was a mere couple of pounds away from his target with almost a fortnight to go. The by now sylph-like bassist was so certain he would win the bets that he had a huge meal to celebrate his triumph. He was immediately overwhelmed by an avalanche of calories and soon regained every ounce he'd lost – we heaved a sigh of relief.

For someone as restless and metropolitan as Ken, touring could bring its problems. Time hung heavily for him in quiet country towns so he devised a novel way of occupying himself. He would visit a local estate agent, express an interest in buying a property, and thus kill a couple of hours being plied with details of a well-appointed vicarage or a run-down farm. Married three times (with five children), he had led an interesting life that included success as a child actor and national service as a commissioned RAF navigator. He enjoyed some success as a composer but his prowess on the bass gave him his musical reputation. His performances were uniformly splendid and he radiated happiness from the moment he stepped on-stage for the 'show'. His sense of stagecraft was admirable (he was, as he frequently reminded us, a fully paid-up member of Equity) and his years of experience made him well able to combat George's fly-catching (extravagant gestures devised to attract an audience's attention). These movements regularly surfaced during Ken's solos, but the bassist's winning smile, talent and stage presence quickly reclaimed the crowd's interest.

A frequent source of angst for Ken was the persistent mislaying of things large and small. The entire band would be asked to trawl for a missing object: all the sofas, cushions and carpets in a hotel lounge would be moved in an effort to locate a missing bunch of keys. Then, just as desperation was about to set in, a jingling sound from Ken's back pocket would bring the search to an end. Diaries, scarves, briefcases, double bass bows all vanished temporarily, causing consternation almost every time we assembled.

The 1990 trip to Australia, New Zealand and Hong Kong was a happy one. There were slight headaches for Ken and Chuck because they had to hire a double bass and drums at each city we played in, but this saved money and also prevented their own equipment from being damaged in transit. The two concerts we did in Wellington, New Zealand, were very enjoyable and all of us were delighted with that city and its people, which led me to say that if Wellington was where Gibraltar is, I would emigrate there without delay.

The one blip on that leg of the tour only affected Chuck Smith and me. A local radio disc jockey, on finding out that we were cricket fans, came to our concerts with two free tickets to the members' enclosure for a test match between New Zealand and India in Wellington. We asked what we should wear for the occasion. 'Just come as you are,' said the kind man. We took this to mean we could wear casual clothes, but within a minute of us taking our places in the hallowed section we were asked to leave because we were unsuitably dressed. The dee-jay, seeing us in our band suits, with collar and tie, had assumed we dressed like that all the time. 'Just come as you are,' was his literal advice. Happily we saw the game from another part of the ground and I got my first sight of the seventeen-year-old wonder cricketer Sachin Tendulkar before he ever played in England.

During a brief stay in Melbourne we had the pleasure of doing a television show from the studios where some of the popular Aussie 'soaps' are made. One of the stars had pinned up on the dressing-room wall a fan's letter which read, 'I understand that in real life you are dead. Can you please confirm this?'

Perth, Western Australia, was always one of our favourite places, but it was there that we played our most eerie gig. We were booked to play a concert on the side of a beautiful lake, with the audience seated on the other side of the water. We completed a satisfactory sound check in the late afternoon, prior to going on-stage just as darkness fell. We soon realised that nightfall had brought a very strong breeze which played havoc with the acoustics. Every trace of sound that emerged from the on-stage monitor speakers and the amplifiers was blown away before it reached our ears – it was like playing alone in a heavily padded room. We couldn't hear one another at all. Because of the fierce gusts the two-thousand-strong audience seemed to be totally silent as their sound too was instantly blown away. Nor could we see them because our signal for more amplification was misinterpreted as a request for more illumination, and as a result we were almost blinded by the powerful banks of lights being beamed on us. We limped through the set, relying on telepathy – it was the longest hour of my musical life.

We came off-stage, as disheartened as we had ever been, but up popped George's old friend, author Bruce Chatwin, who was unusually effusive, stressing that he had never heard us give a better performance. Knowing that he had recently spent a long time in the Australian outback we surmised that he'd had too much sunshine, but within minutes we were surrounded by dozens of well-wishers saying how much they'd enjoyed the show. Every trace of the vigorous applause they created had spiralled away leaving only a ghostly silence.

Our last gigs of the tour were in Hong Kong where George had a reunion with his old school friend, Sir Peregrine Worsthorne, who had recently reminisced in public about their days together at Stowe, claiming that he had been seduced by George on a sofa in the arts department. George vigorously denied the allegation, saying that if the incident had occurred he would not have denied it, and might even have boasted about it because 'Perry' was older, taller and brawnier. George, never averse to sharing details of his sexual adventures, was unwavering in his denials about the supposed liaison. Nevertheless this piece of false history had surfaced in a gossip column just prior to our tour. George, taking advantage of a chance meeting at the hotel reception desk, buttonholed his old chum, vehemently denying any sexual attachment. Peregrine finally admitted that his memory could well be at fault, and not long afterwards told Sue Lawley on the *Desert Island Discs* radio programme, 'I may have got it all wrong. Anyway we're good friends now.' Even so, a year rarely passes without that story being rehashed in print.

When we had finished our gigs in Hong Kong it was time for us to split up and fly to different destinations. Collin flew to New Zealand (to be reunited with his wife, en route to Sydney), Chuck went off to Melbourne (to link up with his wife), Ken set off for Japan (to visit a Buddhist shrine) and George and I caught the flight back to England. It was the end of a longstanding version of the Feetwarmers, and we all felt sad about saying goodbye, but George, Ken and I looked forward to the fact that we would soon be rehearsing with Eddie Taylor and Ron Rubin in preparation for more tours.

Pianist Ron Rubin, having worked with us on double bass, knew most of the band's arrangements and shared the prevailing sense of humour. Drummer Eddie Taylor was exceptionally quick at grasping routines and memorising them so the 'new' Feetwarmers were soon in shape. Eddie, who had starred with John Dankworth and Humphrey Lyttelton, was a no-nonsense Lancastrian, whose considerable technique never became overbearing, truly a steady Eddie and, like George, passionate about fishing. He sometimes looked dour on-stage but just below the surface there existed a fine comic streak. Years earlier, when Eddie was working in a band aboard the *Queen Mary* liner, the expert eye of American comedian Henny Youngman saw Eddie's comic potential and offered him the chance to join him as his 'stooge' for a booking at the London Palladium but Eddie, far too keen on drumming, declined the offer. He could effortlessly remember hundreds of obscure melodies going back fifty years, so if anyone was stuck in trying to recall a song, Eddie could instantly croon the words and music of the piece. He delighted in playing the glum Northerner and (not always to George's liking) would peep through the stage curtains, just before the show began, and say grimly, 'Not many in tonight,' even when the house was full. Eddie had an endless stock of quaint sayings. A typical one was, 'On your toes rhythm fans,' which he always uttered just before we walked on-stage. He shared with me a fervent interest in sport.

The person who was alongside almost every version of the Feetwarmers was our agent Jack Higgins, who had a vast knowledge of all aspects of show business, having been the right hand for Harold Davison, the principal importer of American stars during the 1950s and 1960s. I first became

acquainted with Jack in the early 1960s when I worked for
the Swinging Blue Jeans. He was often terse and brimming
over with self confidence, proud to admit that he was 'totally devoid of sentimentality'. But he was generous with his
advice and taught me a lot about the business side of music,
which proved useful in countering his wiles during the many
years he was our agent.

Born in 1920, Jack had a distinguished army career during
World War Two. I witnessed his devil-may-care courage one
Christmas Eve in a Soho pub. Jack, myself and Chris Barber's
trumpet player, Pat Halcox, were enjoying a lunchtime drink
when a group of tearaways stormed into the bar. Contrary to
the Yuletide spirit they began to wreck the place, hurling
bottles and glasses indiscriminately at the staff and at the
customers. Pat and I left immediately, without discussion,
but as I charged through the swing doors I glanced back and
saw Jack, seemingly unperturbed, sipping his drink while a
barrage of glasses and chairs shattered all around him.

When we first went on the road as a professional unit we
were under the auspices of Ronnie Scott Directions, an
agency headed by Peter 'Chips' Chipperfield and Brian
Theobald. A year or so after, however, disenchantment set in
on our part because, despite glowing reviews and enthusiastic receptions, we didn't seem to be making any progress.
Enter Jack Higgins who, after a long absence from band
booking and agency work, decided to make a comeback via
Ronnie Scott Directions. His arrival was timely, coinciding
as it did with a boiling over of our discontent. The mood of
a confrontational meeting changed abruptly when Jack
presented us with a huge pile of lucrative contracts at venues
we had been longing to play. Jack's ability to sell an attraction

had triumphed and thereafter the main thing we had to complain about was that we were working too often.

Looking back at my diaries for those busy years I am amazed at the number of gigs, often in far flung places, that we managed to play, middle-aged travellers fulfilling itineraries that could well have bowled over younger, fitter musicians. But during this tremendous surge of activity a clash of personalities within the agency meant that Jack Higgins left suddenly to form his own booking organisation. Although we enjoyed friendships with Chips and Brian at the agency, and with Ronnie and Pete at the club, we were given the stark choice of remaining with an organisation whose driving force was about to depart, or going off with Jack. We chose the latter for what turned out to be an association that lasted for thirty years. To their great credit, Pete King and Ronnie Scott never let their dispute with Jack Higgins affect our bookings at the club and we continued to play there for year after year.

14

A Gig with Slim

'What was your most memorable gig?' is probably the question a touring musician is most often asked. I have mentioned the eerie night concert in Australia and the tipsy frolics that garlanded the live recording of *Nuts*, but the most unforgettable event, by far, occurred on Saturday, 9 May 1987, when my old friend Slim Gaillard deputised for an ailing George Melly at the Newbury Spring Festival. As George was poleaxed by pneumonia, various people who had contracted us to play during the time that he was indisposed agreed to transfer the bookings to a later date. The organisers of the Newbury Spring Festival, however, decided to go ahead with their concert.

So, on a bright afternoon, Slim climbed aboard our band bus carrying his guitar and what looked like the earliest amplifier known to man. No sooner had he settled down than he pulled out a mending kit complete with thimbles, thread and needles and began repairing a pair of trousers. He was obviously highly proficient at sewing and, without being asked, told us how he had learnt the skill. As an adolescent he had travelled aboard the SS *American Legion* with his father, who was a crew member. Unfortunately, dad accidentally left him behind at a port of call on the island of Crete. There, Slim obtained work as a tailor's junior assistant and became an expert needleman. Slim told the tale in a matter-of-fact way as though the calamitous parental lapse of memory was the merest of oversights. Some discreet memories of Slim's friendships with female Hollywood stars followed and were topped by tales of his successes as a master chef. The sixty mile journey passed in a flash thanks to his fascinating anecdotes.

On arriving at the venue (the Clere School in Burghclere, Berkshire) we were greeted by the man organising the evening. He was a jazz fan and as we approached he rubbed his hands with glee at the prospect of meeting and present- ing Slim Gaillard, whose work he had long admired. He made us welcome, then left so we could rehearse the programme and complete a sound check. I got Slim to write out a list of numbers that he wanted to play, with their keys and tempo, and we mapped out a programme that would feature his singing and guitar playing as well as including a couple of numbers showcasing his skills at the piano. The smoothness of the run-through augured well and we (myself on trumpet, Chuck Smith on drums, Ron Rubin on double bass and Collin Bates on piano) left the rehearsal relaxed and happy, and Slim made it clear that he shared our mood.

Like most festival events the concert was sponsored, on this occasion by estate agents, Knight, Frank and Rutley, who invited us to their hospitality tent for food and drinks. Slim, beaming broadly, led us into the marquee. The sight of a tall African American wearing a cream beret and a pink Edwardian frock coat and sporting an excessively curly white beard brought a look of surprise to the genteel servers waiting to dispense refreshments. Their *frisson* of wariness was increased by Slim's opening words, 'Have you any brew please?' However there were soon smiles all round when the organiser said, by way of introduction, 'This is Mr Slim Gaillard – who has taken George Melly's place as the star of our show.' Slim, a natural charmer, raised his clasped hands above his head in the manner of a victorious boxer, then again requested some 'brew'. I explained to the serving staff that this was his way of asking for draught lager (which was not available). The visitor was asked, 'Would champagne or whisky do?' 'A little of each please,' he cheerfully replied. This mention of quantity was merely a show of good manners, for it soon became clear that Slim was a very thirsty man. I had, in the past, seen the effects that draught lager had on him and felt apprehensive as to how his metabolism would deal with a mixture of these upmarket beverages – I was soon to find out.

Holding a glass of champagne in his right hand and a glass of Scotch in the left, Slim sipped steadily at each and when the glasses were empty he gratefully accepted refills – on several occasions. Soon it was time for us to return to our dressing room to prepare for the show. By now Slim was deep in conversation with local dignitaries and the female members of the group were tittering nervously as he flirted with them. Fortunately he read my signal indicating it was time to go so we strolled back to the dressing room together.

It had been arranged that the Feetwarmers would play the first two numbers on the concert. We did so without offending anyone and then I stepped forward to the microphone to tell the audience a few details of Slim's career, mentioning his remarkable successes in films and on record, and as a composer and lyricist who, by sharing his own private language, had helped shape the vernacular of the twentieth century. I announced his name loud and clear but there was no sign of the great man (I found out later that he had slipped back to the fount). Agitation and anxiety began to grip the musicians and the audience until Slim put his head around the side of the stage and offered a smile that brought immediate forgiveness.

He sauntered on-stage but before he reached the microphone his gait became a rubbery glide. The combination of champagne and Scotch had unsteadied what was usually a purposeful stride. Beaming at the audience, he told them how pleased he was to be paying his first visit to Newbury. He lingered over the pronunciation of the town's name and decided to try out some variants: New Buree, New Biry and New Borry. Wearying of this he winked rogueishly at the audience and assured them that they were in for a night of 'F–U–N Fun!' In case anyone was in doubt he repeated his promise three times. Then, perhaps feeling he had ignored his accompanists, he began showering us with blush-making praise, after which he picked up his guitar, nonchalantly strumming a few chords by way of a warm-up. Unfortunately, his ancient amplifier seemed incapable of transmitting the magic created by his fingers. The box rattled and wheezed but failed to produce any musical sounds. Slim half-heartedly twiddled the knobs on his guitar and then kicked the amplifier several times which surprisingly brought it to life. The audience was relieved; they had arrived knowing little of Slim Gaillard but his assault on the sound box put him into a pigeonhole – he was an eccentric comedian who used the amplified guitar as a prop.

Slim's next move restored their confusion. One of his huge hands gently cuffed the strings of his guitar and produced a mellow chord that vibrated throughout the hall; the temperamental amplifier had decided to play a constructive part in the proceedings. He counted in a fast 'How High the Moon' and, though his fingers were not at their coordinated best, he soloed with panache. Full of confidence, he proceeded to the second number, a familiar old standard, 'Oh Lady Be Good', which he decided to play at a different tempo and in a different key from the arrangement we had previously agreed upon.

The accompanists broke into a light sweat which developed into an obvious sheen as Slim unleashed his next musical experiment. It was a total revamping of his 'Cement Mixer' hit, this new version having the dubious benefit of a series of out-of-tempo interludes during which he expounded far-out philosophical ideas. The planned running order was abandoned as he delved into his repertoire and dusted off numbers he had perhaps not thought of for years. A reviewer from the local *Newbury Weekly News* was fortunately on hand to give details of the fiasco: 'Between reassuring us that he was in favour of F–U–N and recommending a diet of Ovaltine and Benzedrine he regaled us with music from time past, but somehow it all failed to make much impact on the audience.'

Slim's performance was certainly making an impact on the Feetwarmers. The experience was too nerve-racking for us to offer any smiles, which led the on-hand reviewer to comment that Ron Rubin was 'ashen-faced'. Undeterred by a lack of response from his listeners, Slim sailed through the two numbers that preceded the interval. He made his exit by reviving a dance step called 'truckin'', enabling him to demonstrate a spectacularly loose-limbed way of leaving the stage. Back in the dressing room, Slim's high spirits were unabated. He praised the warmth of the audience, the sympathetic accompaniment, the acoustics of the hall – everything was wonderful. But his joy was not shared by the organiser of the event, who entered the dressing room grim-faced and called me aside to see if we could devise a battle plan to satisfy an audience which was rapidly becoming disgruntled. Deep in conversation we took our eyes off Slim at the very moment a thoughtless benefactor whisked him away to the temptations of the hospitality tent. I got there as fast as I could, just in time to see Slim speedily downing a half pint glass containing a fifty-fifty mixture of whisky and champagne. The blend proved to be as potent as it looked.

Back in the dressing room he was so happy it seemed heartless to dwell on the woes of the first half, but together we mapped out a list of Slim's favourites. The plan was to begin his second set with 'Flat Foot Floogie', which had been a worldwide success for him with his partner Slam Stewart. The Feetwarmers opened with a series of feature numbers for each individual and gradually the audience settled down in a mood that was moving slowly towards contentment. I announced Slim, who slowly trudged on-stage, but there wasn't a hint of gloom or doom on his face. In fact he was giggling loudly. I realised that the careful planning during the interval had been in vain when he struck up a number that he had already performed in the first half. By now it was for Slim another night, another place, or perhaps he had convinced himself that he was playing to a second-house audience.

He had been scheduled to demonstrate his pianistic skills towards the end of the concert, but two numbers into the second half he decided it was time to perform at the keyboard. One of Slim's many gifts was his ability to play a piano feature with the backs of his fingers and, to let the audience know what he intended to do, he turned his palms upwards with a flamboyant gesture. This rare art was difficult enough for him to perform when he was sober, but it was pretty well impossible when he was inebriated. Nevertheless, the audience responded kindly to his topsy-turvy, just recognisable, rendering of Duke Ellington's 'Satin Doll'. Greatly encouraged, Slim reverted to the normal method of fingering and thundered out some ideas for a piano concerto that were, to put it mildly, not fully formed. The crowd's attention began to flag as he then played a medley of songs, none of which was ever finished.

Slim was only scheduled to do two numbers on the piano but, instead, he drastically overran his time at the keyboard. Our pianist, Collin Bates, coughed forcefully and repeated-ly from the wings in the hope of providing Slim with a cue that would signal his time was up, but he sat tight. I signalled for Collin to come forward, hoping his arrival would shift Slim, but Slim simply looked at Collin as if he were a total stranger who had mistakenly wandered on-stage. The mist cleared slightly and Slim invited Collin to share half of the piano stool, which he did. But before a duet could be organised Slim leapt to his feet, charged across the stage and, without a word of warning, launched into singing a frantic version of 'Yes Sir that's my Baby'. When this number staggered to its conclusion he stood

silent and motionless at the centre of the stage, obviously
deep in thought. Inspiration soon took over and, turning to
me, he said, 'John, I've got a great idea. I saw it done at the
Apollo Theatre in New York and it was a WOW!' The
enthusiastic emphasis placed on the final word had a manic
ring: I was distinctly anxious.

Slim grabbed the microphone and said, 'Ladies and
Gentlemen, we're going to have some more F.U.N. All I
need is a few volunteers to join me on-stage.' Nobody
moved. Undaunted, he descended into the audience and
managed to persuade two men and a woman to return with
him into the limelight. Pretending to be hurt by the lack of
response Slim said, 'We can't start with an uneven number.'
An elderly woman showed some interest, allowing Slim to
pounce like a hungry lizard on a slow fly, and she joined
the other three volunteers. Four aboard, all standing
awkwardly at the back of the stage. 'We must have something for these good people to sit on,' shouted Slim, so
drummer Chuck Smith went off and returned with a clus-
ter of small chairs, the dimensions of which were modelled
for the children who attended the school. Slim instructed
the four bulky adults to lower themselves on to the unsuit-
able seats, then appealed to the audience saying he needed
more people on-stage. By a mixture of guile, charm and
press-ganging he gradually got the required quorum. Chuck
went for more chairs and one by one the new arrivals
settled on tiny perches.

A commotion soon broke out among those seated on-
stage when the elderly woman who had been one of Slim's
early selections began calling anxiously to her husband in
the audience, telling him not to worry. The partner, a very
old man, ignored the advice and started tottering towards

the stage. Slim saw him approaching and decided he would demonstrate his strength by leaning down and grasping the man's hands to pull him bodily up to the platform. But the old man was much heavier than Slim had realised, and furthermore he did not want to be lifted like a sack of potatoes, so he began resisting as best he could. For one terrible moment it looked as though the old fellow would tumble backwards and crack his skull. His partner screamed, and three men leapt up from the audience and supported the old man's back, gradually pushing him up into Slim's grasp. Safely on-stage, the old man angrily attempted to get his breath back, spluttering, 'This is diabolical.' Unfortunately these words came out so indistinctly that Slim thought the man was talking Spanish, so he began to speak rapidly in that language to the utter confusion of the old gent. Another chair was brought and placed so that the newly arrived member of the cast could sit next to his weeping wife – the two clutching each other as though they were on the deck of the *Titanic* during its last moments afloat.

Slim broke into a broad smile, happy that he now had enough people on-stage to carry out the great plan. With eyes shining like a wild pirate he bellowed, 'I *shall* be your dancing master.' What this enigmatic phrase might involve sent a shiver of apprehension through his captives. Perhaps this revelation of terpsichorean ambition had been part of the routine that had so pleased Slim long ago in distant New York; we never found out. I looked at him to see what was going to happen next and realised from the blank, bemused look on his face that he knew no more than I did. He had totally forgotten every vestige of the idea that had seemed so appealing fifteen minutes earlier. Here he was with a cast twelve-strong and no plot in sight. There seemed to be only one way out. Slim left the visitors where they were and began singing a multilingual version of his celebrated 'Dunkin' Bagels': one chorus in Greek, one in English, one in Yiddish and one in Spanish (complete with a knowing nod to the old man). He asked those on-stage to join in but there were no takers. The *Newbury Weekly New*s accurately described the situation: 'As the members of the audience on-stage began to outnumber the musicians and space was at a premium, so his anecdotes fell flatter.'

Somehow we managed to conclude the concert by linking 'Dunkin' Bagels' with an up-tempo blues, and Slim departed from the stage by again reviving his 'truckin'' steps. The reviewer faithfully reported the farewell scene: 'Slim announced it was time to depart to do some serious drinking.' There was no question of an encore. I looked round and saw that the on-stage volunteers were in a state of shock; their eyes glazed over as they talked to one another in choked voices, like survivors of a major disaster.

I walked into the dressing room totally drained. Slim was packing his guitar away, singing cheerful little phrases as he did so. 'I sure could do with something to eat,' he said, and the statement was his way of consigning the events of that evening to the deep locker of gigs over and done with. He would probably never think about the concert again but we four musicians remembered every aspect of that amazing evening. Ever after, if we encountered a rotten gig or a misery-making situation, it took only six words, 'I *shall* be your dancing master,' to send our spirits soaring. Although it was a mighty uncomfortable experience at the time, we had been part of an unforgettable night of spontaneous anarchy and I still lament the passing of its perpetrator, one of the greatest characters the jazz world has ever seen, the late Bulee 'Slim' Gaillard.

15

The Good Old Wagon
Stops Rolling

In the early 1990s I was still able to combine writing and touring. My main project during this period was a biography of Louis Jordan (which was published as *Let the Good Times Roll*). Jordan, it seemed to me, was a very important link between the small band jazz of the 1930s and the beginning of rhythm and blues groups and, despite the fact that his records sold well, his work as a musical pioneer was rarely acknowledged. His records continued to be played regularly on the radio long after his death and a show titled *Five Guys Named Moe*, featuring many of his hits, enjoyed success all over the world. Even so, his lithe alto saxophone solos and his rhythmic, mellow singing were taken for granted. The fact that he was a master showman somehow blocked out appreciation of his jazz artistry. Despite his consistent record sales very few biographical details about him were known by the general public.

I did my best to counter this situation by going off to various towns in his home state, Arkansas. I succeeded in following Louis' path from humble beginnings to success in Hollywood and managed to find many people whose friendship with Louis Jordan spanned the duration of his illustrious journey. My last stop during my research trip was Las Vegas where I met Louis' widow, Martha, who could not have been more helpful.

It was just as well that I had carried on with my writings, because almost imperceptibly our band bookings began to diminish. We had been touring relentlessly for almost thirty years but, because we were less able to pick and choose our jobs, the distance between gigs slowly increased. I didn't like the wear and tear of longer journeys, but George was one of nature's travellers, never happier than when he was on the road, and the prospects of travel gave him the incentive to bounce back from some fairly serious bouts of illness. During the years we were together he suffered a number of health setbacks and accidents but he always made light of them and was back in action in an astonishingly brief time. On one occasion he collapsed bleeding in a dressing room at the Mercury Theatre, Colchester – an ambulance took him to hospital where a burst ulcer was diagnosed. The doctors forecast that he would be out of action for weeks but within days he commanded himself to play a concert at the Hexagon, Reading. That was followed the next day by our appearance on Noël Edmonds' ghastly but ultra popular *House Party* television show – Doctor Footlight had again worked wonders. Early in the band's history George was mugged in Soho and smashed to the ground by blows from his own walking-stick, but he picked himself up and made his way to Birmingham to play a university gig. In Australia he was so badly bitten by mosquitoes that a local doctor advised him to take a complete rest for a few days, and George simply brushed the advice aside. On various occasions I saw him hospitalised with pneumonia, by the effects of a bad fall, and by a severe bout of bronchitis. Each time I was tempted to think that these calamitous health problems could well mark the end of George's touring days, only to see him back on-stage within the week – such things as cracked ribs were laughed off. He was a great trouper. On the very rare occasions that he was down in the dumps he was soon restored to good humour by the presence of his long-time friend Alex (affectionately known to the band as 'Squeaky' because of the unusual sound of her high-pitched voice).

But extensive touring took its toll on Ron Rubin, for whom every long journey meant the recurrence of a debilitating backache, and he left the band in late 1992. After much deliberation we decided to ask pianist Jonathan Vinten to take Ron's place. Our hesitation was not because of any doubt about Jonathan's musical ability. It was his age that caused us to vacillate since he was only twenty-nine, half the age of anyone else in the group, and whenever we had featured 'youngsters' in the past we had encountered problems. Our offer meant that Jonathan became a full-time musician for the first time. He had no experience of touring, having become a teacher, playing many semi-professional gigs. Happily, he proved socially flexible and soon struck up a firm friendship with Eddie Taylor.

Jonathan possessed a good technique with an impressive command of 'stride piano' which allowed him to play forceful left-hand phrases in the manner of Fats Waller. Bassist Ken Baldock (himself an adept pianist) took a while to accept the newcomer's approach to music – stride playing didn't jell with Ken's concept of cohesion in a rhythm section, and for a while the two of them seemed to be fighting for possession of the same notes. But things settled down with Ken offering pointers to Jonathan that enriched his harmonic vocabulary.

Jonathan's first trip with us was to Dubai where we played for a week in the luxurious Royal Abjar Hotel. The four Feetwarmers made the usual tourist trips, but the desert sands had no appeal for George, who didn't leave the hotel throughout the entire stay. On our return to England, Jonathan was allocated a seat in the band bus and soon took to life on the road, even though he sorely missed his family. Foreign trips during the 1990s were something of a rarity but we regularly took part in tours of the UK in a package show that featured us alongside Kenny Ball's Jazzmen and Acker Bilk's Paramount Jazz Band. These shows did good business, entertaining predominantly middle-aged audiences nostalgic for the days of trad jazz. Backstage there was always a happy atmosphere, with no trace of rivalry or upstaging, even though the show ended with what most jazz musicians dread, a mass jam session on-stage including everyone who had taken part in the concert. But even these cacophonous gatherings were performed in a good spirit.

The only disharmonious aspect of these tours concerned the enormous amount of time that Kenny Ball spent warming up by practising long and loud before each concert. In all other respects Kenny was a generous and considerate fellow and, like Acker Bilk, easy to work with. Acker never let success go to his head and he remains one of the most popular men in the jazz world, both with the general public and his fellow musicians. He is a totally unaffected West Country yeoman, genuinely modest and possessing a charming rustic humour.

We also took part in a long-running series of concerts entitled *George Meets Humph*, sharing the bill with

Humphrey Lyttelton's band, and here too the backstage camaraderie was warm and friendly. Most of the musicians from both bands went to the nearest pub after completing their sound-checks, leaving Humph and me to share dressing-room conversations about jazz, which invariably ended with both of us talking with the ardour of schoolboys about the genius of Louis Armstrong. All the shared dates with Humph, Kenny Ball and Acker Bilk were stage shows, so even when musicians we had known for many years came to visit us there was no question of them sitting in. However, during our long stays at Ronnie Scott's we welcomed several visiting singers to the stage to share a number or two with George and the band, notably Jimmy Witherspoon, members of Manhattan Transfer and Carrie Smith. Multi-talented Slim Gaillard successfully (this time!) deputised for George, laid low by painful kidney stones, during one of our Christmas seasons at the club.

At the other end of the scale an uninvited 'sitter-in' almost sabotaged a concert we did at the Barbican. In the middle of one number a figure suddenly emerged from the wings wearing an apron and holding a soprano saxophone. It would be an exaggeration to say he was playing the saxophone; he was simply blowing a series of horrendous bleats on the same note. We were flabbergasted, as was the great American guitarist, Barney Kessel, who was guesting with us. The intruder got in front of the microphone and blew and blew his harsh, monotonous note. The audience's initial amusement soon turned to unease and we began to feel increasingly hostile. To save the day I gripped the interloper's arm as tightly as I could and forcibly led him off-stage where he was immediately apprehended by the security staff. Apparently he worked at the Barbican and carried out his one and only musical performance for a bet. Although he had virtually ruined the atmosphere of that concert we wished him no lasting harm, but the authorities at the Barbican took a different view and sacked him.

On-stage surprises are not generally welcome but if one is in on the secret it's interesting to see how reactions differ when performers are faced with an unplanned situation. I had a golden opportunity to observe this when, in 1993, George Melly was the subject of a *This Is Your Life* television show. Earlier that evening we had played a concert in Liverpool, where compere Michael Aspel had confronted George with the celebrated book. George's wife, Diana, and I were the only two in on the secret. None of the band knew anything about it, a fact borne out by their dumbfounded looks when Michael Aspel walked on-stage. From Liverpool we made our way to the Granada studios in Manchester to link up with the participating guests, the most illustrious being the American singer-actor Elizabeth Welch. The show went off smoothly as did the subsequent studio party. The band finally left the building via the property department where we spied a clutch of zimmer frames. The temptation to try them out proved too much for us, so three of us (Eddie, Ken and me) had a zimmer-frame race. 'That's right, get some practice in, you'll soon be needing them,' said a droll northern scene-shifter. Not long after this television show we played our annual booking at London's Pizza on the Park and unbeknown to us Elizabeth Welch was in the audience. During our rendition of a 1920s show tune 'Doin' the New Low Down', she began to sing with us from where she sat. The clarity and feeling of her impromptu vocal produced an ethereal effect that was unforgettable – how I wish that moment could have been captured on record.

Over the years we played at several Labour Party gatherings, none more dramatic than the night in May 1994 when we performed for a gala dinner at London's Park Lane Hotel. Our task was a relatively simple one involving the playing of one cabaret set, scheduled to follow a speech by the party leader, John Smith. We assembled backstage with some minutes to spare and stood listening to John Smith's inspired oratory; I had heard him speak on several occasions but had never been so impressed by the force and majesty of his delivery. There was no question of him keeping to the previously agreed duration, it seemed vital for him to get his impassioned thoughts over to the audience, come what may. He overran by at least fifteen minutes, but we were not in the least put out, as listening to him was a sublime experience, which caused Ken Baldock to ask there and then if he could obtain a copy of the speech. Eventually John Smith left the rostrum to tumultuous applause. My family were still up when I got home and I tried my best to convey just how remarkable the speech had been. Next morning I switched on the radio and learnt that he had suffered a fatal heart attack. In creating such inspiring oratory he had completely overtaxed himself.

Politicians did not play a big part in our work, though we were always happy to see David Steele at our seasons at Ronnie Scott's (later Charles Kennedy carried on this Liberal Democrat tradition). David Steele pleased us greatly by choosing one of our records for his *Desert Island Discs* selection. Fortunately, Margaret Thatcher never made the effort to see us at Scott's – had she have done so it would have been very awkward as we had vowed never to perform if she was under the same roof.

Memories of the many seasons at Ronnie Scott's tend to roll into one another, but the events of December 1996 are etched deep. It was our twenty-third year there, and it began with Pete King calling me aside on our opening night to say that Ronnie was under the weather but would continue to compere. By this time, problems with his teeth made it difficult for him to play the saxophone and the deprivation made him deeply unhappy but, no matter how variable Ronnie's moods were in the past, it was unusual for him to visit the band's dressing room before the show. Yet in the early part of that 1996 season he called in to see us every night. He would sit down, light a cigarette and begin reminiscing about veteran musicians, unusual gigs, regrets, happy days and grievances. But even during the more sombre moments he would suddenly say something hilariously funny. Another change occurred during the band's interval: Ronnie would call me, Ken Baldock or both of us into the office to chat, but sometimes these conversations took a morbid turn.

Ken, who had worked in Ronnie's band for years before he joined us, had often seen him in these downcast moods and I also had experience of them. On one particular occasion, years earlier, I called in the office to leave my trumpet in safe surroundings while I went out for a meal. Ronnie was seated behind his desk staring fixedly at his wrist, in the manner of Hamlet examining Yorick's skull. He made no effort to change his pose and said to me in a desperate voice, 'What shall I do with this German band?' (Cockney rhyming slang for hand). I was nonplussed and said something fatuous about things looking better in the morning.

Within twenty-four hours he was in a nursing home receiving treatment for dementia. That catastrophe was caused, like a lot of Ronnie's depressions, by a broken romance. An avid gambler, he could and did nonchalantly shrug off huge losses on the horses, but the loss of a girlfriend, even when the breakup was his choice, pitchforked him into melancholia.

In December 1996 his behaviour seemed unusual, but the arrival of his daughter Rebecca and her mother Mary, both over from New York, seemed to have a calming effect on him. However, on Monday 23rd December, just as we were getting ready to play our first set, the dressing room door swung open. We looked up, expecting Ronnie to enter. Instead it was Pete King with the tragic news that Ronnie had been found dead in his flat. Pete said he didn't want the audience to be told the sombre news until the end of the evening, so we went on-stage trying our best to suppress the sorrow we felt, and it was the hardest gig we ever played.

At the obligatory inquest the coroner, after hearing that Ronnie had overdosed on barbiturates, brought in a verdict of death by misadventure. Some months later a huge memorial service was held at St. Martin-in-the-Fields, but the most lasting tribute to his memory was that Pete King, until his retirement in 2005, continued to run the club in the way that he and Ronnie had always done.

There were no dramatic changes in our working life during the 1990s. We continued to tour to all parts of Britain but made few overseas trips, the most notable jaunt being a trip to Hong Kong in 1997, just before the handover to the Chinese authorities – the new regime never invited us back. On my last day there, I was stopped by an old woman in the street, who, with an air of confidentiality whispered, 'Never buy a Chinaman a clock' – something that I had never considered doing.

By this time we realised that there was little chance of achieving international success. We had built up a loyal following in Britain, one that was unlikely to expand, but the jazz evangelising spirit still lurked within us and it was always gratifying when young people came backstage to ask about Louis Armstrong, Bessie Smith and Duke Ellington. George's appearances on television and radio stimulated bookings but we rarely broke new ground.

We gradually dropped 'Frankie and Johnny', which had been George's speciality number for years, from the programme. In this number he would hurl himself off the stage as he sang the word 'fell', amazing the audience by leaping back to his feet the instant he hit the ground. But the passage of time made this a dangerous manoeuvre. We tried it with George simulating a couple's passionate embrace by winding his arms around his torso and clutching his backbone, but his increased girth meant this tactic was less than convincing, and the number was quietly retired.

Certain risqué songs were also consigned to the deep. This wasn't because we had suddenly become prudish. George as a middle-aged *boulevardier* delighted his audiences by singing saucy songs, but when, as an old age pensioner, he warbled these same offerings people were less amused; it was something like a recurrence of the 'Georgina' situation of earlier years. To compensate for the dropping of these songs some of the jokes became even broader. This tactic occasionally brought forth a few letters of protest (in the manner of 'Disgusted of Tunbridge Wells'), but in general the grumblers were in a distinct minority. One killjoy wrote to say he had intended to walk out halfway through our performance but was prevented from doing so because everyone else in his row of seats was helpless with laughter.

One person who firmly agreed with the complainants was our agent Jack Higgins, who maintained that this bold approach precluded us from getting return bookings in the more staid theatres and civic halls. This led to verbal battles between George and Jack over the use of 'blue' material. I attempted to act as mediator, but I was biased because I regularly heard the uproarious laughter that George was creating. The dispute led to George writing to Jack saying how much he admired the great musical hall artistes of the past and 'their love of life, outrage and success', adding, 'I prefer to go down with all bawdy flags flying.' Jack countered by saying the great comedians of the past relied on innuendo. Eventually a 'horses for courses' compromise was reached whereby I advised George which jokes to include that night and which ones to leave out.

Gradually we accepted more and more single-gig long distance bookings to bring in the revenue to pay the musicians, our secretary, our accountant and the general running expenses. The weariness caused by playing these distant gigs led to a complete change in our method of travel. The band bus was coming to the end of its life and we decided it was not worth buying a new one, particularly as traffic jams on the motorways meant anxious journeys to reach engagements by the contracted time. George and I decided to travel to gigs by train, allowing the three musicians to drive to engagements in their own cars, with recompense paid on a mileage basis plus subsistence for hotel expenses. My lingering concern was that travelling separately might diminish the camaraderie that travel by band bus had nurtured.

Both George and I had always put band engagements before writing assignments, but the lessening number of gigs allowed us more time to write, so I was able to complete two projects that I had set my heart on years earlier: writing biographies of two great jazz trumpeters, Henry 'Red' Allen and Roy 'Little Jazz' Eldridge, who were both heroes and friends of mine. My tributes to these two men were posthumous, but over the years I had spent many hours enjoying their company. I was delighted that my efforts as an author were rewarded when I was voted 'Jazz Writer of the Year' in 2000.

Two particular non-playing excursions were unforgettable. They involved trips to New Orleans to lecture under the auspices of the University of New Orleans. The first, in 1997, was to celebrate the centenary of Sidney Bechet's birth, a thrilling occasion that allowed me to experience the warmth and friendliness of various of Bechet's relatives. During this trip I was proud to be made an honorary citizen of New Orleans. The second visit, in August 2001, was to commemorate the centenary of Louis Armstrong's birth (which had long been mistakenly given as July 1900). On this occasion Teresa made the trip with me. We had a hugely enjoyable stay in New Orleans, which included a happy reunion with Louis' long-time bassist, Arvell Shaw, who was staying at the same hotel as we were. Arvell (alas, by then almost blind) sat through most days by the swimming pool, reminiscing with great affection about his tenure with Louis. Two good friends of mine, Dan Morgenstern (curator of the Institute of Jazz Studies) and Jack Bradley (jazz historian and photographer) had also made the trip to New

Orleans and I count the informal hours we spent sharing personal memories of Louis among the highlights of my jazz life.

In the late 1990s, when George and I, waving our senior rail cards, began travelling to gigs by train, the British rail system almost fell apart through a series of accidents, track repairs and cancellations. Unfortunately, neither of us had ever learnt to drive. Journey after journey was delayed and train after train failed to keep to schedule, sometimes with very little warning. Occasionally a last train failed to materialise, giving us the expensive and difficult task of finding and persuading a taxi driver to take us many miles back to London. To add to the difficulties, George was having severe problems with his eyesight: a detached retina meant an emergency operation, but no sooner was that damage repaired than the same condition afflicted the other eye. His notable powers of recovery didn't fail him but he had to wear a patch over one eye while relying on restricted vision in the other.

Going to gigs in the Home Counties, we often travelled in trains loaded with commuters. To save time, in case of delays, George took to travelling in the bold suits that he wore on-stage. I felt that this made him into a modern-day Prince Monolulu (a famed African-born racing tipster) who wore dazzling traditional clothes when travelling to race meetings. Monolulu, real name: Peter McKay, whose slogan was 'I gotta horse', achieved fame by his outlandish appearance, basking in pleasure when he was recognised – rather as George did. However, the sombre-suited suburban travellers were clearly not delighted by George's turnout and a good percentage of them, having just completed a trying day at the office, obviously deplored the sight of George disguised as a deckchair. Hostile stares and grumbled comments were common, but fortunately George didn't hear or see any of them.

Parting with the band bus meant the end of a ritual involving a framed reproduction of George Stubbs' 'Monkey' painting, which hung in the vehicle. Ever since our first tour, any purchase of something that was totally unnecessary had to be shown to the Monkey who (we fantasised) greatly approved of wanton spending. A pair of ornate and impractical shoes, a bomber jacket designed for someone forty years younger, or a tie too ghastly ever to wear, were all proffered to the little creature, though less often after various free-spending Feetwarmers departed.

The Monkey was a relic of the 'old' band, as was the playing of jazz cassettes throughout our journeys. During the latter days of the band bus the sound of jazz rarely accompanied our travels and instead the air was filled with snoring and sighing. Other than gathering for the sound-check and playing the gig, George and I saw less and less of the band during the post-band-bus period. The separate travelling changed attitudes and, instead of frivolity and laughter, earnings and mileage payments seemed to be the subject of most of the dressing room parleys. One thing that never changed was George's fastidious reaction to untidiness. We arrived at a gig in East Grinstead to find our changing space in a filthy condition, even though it boasted a sign saying, 'Leave the dressing room as you found it'. Before we departed, George, in beautiful lettering, added: 'like a shithouse'.

Throughout my years with George I kept in close contact with my two brothers. Ron retired from his position in the publishing world to lead a quiet life in the countryside, but for Tom early retirement was a signal for him to do many of the things he had dreamt about while fulfilling the long-time role of landlord in a Sussex pub. In succession he became the driver of a small train that whistled its way along the Brighton seafront, then a glass engraver on the pier, a security guard in a bank, a solicitor's clerk and finally a private detective. None of these activities was connected with his original profession, which was reviewing films for a cinema trade magazine and devising trailers and slogans.

As a temporary respite from the problems of road and rail travel in 2001 the band played aboard a couple of cruise liners. The *Saga Rose* took us to the Channel Islands, France and Belgium, while the other voyage, on the huge P & O *Aurora*, was scheduled as a trans-Atlantic journey. The *Saga Rose* radiated a peaceful and relaxed atmosphere and for once we were playing to an audience almost as old as we were, but the *Aurora* sailing was fraught with problems, all of them connected to the fact that it coincided with the September 11 attack on New York. We were supposed to fly out to link up with the liner in New York harbour, but all flights and sailings were cancelled. After days of kicking our heels in London we finally got an Air Canada flight out of Heathrow to Halifax, Nova Scotia, where the *Aurora* was then docked. Security was naturally tight but some aspects were difficult to comprehend. I was informed that I couldn't take my trumpet as it could be used as a weapon and Ken Baldock's bass strings were not allowed to travel because they could be used to strangle the pilot. Having waited about for day after day, Ken and I were more than willing to debate this issue. Fortunately a concierge from Air Canada, who told us that she came to Ronnie Scott's every year to hear us, took responsibility for allowing us to board the flight with our 'lethal' equipment.

The flight passed uneventfully but once aboard the liner we found that most passengers were apprehensive about the voyage and were understandably slow to share a spirit of revelry. The accommodation and the food were excellent but the international situation meant there were no ports of call, so the *Aurora* left Canada and sailed straight back to England through some of the roughest seas I've ever experienced. Playing the trumpet while being hurled across the stage by the impact of huge waves was nearly impossible.

It is difficult to pinpoint when George and the Feetwarmers began to lose the zest with which they had previously approached every gig but from late 2001 it seemed that almost every job we played was riddled with a feeling of discontent. Travel difficulties and tightening of the belts were at the root of the malaise, but so too was the fact that a repetition fatigue had set in. I used to programme the numbers in a way that switched old favourites and added fresh numbers for each of our return visits to venues we played regularly. With dozens and dozens of songs in our repertoire permutations weren't difficult, but having to tax George's memory by asking him to remember the lyrics and routines for all these numbers when we weren't working as regularly as we had in the past was like asking a chef to watch a hundred pans of milk on a hot stove. To maintain our previous standards we tended to play a similar programme whenever we worked, hence the repetition fatigue. Performing similar set lists created a challenge to add variations by improvising fresh solos, but it is easy to be shoe-horned into repeating note clusters and phrases that fall easily under the fingers.

I felt the end of the group was almost in sight. We had, after all, enjoyed almost thirty years of reasonable success without being fuelled by any big-selling recordings. Pianist Jonathan Vinten, married with two young children, naturally felt the economic pinch the sparser itinerary brought. He assessed the situation and decided to resume his previous profession as a teacher, but continued to work with us as often he could. This meant that during the last year of the band's existence we sometimes used deputy pianists including our old stalwart Ron Rubin, Humphrey Lyttelton's pianist Ted Beament, and John Critchinson (ex-Ronnie Scott's band). Finally, even George's steadfast cheerfulness wavered. At the end of a distant gig fraught with travel problems he said, 'I think I've had enough of this.' I replied without hesitation, 'I certainly have.' So in March 2002 we called a meeting of the band at which George announced the break-up. The musicians took the news as though they were expecting it, and we decided to disband at the completion of our December 2002 season at Ronnie Scott's.

During the nine months between that meeting and the finale George got back his appetite for travelling and began developing the idea that he would go on the road with his own one-man show (accompanied by Ron Rubin on piano), lecturing and singing. But agent Jack Higgins wisely and emphatically pointed out that there would be more opportunities available if George worked with a band rather than if he went solo. He suggested that from the end of 2002 George should use Digby Fairweather's Half Dozen as his regular accompanists. The prospect of not appearing in public had no appeal whatsoever for George and even though it meant he would resume extensive touring, he went along with the idea knowing that under the new regime he would be collected and delivered to his own front door. The change gave him a new lease of life.

By September 2002 it was general knowledge throughout the jazz world that we were all going our separate ways. We were touched when followers of the band travelled many miles to say farewell. A December 2002 concert in Norwich was our final out-of-town gig and it ended with a standing ovation. Then we began our final season at Ronnie Scott's where saying goodbye to the staff was a real wrench. Sadly, a whiff of acrimony drifted through the dressing room on the last night when George announced that there was no money in the kitty for golden handshakes, but this was soon replaced by cheery goodbyes.

My immediate task as a freelancer was to prepare a revised edition of the *Who's Who of British Jazz*. I was offered solo dates and guest spots with other bands but I declined any of them that involved long journeys. My parry was to say I would only work where the London red buses go.

However, I was not musically inactive for long. In what was an amazing reenactment of an incident thirty years earlier, I bumped into Wally Fawkes in a street near Broadcasting House and, just as he had done decades earlier, Wally invited me to blow with him at a couple of weekly pub residencies, both well within the London transport boundaries. It was as if the clock had been magically put back to the pre-Melly era. I took up his offer and within days I was playing alongside the sounds of his wonderfully inspirational clarinet and soprano saxophone; the pianist was an old colleague from Mike Daniels' band, Doug Murray. Not a grain of commercialism entered the performances as we recreated old blues themes, neglected stomps and obscure jazz compositions. To our joy the listeners even clapped the ensembles.

The wheel had turned a full circle and I was content that I would never again have to play a one-night stand far from home. I could look back on hundreds of gigs I had enjoyed playing in various parts of the world. Even when I recalled some engagements that had been less than exhilarating I could console myself with the knowledge that they had played a part in providing the funds that allowed each member of my family – Teresa and our children, Jenny, Martin and Barney – to study for and gain their university degrees. Jenny also passed all her grades on clarinet and went on to be a teacher, Martin became sports editor of the *Evening Standard* and Barney created his own successful football magazine. Quitting the touring life gave me many more chances to see my delightful grandchildren grow up, and to hear them progress on cornet, alto sax, trumpet and piano. It also allowed me time to begin reading the hundreds of books I gathered during my travels, supplementing that pleasure by listening as avidly as ever to jazz records old and new.

Index

100 Club, London, 110, 112, 165, 181-2
Acheson, Merv, 86
Adelaide, 51, 85, 169-70
Aden, 84, 86-7
Ali, Muhammad, 154
Allen, Dave, 61
Allen, Henry 'Red', 114, 251
Allen, Ron, 20-1
American Forces' Network, 65
American Legion (ship), 229
Amis, Kingsley, 156
Amis, Martin, 130
Archer Street, London, 82
Armatage, John, 59, 72, 76, 97
Armstrong, Louis, 28, 52, 55-6, 118-19, 123, 144, 196-7, 199, 208, 210-13, 244, 249, 251-2
Aspel, Michael, 245
Association for Recorded Sound Collections, USA, 191
Atterton, Jeff, 141
Aurora (liner), 254-5
Bailey, David, 130
Bailey, Derek, 131
Baldock, Ken, 218, 220-2, 225, 242-7, 254
Ball, Kenny, 70, 243-4
Barber, Chris, 70, 227
Barbican Concert Hall London, 244-5
Barbieri, Gato, 138
Barnard, Bob, 172

Barnes, John, 145
Basie, Count, 102, 111, 194-5, 201-2
Bates, Collin, 72-5, 85-6, 93, 121-2, 126, 138-9, 149, 153, 171, 189-90, 216-18, 220, 225, 230, 235
Batley, 144
BBC, 93, 106, 111, 121, 127, 164, 185
Beament, Ted, 256
Beatles, 102, 105, 108, 123, 126
Beaulieu Jazz Festival, 92
Bechet, Sidney, 27-8, 38, 121, 165, 191, 205, 251
Beijing, 174
Belfast, 210
Bell, Graeme, 172
Bell, Madeleine, 185
Bennett, Dave, 214
Bennett, Les, 80
Berigan, Bunny, 172, 177
Berk, Sam, 200
Betts, Simon, 185
Bigard, Barney, 92
Bilk, Acker, 70, 121, 185, 218, 243-4
Birmingham, 65-6, 136, 241
Bloomsbury Book Shop, London, 115-19, 125
Blue Oyster Cult, 137
Boardman, Bruce, 166, 219-20
Bown, Vernon, 79
Bradley, Jack, 251

Braff, Ruby, 122, 203-6
Braid, Les, 104-6
Bray, Jim, 76, 81
Brisbane, 170
British Film Institute, 96
Bron's Orchestral Service,
    London, 37
Brooker, Frank, 111
Brooks, Michael, 74, 140-1
Brown, Geoffrey, 20
Brown, Pete, 92
Brown, Sandy, 98
Brown, Terry , 67, 153
Bruce, Lenny, 188
Buckner, Milt, 122
Burrows, Don, 172
Bury St. Edmunds, 166
Burton Latimer, 7-13
Butlin's holiday camps, 58-66,
    78-81
Butterfield, Billy, 122, 192
Byas, Don, 196-197
Byng, Douglas, 130
Calloway, Cab, 200
Cambridge, Massachusetts,
    142-3
Cameron, James, 147
Canberra, 170
Cannock Chase, 39
Carlisle, 155
Carmichael, Hoagy, 153
Carter, Benny, 92, 195-6, 200
Cash, Tony, 106
Cavett, Dick, 147
Central School of Dance
    Music, London, 50
Chamberlain, Neville, 6, 9
Channel Islands, 156, 254
Chapman, Graham, 130
Chatwin, Bruce, 224

Chicago, 66, 115, 203, 207
Chilton Book Company, USA,
    119
Chilton, Barnaby, 116, 164, 258
Chilton, Eileen, 2
Chilton, Jennifer, 100, 113, 115,
    164, 258
Chilton, Martin, 113, 115, 164,
    174, 258
Chilton, Ron, 1, 6, 16, 19, 21,
    25, 32-3, 38, 56, 253
Chilton, Teresa, 74, 100, 105,
    113, 115-18, 125, 135, 164, 172,
    201, 251, 258
Chilton, Thomas (father), 1, 26
Chilton, Tom (brother), 1-2, 6,
    13, 15, 19, 32, 54, 253
Chipperfield, Chips, 128, 142,
    227-8
Christie, Agatha, 189
Circlorama Cavalcade (film),
    106
Clacton, 78-81
Clayton, Buck, 111, 141
Colchester, 241
Cole, Cozy, 200
Coleman, Bill, 111, 122, 197
Coleman, Ray, 123
Coles, Frank, 54
Columbia Pictures, 145
Compton, Denis, 32
Constantine, Learie, 33
Cook's Ferry Inn, London, 36
Coward, Nöel, 171
Crane, Ray, 101
Crisp, Quentin, 163
Critchinson, John, 256
Crosby, Bing, 165
Crosby, Bob, 165, 191-2
Crump, Rodney, 82

Dads' Army (TV show), 149
Daily Express, 106
Daily Mail, 120, 122
Daily Mirror, 17, 172
Daily Telegraph, 53-7, 67
Daily Worker, 89
Dance, Stanley, 141
Daniels, Mike, 110, 257
Dankworth, John, 226
Darnley, John, 128, 133
Davis, Miles, 102
Davison, Harold, 114, 226
Davison, Wild Bill, 38
Dead of Night (film), 88
Delmar, Elaine, 185
Dempsey, Jack, 210
Desert Island Discs (radio show), 225, 246
Devis, Arthur, 23
Diana, Princess, 172-3
Dickenson, Vic, 114
Dillon, Barry, 153, 165-6, 192, 217, 220
Dinely Rehearsal Studios, London, 58
Dingwall's, London, 144
Dobell, Doug, 96, 203
Dodd, Ken, 187
Driberg, Tom, 130
Dubai, 243
Dulwich, London, 67
Edinburgh, 135, 165
Edmonds, Noël, 241
Eldridge, Roy, 122, 197, 251
Ellington, Duke, 70, 114, 123, 206, 235, 249
Ellis, Ralph, 104
Elsdon, Alan, 208-9
Ennis, Ray, 104, 109
Equity (trade union), 222

Escorts (band), 103
Evans, Will, 93
Evening Standard, 258
Everett, Betty, 109
Fagg, Steve, 121, 126, 129, 132-3, 153, 216-17
Fairweather, Digby, 256
Fame, Georgie, 185
Fauria, Beansy, 207
Fawkes, Wally, 98, 120-3, 125-6, 132, 205, 257
Fazola, Irving, 165
Feather, Leonard, 99, 119
Feetwarmers, 114, 121-191. 199, 216-231, 233-9, 242-57
Feldman, Marty, 110
Felix, Lennie, 204
Fitzgerald, Ella, 185-6
Five Guys Named Moe (theatre show), 240
Flemming, Herb, 207
Foster, Vivian, 93
Foxx, Redd, 188
Foy, Tom, 93
Freeman, Arnie, 202
Freeman, Bud, 114-15, 202-3
Gaillard, Slim, 185, 209-10, 229-39, 244
Gaines, Charlie, 143
Gaines, Will, 185
Gallipoli (film), 169
Gardner, Ava, 148
George Meets Humph (concerts), 243-4
Gershwin, George, 3
Gillingham, Sid, 55
Glasgow, 136
Glenroy, Leslie, 93
Godbolt, Jim, 69, 88, 98-9, 101, 103-4, 111, 114, 201

Goffe, Toni, 72
Gold, Jack, 96-7
Good Time George (TV show),
   183
Goodman, Benny, 37, 70
Granada Television, 130, 148
Granz, Norman, 186
Grappelli, Stéphane, 206-7
Greene, Graham, 117-18
Greenow, Bill, 121
Greig, Stan, 153, 218
Grimsby Jazz Club, 74
Grosvenor Hotel, London, 185
Hager, Fred, 214
Haggart, Bob, 192
Hall, Edmond, 114, 207
Hamburg, 107
Hamilton, Duncan, 121
Hammersmith Palais, London,
   160
Hammond, John, 141
Hampton, Lionel, 205
Handscombe, Les, 121
Hardy, Thomas, 94
Harrison, George, 126-7
Hastings, Lennie, 214-15
Hatfield House,
   Hertfordshire, 173
Hawkins, Coleman, 159, 191
Hayes, Gabby, 177
Heath, Edward, 131
Heifetz, Jascha, 21
Hi-Lo's, 61
Hickcox, Sleepy, 194
Higgins, Jack, 114, 174, 226-8,
   250, 256
Hines, Earl, 113-14
HMV records, 28, 104-5
Hodes, Art, 214-15
Hodges, Johnny, 92

Hoffman, Dustin, 179
Holborn Empire, London, 2
Holiday, Billie, 126, 140-1
Holland, Dave, 197
Hollywood, 44, 54, 96, 142,
   177, 192, 208, 240
Hong Kong, 84, 86, 166-7, 216,
   223, 225, 248
Honolulu, 86, 211
Hope, Bob, 99
Horton family, 16-18, 22-3, 26-
   9, 32-3
Horton, Roger, 110
Howard, Darnell, 195
Howerd, Frankie, 186
Hubbard, Freddie, 212-13
Hubble, Eddie, 122
Hull, 73-4
Iberia (liner), 82-5, 88, 166
Imhof's (record store),
   London, 37
Ind, Peter, 214
Institute of Contemporary
   Arts, London, 68
Institute of Jazz Studies, USA,
   251
IPC Magazines, 25
Ireland, Jim, 73, 101-3, 106-7,
   109-10
It's George (TV show), 130-1,
   145
Jackson, Preston, 207
Jacques, Hattie, 94
Jazz Club (TV programme), 111
Jazz Horizons (company), 114
Jersey, 156-7, 194, 200
Johnson, Jack, 54
Johnson, Malcolm, 20-1
Johnston, Sue, 105
Jones, Brian, 108

Jones, Elvin, 128
Jones, Eric Clayton, 20-1, 29, 32
Jones, Jonah, 122, 197-201
Jones, Max, 118-19
Jones, Paul, 185
Jordan, Louis, 143, 240-1
Joyce, James, 116
Juke Box Jury (TV programme), 105
Kaminsky, Max, 138
Kansas City, 112, 194
Kemp, Geoff, 120
Kendall, John, 100
Kenley, Surrey, 47-50
Kennedy, Charles, 246
Kenton, Middlesex, 26, 31-2, 36, 45, 49-50
Kentucky, 201
Kessel, Barney, 244
King, Pete, 127-8, 176, 178-9, 228, 247-8
Kingswell, Don, 201
Kinnell, Bill, 73
Kinnock, Neil and Glynis, 172
Kirby, John, 113
Klein, Manny, 192
Konitz, Lee, 92
Kuala Lumpur, 170
Kuhlke, Norman, 104
Labour Party, 17, 246
Langan, Peter, 166
Larkin, Philip, 119, 125
Las Vegas, 209, 241
Laveau, Marie, 156
Lawley, Sue, 225
Lawson, Yank, 192
Lee, John, 111
Leeds, 91, 157
Lemmon, Jack, 185

Lennon, John, 102
Lewis, Linda, 185
Lindsay, Ken, 96
Lister, Eric, 215
Liverpool, 39, 73, 101-4, 108, 139, 144, 162, 217, 245
Living Jazz (film), 96-7, 100
Lloyd, Harold, 118
London Jazz Club (see also 100 Club), 36, 181
London Palladium, 37, 63, 144, 226
London Weekend Television, 130
Los Angeles, 86, 137
Loughborough, 174
Louis, Joe, 210
Lovell, Alan, 96
Lowe, Arthur, 149
Lowe, Rob, 145
Luard, Nicholas, 119
Lunceford, Jimmie, 211
Lyttelton, Humphrey, 36, 67, 98, 181, 218, 226, 244, 256
MacColl, Ewan, 76
MacDowell, Andie, 145
Macmillan (publishers) 119
Man, Woman & Bulldog Ltd, 134
Manhattan Transfer, 244
Manning, Bernard, 186-7
Manone, Wingy, 114-15, 208-9,
Marsden, Boz, 46, 59, 76
Marsh, Terry, 44
Martin, George, 103
Marx Brothers, 61
Matcham, Frank, 166
Matlock, Matty, 122, 192
Maxwell, Robert, 172
Mayflower (ship), 119

McCorkle, Susannah, 125
McKay, Peter (Monolulu), 252
McKinnon, Duncan, 69
Melbourne, 85, 169-71, 216,
    224-5
Melly, Diana, 161-2, 178, 183,
    245
Melly, George, 98, 114, 122-91,
    209, 216-7, 219-257
Melody Maker, 58, 87, 119, 123,
    141
Menuhin, Yehudi, 21
Mickleburgh, Bobby, 76
Mildenhall, 40-4, 47
Miller, Eddie, 192
Miller, Max, 187
Milligan, Spike, 131
Milligan Meets Melly (TV
    show), 130-1
Mills, John, 148
Mister Kofi and his Rhythm,
    58
Mix, Tom, 54
Moore, Demi, 145
Morgenstern, Dan, 195, 251
Morning Post, 53
Morton, Benny, 122
Morton, Jelly Roll, 27, 37, 123,
    130, 154-155
Mulligan, Mick, 98, 145, 160,
    181
Mumford, John, 72, 94, 98
Munich, 6, 156
Murray, Albert, 195
Murray, Doug, 257
Musicians Union, 57, 209, 212
New Merlin's Cave, London,
    120-22, 124-25, 127, 199, 205
New Orleans, 41, 70, 156,
    164-5, 207-8, 251

New Statesman, 217
New York, 70, 137-41, 143, 147,
    162-4, 191, 197-200, 202,
    205, 213, 219, 236-7, 248, 254
Newbury Festival, 229-39
Newcastle upon Tyne, 149
Newport Jazz Festival, 140,
    164, 219
Nichol, Bill, 53-4
Nichols, Red, 177
Nimmo, Derek, 147
Noakes, Alfie, 50
Norwich, 47, 257
Nottingham, 73
Nova Scotia, 254
Nuffield Centre, London, 51
Nuts (album), 124, 127, 174, 229
Observer, 122
Okeh Recording company, 213
Oliver, King, 208
One Mo' Time (TV show), 219
Oslo, 95-6, 196
Owens, Jimmy, 200
Paris, 158, 204, 206, 212
Park Lane Hotel, London, 246
Parker, Charles, 76
Parker, Charlie, 92
Parker, Johnny, 120, 122
Parkinson, Michael, 147
Parnell, Colin, 121
Parsons, Nicholas, 146
Peerless, Brian, 126, 191-2
Peppiatt, Andrew, 221
Perth, 85, 167, 169-70, 224
Peterson, Oscar, 221
Philadelphia, 142-3
Phillips, Lloyd, 122
Picard, John, 98
Pizza Express (Dean Street),
    London, 212

Pizza On The Park, London, 182, 205, 214, 245
Porter, Cole, 130
Powell, Sandy, 188
Price, Sam, 200
Priestley, J.B., 161
Punch (magazine), 162
Pye Records, 153
Python, Monty, 130
Queen Mary (liner), 226
RADA, 97
RAF, 6, 13, 15, 19, 32, 38-40, 42-52, 222
Reading Festival, 126-7
Reinhardt, Django, 207
Rendell, Don, 73
Rhys, Jean, 183
Richards, John, 82
Richardson, Johnny, 215
Riddle, Nelson, 185
Ridley, Wally, 104-5
Rogers, Ted, 186
Rohde, Shelley, 148
Rolling Stones, 108
Romero, Chan, 104
Ronnie Scott Agency, 128
Ronnie Scott Directions, 227
Ronnie Scott's Club, London, 124, 127-31, 162, 165-6, 173, 176-7, 180-1, 183, 211, 244, 246-8, 254, 256-7
Rosolino, Frank, 128
Royal Navy, 5, 15, 162
Rubin, Ron, 216-7, 221, 225-6, 230, 233, 242, 256
Ruislip, 44-6
Russell, Pee Wee, 86, 92, 204
Russia, 5, 41, 105-6
Russo, Bill, 58
Saga Rose (liner), 254

Samson Clark and Company, 35, 37-8, 52
Scott, Ronnie, 127-8, 176-80, 228
Scruggs, Earl, 142
Seeger, Peggy, 76
Shand, Tom, 142
Shapiro, Helen, 185
Shavers, Charlie, 112-13
Shaw, Artie, 70
Shaw, Arvell, 251
Shaw, George Bernard, 186
Shearman, Don, 59, 82
Shipton, Alyn, 126
Simmen, Johnny, 118
Singapore, 84, 170
Six Bells, London, 88, 111
Slim, Memphis, 185
Smith, Bessie, 36, 123, 154, 160, 249
Smith, Brian, 171
Smith, Carrie, 244
Smith, Chuck, 76, 79, 111, 113, 121, 126, 133, 165-6, 169, 171, 189-90, 216, 218, 223, 225, 230, 236
Smith, John, 246
Smith, Mamie, 213
Smith, Ray, 120
Smith, Ronnie, 77-9
Smith, Stuff, 198-200
Son of Nuts (album), 127
Southampton, 150
Spectator, 217
Spivey, Victoria, 196
St. Clement's Press, 25, 33-5
St. Elmo's Fire (film), 145
St. Ives, 175
Staff, Freddy, 50
Stage (magazine), 93

Stapleton, Cyril, 92-3
Steele, David, 246
Steinbeck, John, 116
Stewart, Al, 142
Stewart, Rex, 114-15
Stewart-Baxter, Derrick, 201
Stewart, Slam, 234
Stockport, 187
Strachey, Lytton, 115
Strand Palace Hotel, London,
     195
Strange, Pete, 98
Strayhorn, Billy, 206
Stubbs, George, 253
Sutton, Ralph, 122, 185
Sweden, 99
Swing Kings, 110, 115, 197
Swing Music (magazine), 195
Swinging Blue Jeans, 102-9,
     227
Sydney, 85, 169-72, 216-17, 220,
     225
Tasmania, 86
Tatum, Art, 205
Tayar, Graham, 121
Taylor, Derek, 123, 126, 128,
     135-8
Taylor, Eddie, 216, 221, 225-6,
     242, 245
Taylor, Sid, 59, 76, 79, 82-4
Teagarden, Jack, 196, 206
Tendulkar, Sachin, 223
Thatcher, Margaret, 246
Theatre Royal, London, 209
Theobald, Brian, 227-8
This is Your Life (TV show), 243
Thompson, Pat, 86
Tilbury, 82, 88
Time-Life Corporation, 119,
     180

Toronto, 164
Townsville, Australia, 170-1
Turner, Bruce, 67-76, 78-9,
     81-2, 85-6, 88-102, 121, 123,
     125-6, 145, 153, 184, 187, 204,
     206, 214-15, 219
Tynan, Kenneth, 130
Vaughan, Roy, 111
Venuti, Joe, 206
Vinten, Jonathan, 242-3, 256
Waller, Fats, 143, 153, 242
Wallis, Bob, 101
Walsh, Mike, 171
Warner Brothers (company),
     123-4, 127-8, 134, 137, 140,
     145, 153
Warrington, 39
Washington, Al, 212-14
Watts, Charlie, 108
Wavendon, 158
Wayne, Cecil, 56-7
Webster, Ben, 111-12, 199-200
Weir, Peter, 169
Weist, Gil, 163
Welch, Elizabeth, 245
Wellington, 223
Wells, Dicky, 114-15, 201-2
Welsh, Alex, 110
Wembley, London, 50, 56
Wesker, Arnold, 39
Weston, Charlie, 23-4
Weymouth, 92-5
Whanel, Paddy, 96
Wheeltappers and Shunters' Club
     (TV show), 186
Whiteman, Paul, 206
Whittle, Tommy, 145
Wilber, Bob, 122
Williams, Roy, 145
Wilton, Robb, 188

Witherspoon, Jimmy, 244
Wogan, Terry, 147
Wooding, Sam, 207
Woolf, Virginia, 115
World War One, 1, 93, 169
World War Two, 6-31, 39, 84,
     227
World's Greatest Jazz Band,
     192
Worsthorne, Peregrine, 225
Wyndham, Francis, 183
Yardley Gobion, 16-33,
Yentob, Alan, 164
Young, Trummy, 210-11
Young, Lester, 194
Youngman, Henny, 226
Zaidins, Earle Warren, 141
Zola, Emile, 116-17

Join the Northway Books mailing list to receive details of new books about jazz, as well as events and special offers. Write to Northway at 39 Tytherton Road, London N19 4PZ or email info@northwaybooks.com

We do not pass information from our mailing list to other organisations.

Doggin' Around

by Alan Plater

with illustrations by the author

2006   £6.99

Described by the author as: 'memoirs of a jazz-crazed play-wright – some of the stories are autobiographical and some of them are true.'

'rich throughout with smart lines and offbeat observations,' *Guardian*.

'a very, very, readable book,' Michael Parkinson, Radio 2.

'terrific price, terrific read. It kept me turning pages like mad,' Campbell Burnap.

'masterly in its knowledge and poetic communication... Don't hang about, go out and buy it,' *Jazz Journal*.

'illustrated by some extremely funny cartoons... and imbued with the humane wisdom that has made him famous...' *www.vortexjazz.co.uk*

212 pages

ISBN 978-0955090806

I Blew It My Way

by Vic Ash

with Simon Spillett and Helen Ash
Preface by Michael Parkinson

2006 £11.99

Vic Ash, saxophonist and clarinettist with the great popular musicians and entertainers, tells of touring with George Shearing, Shirley MacLaine, Fred Astaire, Ray Charles, Tony Bennett, Liza Minnelli and many others – and for more than twenty years with Frank Sinatra. He has worked with the stars of British modern jazz – Tubby Hayes, John Dankworth, Ronnie Scott and others – and is busy today with his own group and the BBC Big Band.

'a fascinating book covering not only Vic Ash's personal story but the changes which have come about in Britain's jazz scene during the last sixty years,' *Jazz Journal*.

'an unusually rich variety of musical reference and insights,' *Jazz Rag*.

'nicely written with plenty of good photos... A good read,' *Crescendo and Jazz Music*.

170 pages

ISBN 978-0955090820

A History of Jazz in Britain 1919-50

by Jim Godbolt

revised edition with new illustrations

2005   hardback, £16.99

This book covers the visits of American trail-blazing artists
of the twenties and thirties, their influence on British musicians, the emergence of specialist magazines, rhythm clubs,
discographers and pundits, and the fascinating cloak-and-
dagger plots to defy the Musicians' Union ban.

'As breezy as a riverboat shuffle, ever on the lookout for the
preposterous detail and the opportunity for raffish reminis-
cence,' *Times Literary Supplement*.

'Enlivened throughout by the author's passion for the music
itself and his sharp eye for human failings,' George Melly.

'If you have not bought this book, I urge you to do so – now!'
Humphrey Lyttelton, BBC *Sounds of Jazz*.

285 pages

ISBN 978-0953704057

All This and Many a Dog
by Jim Godbolt

reprinted with new illustrations

2007   paperback, £12.99

Jim Godbolt's memoir is packed with hilarious anecdotes and vivid portraits of British jazz stars such as George Melly, Sandy Brown, Humphrey Lyttelton and Ronnie Scott. His story encompasses the trad boom of the 1950s as well as the pop revolution of the early sixties when he was the agent of the Swinging Blue Jeans. He also recalls his years working as an electricity meter reader while struggling for recognition as a writer. The final chapters chart his return to the jazz scene as a published author and editor of *Jazz at Ronnie Scott's*.

'A warm, human autobiography... Godbolt writes with great insight about both the musicians and social changes of those heady times,' *Listener*.

'Highly intelligent and articulate... He has an excellent eye and ear for the quirks of others... irresistible.' George Melly, *Guardian*.

'His book gives us the whole spectrum of post-war pop music – the explosion of the Beatles and the demise of the big bands, written in an easy conversational tone,' Spike Milligan, *Mail on Sunday*.

248 pages
ISBN 978-0955090844

Other books about jazz
published by Northway

Ronnie Scott with Mike Hennessey
Some of My Best Friends Are Blues

Alan Robertson
Joe Harriott – Fire in His Soul

Coleridge Goode and Roger Cotterrell
Bass Lines: A Life in Jazz

Peter Vacher
Soloists and Sidemen: American Jazz Stories

Harry Gold
Gold, Doubloons and Pieces of Eight

Digby Fairweather
Notes from a Jazz Life

Ron Brown with Digby Fairweather
Nat Gonella – A Life in Jazz

Forthcoming books about jazz
from Northway

Chris Searle

*Forward Groove: Jazz and the Real World
from Louis Armstrong to Gilad Atzmon*

Derek Ansell's
biography of Hank Mobley

Mike Hennessey's
biography of Johnny Griffin

Peter King's
autobiography

Ron Rubin's
musical limericks